PHOENIX
The Rise
A PHI ATHANATOI NOVEL

EFTHALIA

ISBN: 978-0-6487854-4-6

DEDICATION

To my father, Taxiarchis, you left the stamp of kindness behind.

PROLOGUE

"The scales of battle turned. But until then, they attacked each other, fighting furiously in fierce combat." ~ Hesiod Theogony.

Francis Marion National Forest; Charleston, SC
Evening, mortal realm

"Etimos." Hades whispered the word to signify his readiness as he watched the battle below from a hill in the forest. He knew the outcome as he had foreseen it. The winning team was required to make a sacrifice in his honor. He recognized his sibling's signature before he made his appearance.

"Brother." Hades turned his head in greeting.

Zeus slapped him on the back. "Not bad seating."

"If you could call standing in the forest a good view."

"Cheer up, Hades. You know we both enjoy a splendid victory." Zeus gave him another clap between his shoulder blades.

Everyone thought the all-seeing Zeus was serious, but Hades knew better. His sibling could be quite the jokester, and his humor transcended to the mortal realm where he had forbidden any of the gods and goddesses to frolic and intervene. Save for when Zeus, the most powerful of gods, had the urge to shift the balance. His grand-daughter, Carissa Alkippes, triggered events that brought Zeus on high alert for a prophecy that had been all but forgotten for two millennia. Everything that had transpired recently only confirmed that Carissa and the vampire Xen Lyson, who she was engaged to, would both be instrumental in how everything would play out.

"I take it you are going to lend some power in this war."

"I don't think it's necessary. We both know who is going to win."

Two factions of demons were already in the heat of battle. The *eudemonia* and *kakodaimones* were once one entity that walked the earth and spread fortune to those worthy and misfortune to those who were not. When it all ended, the earth opened and swallowed them into the underworld. There they were split in two segregated groups. They battled for many millennia until a few centuries ago when Lox, the leader of the *eudemonia*, worked on a way to break the curse that kept them bound to the underworld. Now they fought in the mortal realm and Zeus, the god of thunder and storms, wanted to see it for himself.

"Watch closely, Brother, for in the fray of battle important details are often missed."

Hades turned his gaze toward the skirmish. The perk of being a god meant you could zoom your view in from any location. He focused on the perimeter where the *kakodaimones* stood ready to fight the oncoming onslaught of the *eudemonia*. His head followed the lines of men, and just at the fringes, he caught something. A portal. Demons exited by the dozen into the mortal realm. "Are you seeing this?"

"Crystal clear color," Zeus answered.

"We know how this ends. You can stay and view the rest, but I need to close that portal for Hekate." Hades turned to his brother, eyes burning like torches. He tilted his head and dematerialized.

Zeus watched from his position. He wanted to witness this small victory for the *eudemonia*. Long ago it wasn't only their name that stood for happiness, they were the givers of happiness, and that had allowed humans to flourish and prosper.

His chess pieces were in place. One more action was required to be taken after the battle ended. He watched Lox carve his way through the *kakodaimones*. Hades had done the *eudemonia* a favor by removing the glamour that made the *kakodaimones* look like ghastly reptiles when they stepped from the underworld to the human realm. Their sulphury odor permeated the air. Without their glamour they no longer looked identical. Zeus saw Lox lock into the leader and head straight for him. His men were well-oiled killing machines, and Zeus needed to make sure his granddaughter, Carissa, had these men on her side.

The *eudemonia* cut their opposition down without raising a sweat. It appeared the skirmishes they fought before freeing themselves were a test of endurance and skill.

There was only one more thing Zeus needed to see and that was the fulfilment of the *orkos* Lox had sworn to Hades.

He watched as they prepared the sacrifice with a temporary altar. A sheep was dragged along for the offering.

Zeus transformed himself to a mist and surrounded the site where the oath would be sworn.

Lox stepped forward with a knife in hand. "I swear to Zeus, Athena, Apollo, Demeter and the Styx that I will ally myself and my men to the *Phi Athanatoi* and Carissa, the daughter of Ares. I have sworn this to Hades."

The knife slit the throat of the sheep and blood was gathered in a vessel. "Whoever is to do wrong by this oath, let their blood flow to the ground like this wine." He poured wine to the ground.

All the necessary libations were poured, and prayers were said.

Satisfied by the sworn *orkos*, Zeus dematerialized back to Olympus. The drama had commenced, and he would watch it unfold from the comfort of his throne.

ONE

"We know nothing for sure: truth is hidden at the bottom of a well." ~ *Diogenes Laertius*

Francis Marion National Forest; Charleston, SC
Evening, mortal realm – Day 1

"*Skata*, this is bad." Carissa rolled her shoulders. It was going to be a long night.

"Witch, can you materialize us closer to the men?" Xen, Carissa's fiancé, asked their flame-haired friend Kirke.

They surveyed the open area before them. It resembled a small war zone. Hundreds of demon bodies lay slaughtered.

The thought of these *kakodaimones* being unleashed on innocent and unsuspecting humans sent a shiver down Carissa's spine. Someone had saved countless mortal lives by slaying the demons, or had they? The question bounced around her brain like a ping pong match.

Kirke lifted her hands and Carissa knew what it meant, she had a fraction of a second before they dematerialized. She turned and pulled Xen to her, squeezing him tight.

"I like it when you are forceful, *koukla*."

She rolled her eyes, and her vampire gave her his dazzling signature smile that had its own zip code. His devastating good looks could slay, and he wasn't afraid to amp up the charm when he wanted and needed to. She was sure supernaturals oozed with more pheromones.

Her feet landed on soft grass while still in his embrace.

Several men with swords surrounded them. The thought they were unarmed did not sit well with her. Why hadn't she grabbed her sword before Kirke had zapped them here?

She staggered and straightened.

Xen took a step toward the man whose blade was closest. He had raised his hands in surrender. "Tell Lox, pay attention to your enemies…"

"…for they are the first to discover your mistakes," a deep voice finished from behind them.

Carissa watched carefully from where she stood. Xen spun on the balls of his feet, and his lips turned up in a smile as he assessed the man before them.

That's Lox? She was bonded to Xen, and they could communicate telepathically.

It is, koukla.

He looks like a Viking.

He's not, but I won't argue that he does look like one.

Lox motioned for his men to drop their swords, and he locked arms with Xen in greeting.

"What brings you here, vampire?"

"Several things. We need to talk."

Carissa shuffled closer to Xen.

Kirke had moved in on Lox, her finger poking in rapid succession at Lox's chest. "This is my domain. I want you and your men out of here."

Lox leaned over so his face was directly in Kirke's, a growl low and filled with warning escaped his lips. "We go when I say and the danger is clear."

Kirke raised her hand. Magic swirled.

Carissa stepped in the space between them, and her fingers closed around Kirke's wrist. With one swift move, she removed Kirke's hand and severed the magic she was about to unleash. "No arguing," she scolded her friend.

6

Her witchy friend continued her laser beam glare at the trespasser.

Eyebrow raised, Carissa directed her demands at the Viking. "Lox, I'm sure you've guessed, I am Xen's bonded. I believe you have my friend Kelly, and we have come here to retrieve her, whatever the cost."

The mountain of a man let out a laugh.

"Nice to meet you, demi-god daughter of Ares."

"How did…" The question died on her lips.

"I have my sources too."

"Let's not get sidetracked here. Kelly?" she asked again.

"Kelly is safe and well."

"I will be the judge of that when I see her myself."

"Carissa." A soft familiar voice sounded from behind her.

She twisted around and ran toward her friend. They collided in a tight hug full of joy. When Carissa hugged her friend long enough, she stepped back. "Are you okay? Have you been harmed?" She scanned Kelly's face and then did a quick assessment over her body.

Kelly held her hand up to stay her questions. "I'm more than fine."

"But you've been missing, and we feared you were kidnapped and held against your will or even far worse. Even Ligi has been going out of her mind."

"Carissa. I'm here because I want to be." Her friend leaned in and gave her another hug. "Come, let's catch each other up on what's been happening." Kelly motioned for them to enter the large tent she had come out from.

Carissa looked over to Xen and Kirke. Xen had already entered a deep discussion with Lox. Kirke's face wore the marks of disdain and anger. She waived to Kirke to come and join them. "There's someone I want you to meet."

Kirke dematerialized before them. "Couldn't just walk over, could you," Carissa said with a gentle nudge of her shoulder to her friend.

"Walking is overrated." Her witchy friend winked.

"Kirke, this is Kelly."

Carissa watched as Kelly took Kirke's hand and squeezed. "I'm judging that I've missed a lot while I was gone."

"You have indeed," Kirke replied and they stepped into the tent.

Carissa's jaw dropped when she saw the depth and opulence inside, it had been decked out in luxury items. A king bed with side tables sat at the back end. To their left was a plush sitting area, and the far right had a dining area. It resembled a Boudin tent. "Are all the tents like this?" she asked.

"Pretty much."

"How did they manage to set all this up?"

"We realized this area was glamoured, so Lox, with the help of his men, thought it would be the perfect spot."

Carissa looked to Kirke.

"This is my spot and my spells that keep everything hidden." Kirke pointed a finger outside. "Those men are trespassing." Kirke's temper rose again.

Carissa had to diffuse this until they all came to some agreement.

"Kirke, let's sit down and hear what happened first."

"Yes, let's," Lox said as he stepped into the tent with Xen." He moved toward Kelly and her friend knew that look. Kelly belonged with him and he with her.

Xen moved to Carissa's side. "Kelly, this is Xenocrates Lysandros.

"Just Xen Lyson. No need for full formalities."

Kelly swung her head to Carissa. "We really do have lots to talk about."

"But that can wait," Xen replied. Then he turned a steely gaze to Lox. "I need details, that war field out there will take a lot of effort to clean up."

"That field is my business, and as you can see we're cleaning up."

"Your business just tangled too close to the ordinary world, and that mess will take some time to clean. You can't bury and burn all the bodies in deep trenches. It will only bring attention to the police and fire brigade. Need I remind you that you are in the middle of

Francis Marion National Forest. A forest that has plenty of human people during the day."

"I don't need the reminder, Xen. It's our mess."

"Normally I would agree, but this is too much and requires more sophisticated methods."

"And how would you remove the bodies if not with fire?"

"I have more than one method for this." He pointed to the carnage outside. "You need help." Xen was the head of the *Phi Athanatoi*, a group of immortals that protected humans from unearthly creatures. He had the necessary resources to remove any trace of otherworldly evidence from the mortal realm. Lox needed him.

Lox shifted on his feet. "I normally take care of my affairs."

"You know this time you have to ask for help."

"I don't like being indebted to others," Lox finished.

"Lox, this isn't about how you are feeling." Carissa threw a thumb gesture over her shoulder. "Xen is offering assistance for that hell basket body dump out there."

"Again, that's my business."

A tick started at her temple. Lox was huge in size, but Carissa was starting to wonder whether he could see past his own issues to allow the *Phi* to help him clean up in Kirke's backyard. She knew the witch well enough to know she didn't share her turf with anyone. Witches liked their anonymity, and right now Lox and his band of merry men were trespassing on Kirke's stomping ground.

"You risk much."

"It's my problem," he cautioned.

"One, that chaos out there is in my friend's domain, and two, I'll repeat what Xen said in case it didn't sink in. You risk exposure if you keep lighting those bodies up. That's like flashing neon signs saying H.E.L.L.O." Heat fused its way through her body. She did not like his stubbornness and lack of reasoning. Her fingers started to tingle.

Lox let out a growl.

Xen's fangs elongated.

Lox made to take a step forward. Kelly's arm shot out and she pulled him back. "Boys," she hissed through gritted teeth.

The anger radiating and bouncing around the tent only fueled Carissa more. The storm inside her rose. Her fingers tingled and her power began to pulse out of her, knocking some of the smaller items in the tent to the ground. Air lashed and whipped around her.

Calm koukla. Xen's words embedded themselves in her furious mind. She knew the damage she could inflict on everyone around her because her power was erratic.

Rigos. She spoke the spell internally to contain her power, but her anger did not want to be constrained. It wanted to lash out and rip everything to shreds.

TWO

"Of Pallas Athena, guardian of the city, I begin to sing. Dread is she, and with Ares she loves the deeds of war, the sack of cities and the shouting and the battle. It is she who saves the people as they go to war and come back. Hail, goddess, and give us good fortune and happiness!" ~ *"Homeric Hymn 11"* to Athena

Francis Marion National Forest; Charleston, SC
Evening, mortal realm – Day 1

The air shifted.

Carissa recognized the familiar presence. Behind her friends stood the goddess Athena with flashing red eyes that ebbed and turned her usual shade of gray.

Stay your hand, Niece, she said to Carissa's mind, and a wash of calm settled over her. *Keep my presence concealed.*

Xen squeezed Carissa to his side. Her vampire sensed the omnipresence of someone. His heightened senses would have alerted him before Athena materialized. She sent a message through their bond. *It's okay.*

He didn't provoke her for an answer. It was one of the many attributes she loved about Xen. He knew when not to probe or ask too many questions.

Kelly tried to calm Lox. She hadn't picked up on Athena's presence, but Kirke had done so without fail. She gave her and Xen a once over and didn't ask either.

"If you'll excuse me. I need to get some air."

"Wait, Carissa. I'll come with you," Kelly offered.

"No. I need five minutes to myself."

Xen dropped his arm from around Carissa's waist.

She flashed Athena a look and made her way out of the tent. Outside Carissa moved to where there was less activity and men. When she was secure the goddess appeared.

"Niece."

Carissa bowed. "Athena."

"No need to bow."

Carissa straightened. "Is something wrong, is Father…"

"Ares is fine and putting out other fires on Olympus. Never a dull moment where the gods and goddesses are concerned," Athena said, smiling.

A laugh escaped Carissa's lips. "You're not mistaken there, but won't your presence here irritate Zeus?"

Athena waved a hand. "I can handle my father," she said with a wink. "The reason I am here is that you need to control your anger with Lox. Whatever minor arguments you have going on here, they are, let's say, insignificant in relation to what is coming."

"Please don't tell me there are more escaped Titans."

"If only it were. There seems to be another foe hiding in the shadows. Even Zeus has foreseen, but this foe, he has magic all around him and is shielding himself. This makes him much more dangerous to you and Xen."

Carissa digested what the goddess had just divulged.

"You're gods, you can break spells."

"Ah… that's where it gets messy."

"How?" Carissa asked.

Athena started to pace. "When another god casts a spell, it is impossible to remove it. It doesn't work the same way as a witch's magic. Ours is embedded in the very fabric of the whole cosmos."

"That still doesn't explain it."

"Patience, Niece."

Carissa's lungs expanded and she pushed air out of her nose. "Is this one of those cryptic things?"

Athena raised an eyebrow at her, and a small smile tugged at her lips. "You know I should not be meddling."

"Then why come here and tell me there is an unknown person shielded in magic?"

"Because that person is here in your mortal realm, and anything you have going on with the demon inside is far smaller than you can envisage. There's a tempest brewing, and you are right in its path."

"Then point me to where this foe is so I can deal with him."

"I'm afraid it's not that simple. The magic surrounding him leaves us blind, we cannot pinpoint him, which makes him even more dangerous. He can move around undetected. There is no telling what he has planned and whether there are others shielded by the same magic."

"How do I find the proverbial needle in the haystack?"

"That I can't answer. I can only give you warning."

"Great." Carissa ran her fingers through her hair then turned her head upward to the dark sky. An epiphany hit. "You said your magic is not like witches' magic in that it cannot be broken or undone, and that the gods' magic is tied into the elements."

"Yes."

"When the gods can't break a spell, what do you do to counteract it?"

"We add a gift to the inflicted to compensate or add to the infliction we want caused."

"But you would have to know who you are gifting or inflicting?"

"Yes."

That line of questioning led her to a dead end. "I would have to find him for you to slow him down."

"Correct, Niece."

"I am none the wiser nor closer to knowing who this foe is and don't know how to help you."

"You need allies, and you need to gather them fast."

Carissa opened her mouth, but the goddess had dematerialized. *Confusing gods and goddesses*, she thought. *Who could understand them?*

No one. The answer came to her mind. It was Xen.

Did you get any of that?

Only your last thought. It was like I was muted from tapping in.

"Ha." She let out a laugh. *Thank the goddess Athena for that,* she sent back to his mind.

She made her way back inside the tent. Everyone stopped talking. Except Xen, who had been talking with her.

"The time for arguments is over," she said to Lox. "Will you work with the *Phi?*"

Xen folded his arms over his chest and Lox stood straighter. "What's in it for me?"

"Carissa, permit me," Xen interposed.

She waved her arm as if to clear the path.

"What you get is training and access to my organization for your men's needs."

Carissa's chest tightened. Xen knew when to interject, and she internally gloated that they were in sync with each other.

Xen gave her a knowing glance, telling her that he had just read her mind.

"Then I will be indebted to the vampire," Lox said.

"You're spending too much time worrying about accepting help because you might have to do a solid for Xen. That is small, based on what Athena thinks."

Kelly jumped to her feet. "The goddess was here?"

"Yes," Carissa answered without flinching.

"What did she want?" Lox asked.

"First, your word that you will accept our help."

"You have my word. I have already sworn it," he grunted.

Xen raised an eyebrow. "Do I need to ask?"

"No. You know I won't go back on my word."

Carissa stepped toward Lox. "Then why are you playing hardball?"

"Because I need to be certain any alliance formed here will not result or end in a bad way because of who you are and who you represent."

Carissa's voice came out clipped and sharp. "I. Am. Carissa. And. I. Represent. Myself."

Kelly thumped him in the arm. "Way to go big guy. Don't piss off my friend."

Lox held up his hands. "I don't mean any disrespect. I just need to be certain."

"There is no need to doubt. You've known me long enough," Xen said. "The question we should all be asking is, what are the gods playing at now?"

Kirke got to her feet and dusted off her long green Camelot looking gown. She had been observing in silence and now directed a digit toward Xen. "What the vampire said. You," she shifted her pointed finger in Lox's direction, "accept the help and remove your men from my domain." She lifted her arms and disappeared.

Carissa stared at the spot where the witch had been a second ago. "She does do that with style."

Kelly walked over to Carissa. "Let's talk."

With Kirke gone they weren't getting out of here any time soon. "Mind if I grab a minute with Kelly?" Carissa asked Xen.

"Take all the time you need, *koukla*. I have a few questions to ask Lox before I call for a few clean up teams."

In short Xen had built quite a few industries over the many hundreds of years. One of them was Phi Technologies that developed and produced a number of weapons to fight against demons. Their latest bullets contained digoxin, polonium and vitamin A in high concentration. This combination was lethal to the demon physiology. Once shot the demon would disintegrate on the spot. Xen's organization also had teams that would clean skirmishes with demons. It was how Carissa met Xen. In the middle of a skirmish. In an abandoned warehouse.

"Why don't you two sit here and we can talk outside," Lox said to Kelly.

"That sounds like a marvelous idea, big guy," she agreed.

The men exited, and Kelly dragged Carissa by the hand to the couches. Carissa dropped her weight in one, and her friend took the one next to her.

Kelly turned in her direction. "Now girlfriend, spill."

"We need a year to cover it all, there's that much. Why don't you start first and commence with the part that Ligi..." she paused then pointed "…and you both knew I was something other than all human and that you're both definitely not human."

Ligi was their siren friend and had been working in the background to locate Kelly. Carissa had been gutted when she learned her friends had not thought to clue her into the fact she might belong to another world for fear she would have thought them to be crazy.

"Carissa, you have to understand that had we revealed ourselves we would have risked you going la la on us. And how on earth would I have said, 'Hey, I'm a harpie. You know, a mythical creature?'"

"Look, I get it but a part of me wishes you both tried to explain. Let's park that and tell me what happened with Lox."

"Well, you know I have a penchant for stolen artifact stories. I was on my way to investigate a story in Romania when I bumped into Lox."

Carissa nodded.

"So you were smitten and vanished."

"Not exactly. I mean I did feel a big kapow when I met him, but he went all neanderthal on me and threw me over his shoulder and in his car. Said something about being fated."

"So, he kidnapped you?"

"You could say that."

"Listen, Kelly, if you don't want to be here, you say the word and I'll get you out."

"It's not like that. I've fallen for him."

"I'd like to get you away from here for a few days to test that. I think you have Stockholm syndrome."

"I don't, and if I'd wanted to get away from him, I could have shifted."

"Wait, shifted to what?"

"As I said, I'm a harpie. I'll let you work that one out." Kelly winked.

"So… you really want to be here with him?"

"I do."

"Then why didn't you send a message at least, so we weren't out of our minds thinking you were lying in a ditch somewhere?"

"One thing led to another and there was no time. Especially with what was going on out there."

Carissa took a moment to mull over her friend's words. Kelly had a point, and Carissa could relate to some degree. She'd met Xen a few months ago, and her whole life had changed. Aside from that she found out she was the daughter of Ares and had fought off a demi-god friend, battled demons, ended up on Olympus, fought off two Titans, both Kronos and Iapetos, and her ordinary world had been turned upside down, and it didn't look like it was going to right itself any time soon.

"Will you come back home?"

"Of course, and Lox wants us to move in together."

Carissa reached over and squeezed her friend's hand.

"What's with you and that gorgeous vampire?" Kelly raised her eyebrows a few times.

"He's my fiancé." Carissa's heart drummed steadily and warmth spread through her chest. With Xen at her side she could do anything.

"What? No way. Already?"

"Uh-huh."

"So…" Kelly didn't finish because a loud familiar voice sounded from outside the tent.

They both knew who that angry voice belonged to. They shot to their feet and bolted in the direction of their yelling friend. Carissa skidded to a stop right in front of Ligi, and Kelly came careening right behind her, smashing into her back and sending her forward onto Ligi.

They all tumbled on the ground in a heap.

THREE

Francis Marion National Forest; Charleston, SC
Evening, mortal realm − Day 1

Loud giggles burst from all three. Carissa's eyes watered.

"I'm supposed to be the clumsy one," Ligi said from under Carissa.

Carissa ceased her laughter for a second. "We do make quite the trio."

"I'll say." Another familiar voice boomed from above them.

Carissa looked up to see amused faces looking down at them and one of those was Tithon—a bounty hunter vampire that had aided her when she'd been kidnapped by her demigod friend Hal. "Gumbo. What are you doing here?" She used the nickname she had given him when they'd met.

Xen held out his hand to Carissa. Lox and Tithon did the same for Kelly and Ligi.

All three were hoisted back to their feet in a fit of giggles. The men shared some of their amusement.

The girls got themselves under control, and Carissa looked between Ligi and Tithon. They couldn't possibly be here together.

They are, koukla, Xen communicated.

The smile from her face dropped. "Gumbo, what brings you here?"

"I believe Ligi was looking for Kelly."

The words left his mouth, but something in her stomach told her there was more to why Tithon was here.

I think you're right, koukla.

Ligi moved over to where Kelly and Lox stood.

Carissa leaned over to Tithon. "Mind if we have a word?"

He tilted his head and paused. "Not at all," he said after a few beats.

Her fingers closed around his arm, and she dragged him away from the others. Her gaze collided with Xen and his eyes flashed with a warning. *Go easy, koukla.*

We both know enough to know he is here to collect a bounty. She sent the message back to Xen through their bond.

"Easy on the arm, Carissa." Tithon chortled.

When they were a safe distance from prying eyes and ears, she gritted her teeth and turned on Tithon. "Spill it."

Tithon put up his hands in surrender.

"You're not here out of a favor to Ligi." She straightened her shoulders. He was taller than her, but his height did not scare her, nor did the fact that he was a lethal vampire.

"I cannot tell you that."

"Are we really going to play this game? I thought you were smarter than that, Gumbo." He had been working on both sides of the fence, and this just raised her suspicion more. She decided to throw another question at him. "What are your intentions toward Ligi?"

"You can say we are involved."

"Don't lie to me. Ligi is a tough nut to crack."

"She's mine." He growled.

"Great, another possessive vampire to deal with." She let out a frustrated breath and rolled her eyes. "But does she know why you are here?"

"I did tell her I was after a thief."

Carissa scratched her temple. "And that thief is here?" She

couldn't see how. The place was riddled with dead demons and Lox's men.

Tithon folded his arms across his chest and widened his stance. "Yes."

"Gumbo, give it to me straight. Who is the thief you're after?"

"Your friend Kelly."

Her eyes widened and she shook her head. "No. That doesn't make sense. Your bounty is Kelly?"

He didn't verbalize anything, just nodded his head in confirmation.

"You can't be serious about this."

"Sho 'nuff. As serious as anyone in my profession could be."

"Tithon, if you do this, you will lose Ligi. Trust me on this. Whatever you have been offered as payment..." She trailed off but only because the slight shift of air alerted her to a known presence that now stood beside her in unification.

"I'll double your bounty fee," Xen said.

Tithon contemplated the idea. "It's not that easy."

"Make it so," Xen countered.

"The guys that commissioned this are tied into politics."

"Give me the names."

"No can do, Xen."

"Tithon. If you pursue this risky assignment it will end with great harm being brought to you."

"I can handle myself."

"I never said you couldn't. Lox has bonded with Kelly. If you try to pluck her out for a mere discretion at some unscrupulous politician's whim then not only will he hunt you down but so will those five hundred men."

Tithon looked up and over to where most of Lox's men were gathered and spread in groups. "I guess you make a good point."

"Listen, you know I would have your back in any situation but with this one, we would be divided," Xen said.

Carissa shifted her footing. "Why exactly do they want Kelly?"

Tithon cleared his throat. "She stole an artifact that doesn't belong to her."

"Then retrieve it and give it back to those who want it," Carissa implored.

"I can't retrieve it without taking your friend. She is the only one who knows where it is," Tithon threw back.

Power tingled beneath her fingers. Her anger ebbed up another notch. "Haven't you heard of communication?"

Calm, koukla. Xen sent the words to her mind.

She mentally shook herself.

"Listen, Gumbo, there is no way you are going to take Kelly anywhere. Read my lips." She pointed to her face. "Not. Happening."

"Lox won't let her out of his sight, and you'd be a fool to think otherwise," Xen threw in. "There is always another way." He stepped forward and into Tithon's space. "Find it."

"I didn't come here for a fight."

"Then choose your next steps wisely."

Tithon took a step backwards. "Point made."

"Good to hear, Gumbo. I really didn't want to kick your ass," Carissa said with a smile.

Tithon raised an eyebrow. "You two amount to quite a force."

Xen's lips lifted in a cocky smile. Her vampire was in tune with her and she with him.

"So, do I get an invite to the wedding," Tithon asked, wiggling his eyebrows.

Carissa mentally slapped a hand to her head. She had the feeling her wedding was going to snowball to ridiculous crowd numbers. "What do you think, Gumbo?" she said, trying to be polite. She looked sideways at Xen. He seemed too amused for her liking, so she whacked him in the stomach. He enjoyed egging her *yiayia* and Aunt Paula on about the wedding.

She turned a burning gaze at Tithon. "I know you care for Ligi. I can pick that up already but be warned. She hates liars and duplicity. The sooner you bring her up to speed with the Kelly situation the better for you."

"I think we should rejoin the others. We've roused enough suspicion."

Ligi, Kelly and Lox were engaged in deep conversation when they got back to them. Tithon put an arm around Ligi's waist and pulled her in. Carissa watched with eagle eyes. There would be friction when Tithon took the man-up approach and told her the truth. He should have been upfront from the beginning.

"What did we miss?" Carissa asked.

Ligi turned toward her "Just boring chit chat."

"Looks like y'all had a lot to discuss," Ligi said.

"We needed to brief Tithon on a certain situation," Xen replied.

Saving Carissa from spilling what she really wanted to say. *Thanks for that.* She sent the words to his mind.

No problem, koukla.

"Well, if it's dangerous, shouldn't you share it with all of us." It didn't look like Ligi wanted to leave that bone alone.

"It doesn't involve everyone, and the only danger is to Tithon," Xen supplied.

"Okay, vampire." Ligi let it drop.

Carissa was grateful her friend didn't push the issue. It was time to go. "I think we need to wrap this up."

"Agreed." Xen fished his phone from his pocket and fired off several texts in seconds. The phone pinged. "Several clean up teams are on the way to help you remove and dispose of the demon bodies. I will be in touch with you as soon as I work out the details of where and how soon we can start moving some of your men to proper accommodation. Including yourself."

"They won't want to be separated," Lox said.

"Then we will find a way to make it work for everyone."

Carissa didn't doubt Xen. She knew he would deliver. This was what he did, this was why he was the *Phi Athanatoi* leader. He led men, and he looked after those who needed it. Right now Lox needed somewhere better than Francis Marion National Forest. Plus, Kirke had dibs on the place, and it wasn't wise to piss off a witch who could cast illusions. She was likely to get them to turn on themselves, or worse.

Carissa would heed Athena's words. "Lox, whatever decision

you make, make the one that sees you and Xen working on the same side. It is the will of the gods."

Lox eyed her for a moment. "Then so it shall be, but know this, if anything befalls Kelly or my men then I will unleash my wrath."

"Noted and I would return it in kind," Xen said.

The two men gave each other death stares and then relaxed their features.

Supernatural people are a strange bunch.

Xen's lips tugged up. *It took you this long to work that out, koukla?*

She mentally rolled her eyes. Her vampire was being a wise guy. "I think it's time for us to leave. She closed her eyes and focused on her power of *anagke*—compulsion. She could call anyone, and they would be compelled to come to her aid. "Kirke," she whispered.

Wind whipped around them. The witch reappeared.

"Think you can give us a ride." Humor lined her voice.

Kirke didn't speak. She gave Carissa a nod and raised her arms.

Carissa grabbed on to Xen and waved to her friends. Kirke dematerialized them.

They landed in the lounge room but with a muted thud.

FOUR

"What we achieve inwardly will change outer reality." ~ Plutarch

Yiayia's house; Charleston, SC
Evening, mortal realm – Day 1

Carissa looked over to Kirke. "That was an unexpectedly soft landing."

"I figured you wouldn't want to wake your grandmother and aunt."

True, she didn't.

"Thank you, Kirke. Where will you go?"

"Back to the forest. I'm not going to let a bunch of redeemed demons hang out indefinitely."

"Lox has agreed to let the *Phi* place his men in proper accommodations. There are a few locations I can spread his men around while keeping them within close distance to each other."

"Any proper lodgings you give them will be better than tents in a forest," Kirke said.

"These men have had it harder than those tents," Xen informed.

"I don't doubt it, but I would like the peace and tranquility of the forest back. That many men will only arouse suspicion with the humans. What then?"

"It is the reason why I have asked him to trust me to house and train his men, so they may better blend. I have a few more calls to make to set that up. Just remember they've been doing things on their own for a long time."

"I'll hold you to that, vampire." Kirke raised her hands in true Endora style from *Bewitched*, flicked her wrists and disappeared.

Carissa turned to Xen. "We should talk about all this, shouldn't we?"

He pulled her close. "We should, but right now I can only think of one thing I want more." His lips crashed to hers in a searing kiss that left her boneless.

When he broke away, she took in a large gulp of air. His kisses always left her dizzy.

"We don't have that much time until my rejuvenation sleep, and I'd rather spend it with you."

"Take me upstairs."

He scooped her up in his arms and raced them both up to Carissa's room. There, he put her down and shut the door then pulled her to him and gave her a scorching kiss. The kind that told her he hungered for her.

She began to undress, and he did too, only he used his vampire speed. "I'm not as fast as you."

"I could help."

"That's not necessary."

He got into bed, and a minute later she threw the covers over her.

He pulled her into the spooning position.

"I won't be staying tonight. I have made flight arrangements for your grandmother and aunt and need to finalize the security of this house."

Carissa's *pappou* had had a whole underground chamber built that was spelled by magic. Carissa, with the help of Kirke, had unlocked it, and it held many artifacts that contained magical properties. Xen planned on fortifying it so it didn't give off magical energy and didn't light her house up like a beacon for other creatures.

Her thoughts drifted to the underground basement at Phi

Technologies, which was the headquarters of the *Phi Athanatoi*. Huge wasn't the right word for it. Gigantic fitted it more accurately.

Xen was thousands of years old, but he hadn't wasted his time over the years. He'd amassed and invested and grown his business interests as well as the *Phi Athanatoi*. Carissa understood there were times where his attention would be needed elsewhere.

"Understandable. I will make sure they are packed and ready on time." She paused. "Do you think it's a good idea letting them go to my aunt's house in Virginia Beach?" She turned her head from their spooning position.

He had already lifted his head to meet her look. "Without a doubt."

"I guess they would be trouble if they stayed here. They'd only get in the way."

"On that point, I have to agree."

Yiayia and Aunt Paula got into all sorts of trouble, and lately it had amplified to the point where they'd decided to go sleuthing on their own. They'd run into some demons, but luckily Xen and his men had intercepted. It could have ended badly. Each, on her own, seemed to be okay, but together they were a force to be reckoned with.

"What do you mean I can't take my favorite pillow," Yiayia screamed down to Aunt Paula who had just taken the last stair and turned up to look at her.

"I have plenty of pillows at my house."

"But my pillow is special."

"There's nothing special about a thirty-year-old pillow. I'm surprised you don't wake up with neck cramps."

"Come to think of it, I think I need to see my chiropractor."

Paula rolled her eyes.

"What are you two arguing about?" Carissa asked, knowing full well they'd be talking about the same thing for the next fifteen minutes. She looked up at her *yiayia* and then over to Aunt Paula.

"Oh nothing, she's stuck on bringing that ancient pillow of hers."

"It's not ancient," Yiayia yelled from the top of the stairs.

"Yiayia, Aunt Paula has enough pillows at her house. Now come down to breakfast and then I'll help you pack after coffee."

"Good, maybe you could talk some sense into her." Paula headed for the kitchen.

Yiayia looked to where Paula had been standing. Her face had fallen.

"I'll help you squeeze it in the suitcase later," Carissa said with a wink.

Yiayia's lips curved into a smile. "I knew I could count on you, *paidi mou.*"

She dropped the pillow and made her way to the stairs. Carissa took two at a time to give her *yiayia* a hand. They descended step by step.

"You won't rat me out?" Yiayia asked.

"Pinky swear. I'll make sure it makes it in, but it will be your job to keep it out of sight."

"Don't worry. I can sneak it into the cupboard every morning. Paula won't catch on."

"She won't be happy if she finds it or that I helped you stash it."

"I will never admit to having had help." Yiayia's lips twitched.

"Oh, I'm sure of that."

They stepped into the kitchen, and Paula asked, "What are you sure about?"

"Carissa was sure you had coffee ready." Yiayia's eyes sparkled.

"I do."

"Well then, ladies, let's get breakfast happening so we can get you to Xen's private plane."

Both women giggled and Carissa rolled her eyes. They were like schoolgirls around him. She couldn't work it out. Maybe it was that whole vampire allure. Carissa pulled out a pan. "Who wants eggs?"

Both women answered in unison.

Carissa cracked eggs in a pan and cooked them to the desired preference. Her grandmother and aunt were seated and ready.

"How long will we be gone for?" Yiayia asked between bites

"Xen said he can have this house secured to his specifications in a week." She'd seen Xen's version of secure, both in his homes and workplace. She trusted him.

"That's pretty fast," Paula said.

It would be, and Carissa guessed he'd probably have vampire and werewolf tradesmen do the work, not regular humans.

"Will you be okay?"

"Yiayia, I'm fine. I'll be with Xen."

"That's right, Vetta. She can look after herself."

"You can't blame a grandmother for worrying."

Carissa reached over and squeezed her *yiayia's* hand. "It's a week. Then you'll be back here, unless you want to spend a little more time up in Virginia Beach?"

"Nonsense, we have your wedding to plan."

And there it was. The wedding talk. The thing she'd been trying to avoid. She really didn't want to envisage what Yiayia and Aunt Paula would be planning. She knew it would be bigger than the super bowl. She cleared her throat. "About that. I want to keep things small."

"Small?" Aunt Paula asked.

"Yes, something personal and intimate."

"Small?" she asked again.

"*Thitsa.*" Carissa used the Greek endearment for her aunt to get her attention good and proper. "That's what I said. You know, as in little." She picked her cup up and took a sip of coffee.

"Oh, you want to have three hundred guests instead of seven hundred."

Carissa's eyes went wide, and she choked on her coffee. Clearly Aunt Paula wasn't getting the brief. When the fits settled down, she steeled her composure. "*Thitsa*, I don't want more than eighty people. I don't even know three hundred people."

"Don't worry, we will fill the tables."

Carissa huffed. "I'll say this one time, I want a small wedding."

"Okay, you want three hundred people, we can work with that. Right, Vetta?"

"Three hundred it is. Three hundred is a good guest army," Yiayia said.

Three hundred? Guest army? They'd gone mad. This wasn't war, it was a wedding list. "This. Is. Not. Sparta." Carissa's voice boomed in the kitchen.

Her *yiayia* and aunt were not fazed, they rolled their eyes at her.

She opened her mouth to say something then closed it again. She was going to tell Xen eloping was her number one option.

"Well, you never know who will turn up and you're marrying a vampire."

"Yiayia, nobody other than you and Aunt Paula know he's a vampire, and I'm not expecting half of the village to crash the wedding."

"True, but what's to stop demons coming?"

"Xen will have his men doing the security detail."

"Oh yeah, the vampire does have his own army."

"Speaking of the village, if we don't invite them, they'll get upset," Paula said.

"I'm not inviting all of Greece, and I'm not having a *Big Fat Greek Wedding*."

"Why not? It was a good movie," Paula countered. "You know I have a bottle of Windex in my room."

Carissa slapped a hand to her head. If she let this conversation go on much longer, it would turn ridiculous. "Okay, enough about armies and weddings." She picked up her cup and downed the rest of the coffee in one go. "I'm going to start packing for you, Yiayia." She got to her feet.

"You won't forget to pack some of my necessities." Yiayia closed an eyelid.

"No, Yiayia. I won't."

"We'll be up shortly," Paula said.

Carissa took the stairs two at a time. Once in Yiayia's bedroom, she made quick work of throwing the pillow that had caused a fuss into a suitcase along with some clothes already on the bed. She moved the suitcase to the floor, sat on it and zipped it up. A smile stretched across her lips. That pillow would spring to life like a jack-in-the-box. She wondered for a split second if her *yiayia* had an ulterior motive for wanting that pillow in the case.

Time to load the cases up and see the women off. Hopefully they'd stay out of trouble up in Virginia Beach, but logic told her there would be some strife.

She piled them into the car and had them at the private landing strip in no time. *Greek aunt and* yiayia *equals drama of epic proportions.* The words danced around in her head, and she squashed them when Xen's private jet came into view. A familiar wolf stood on the tarmac ordering people around.

"Wow. Get a look at that, Vetta," Aunt Paula said to Carissa's grandmother. Aunt Paula was Yiayia's younger cousin and out of courtesy and because Paula had similar aged children, they called her aunt.

"That vampire is a sure catch," Yiayia said.

Carissa rolled her eyes. They liked the perks that came with Xen more than she did. She put the car in park and cut the engine. Before she could exit the doors to the car were opened by *Phi* members to help them out.

"Carissa." Kane Hart, Xen's right-hand man, and wolf, held his hand out to her.

"Good to see you. You think these two can behave on the flight." She tossed a thumb over her shoulder.

"Let's just say they won't be unsupervised."

"You know, they say where there's a will, there's a way." And Carissa knew full well that her aunt and *yiayia* could get into all sorts of trouble without trying too hard.

"What could they possibly get up to on a plane?" Kane's eyes sparkled.

"Kane, I'm going to pretend you didn't just say that."

"You know the assigned men will have eyes on them the whole time."

"And this has stopped them when?"

"Good point. Want me to get the men to strap them in their seats."

She let out a laugh. "That won't be necessary. Just tell them to be on their guard."

The men had removed the luggage from her car and were now loading it on the plane. Kane closed the trunk once they were out of the way. "Consider that done."

"Hey, toy boy," Yiayia yelled at Kane.

"It's boy toy and I'm not your boy toy," he growled.

Carissa raised an eyebrow. "Are you going to tell me why she calls you that?"

"Nope."

Yiayia winked at him. "Here, take my handbag and help me up the stairs." She shoved it at his chest then tugged on his muscled arm.

Carissa watched with interest.

"What about me?" Aunt Paula shouted, coming around to where Carissa was. "Why does she get an escort?"

"Did someone call for assistance?" A gravelly voice had both women turning.

A smile split across Carissa's face. "Adam."

He gave them a flash of his pearly whites.

Paula took a few steps in his direction. "My favorite wolf."

Her aunt and *yiayia* had helped nurse him back to health with soup and other Greek dishes when he was badly injured on a mission to save Zeus, Ares and a group of Greek gods that had been kidnapped by two Titans. Carissa had thought they'd lost him, but to her relief and to all of Xen's men he had survived.

"Where's my favorite aunt?" he said, pulling Paula into a hug. When he stepped back Paula was beaming.

"Rissa," he said, giving her a hug too.

"You know if Xen heard you…" She ran a finger across her throat. "…pfft."

"Well, he's not here, and we can have a bit of fun until the grumpy vampire wakes up."

"He's not grumpy." She had to defend her fiancé. "Maybe a tad brooding at times."

"That too," Adam threw in.

"It adds to that whole sexy vampire thing he's got going on," Paula added.

Carissa's head snapped back to her aunt. Her aunt had a point, but she didn't want to have that kind of discussion with her. Talking about Xen being droolworthy was something she discussed with her friends. Not her aunt. Time to change the subject and get the show on the road.

"Okay *Thitsa*, move it." She used the Greek endearment. "You need to catch up to Yiayia. She'll be sipping cocktails by now."

"Then we better giddy up. No way is Vetta going to have all the fun," Aunt Paula said.

Adam held out his arm to escort her up the stairs, and Carissa followed behind. Once inside Adam walked her aunt to where her grandmother was now seated.

"Get a load of all this space, Paula. I feel like Jackie Onassis," Yiayia said, beaming like a kid who had just been given a sugary treat.

Paula ran her hand over the leather seats in appreciation. "I feel like some socialite."

Carissa's chest expanded with joy. These women were important to her and a huge part of her life. Without them she wouldn't be the person she had become. She owed them and owed Xen for taking the time to ensure they would be not only protected, but to use his resources and private plane to give them a comfortable flight.

"It's time to go." She moved over and kissed her grandmother and then her aunt. "Behave and don't go looking for trouble."

Both women's mouths dropped open. "We don't go looking for trouble on purpose, *paidia mou*," Yiayia explained.

"It usually finds us," Paula added.

"No, seriously, both of you. You will have some of Xen's men nearby. If you see something odd, you contact them. Got it?"

They nodded their heads in understanding.

Yiayia got up and hugged Carissa. "You stay out of trouble too, and we should have all the wedding preparations done in no time."

And there it was again. The wedding talk. "Yiayia, just enjoy your time in Virginia, and we'll focus on that when you get back."

"Nonsense, Carissa. You have to start thinking about wedding dresses."

Shoot me now, she thought. She should leave the plane before this discussion got crazy.

"Okay, Kane, Adam. I think we should be off."

Both men said their goodbyes and followed Carissa out.

"Hey, boy toy. You make sure my granddaughter is looked after," Yiayia shouted to Kane. She then pointed to Adam. "I left some soup for you in the freezer. You need to keep your strength up."

Adam flashed her a toothy smile. "Thanks." Little did Yiayia know that Adam was fine. He had healed quickly after the skirmish, but he played along with both Yiayia and Aunt Paula because he loved the attention.

Back on the tarmac, Carissa took one look back up at the plane. Both women were at separate windows waving down at her. She touched her hand to her lips and blew them a kiss each. They did the same. It was going to be quiet without them.

"So, what's with you and the wedding?" Kane asked.

"Oh no. Not you too."

"Rissa. What's the problem?" Adam questioned.

"They wanted to turn it into a circus, and Xen is just letting them have a field day. It's going to be a big fat Greek supernatural wedding."

"Nothing wrong with that."

"Adam, that's not what I want."

They came to a stop at her car. Kane opened the door for her. "Then tell Xen."

"I can see he gets a kick out of watching my *yiayia* and aunt fuss. I don't want to ruin that for him."

"But if it's not what you want then you need to be clear."

"I hear you. I'll sort it out with Xen."

"Good."

She gave Kane a hug then hugged Adam. He stepped back. "We'll see y'all later on."

She nodded, but a rock formed in the pit of her stomach as she climbed in behind the wheel. Something didn't feel right. She just couldn't put a finger on what it was. Maybe it was her *yiayia* and aunt leaving. As crazy as it got it was nice having them around.

Her thoughts were running rabid and crazy. They'd probably get into trouble.

FIVE

"Ares whipped the fighting spirit in each man." ~ Homer, The Iliad

Yiayia's house; Charleston, SC
Evening, mortal realm – Day 2

A breeze wafted through the open window. The familiar signature danced in the air. Her father's—Ares. One she recognized before he materialized in the room.

"*Kori mou.*"

She stepped into his open arms for a hug. "What brings you here?" she asked when he released her.

"Zeus has summoned us for a final hearing on the death of Hal."

Halirrhothius or Hal, which she called him, was a demi-god like Carissa, who had kidnapped her. During one of his demented episodes, she was hurt and lost her baby. Her father had killed him on the spot. Poseidon wanted to punish Ares for the death of his demi-god son. The gods agreed to a trial. The first god ever to be tried for murder—Ares, her father. Carissa wanted Poseidon to answer for neglecting his son and for his actions against her.

"I hadn't expected it yet." Her voice rose a few pitches higher.

"Nope. It's definitely in line with my father's thinking."

She studied her father for a moment. "I guess you are right."

"Are you ready now?"

"No, she's not." Xen's deep voice sounded from the doorway. He entered the room.

"The question was not directed to you, vampire."

Xen's fangs elongated. "I will not have you whisking her away again without some thought or plan."

"I have had time to prepare for any courtroom drama."

Xen closed the distance and came toe to toe with Ares. "Have you?"

If she let this go on, they would just keep amping it up. She stuck her palms together and slid her joined hands between both powerful beings. Then she pushed her hands outward to nudge them apart. "Enough. Both of you. How many times do I have to tell you I can make my own decisions, and I too can prepare if needed."

They moved a few steps apart and Xen let out a low growl. Then retracted his fangs.

Her father turned his attention to her. "It is your choice if you want to come with me now or you wish me to return when you are ready?"

"Some time would be nice," she said. In truth she wasn't ready yet for another round of godly courtroom dramas but not going soon also delayed the result of her father's pending court case. "How will you know when I am ready?"

Time moved differently between the Olympian realm and the human one. One day with the Greek gods would be equal to three days on the mortal plain.

"Use your power of *anagke,* but only with me, and be very careful when you summon me."

Ah, the power of compulsion. The one thing her father wanted her to control. If the gods all knew she could compel them to do her bidding she'd have an Olympus sized target on her back. Her father had bound her powers of compulsion as a baby because he feared she would be a target. The gods feared anyone with power that could be used against them, especially a demi-god. Ares had given her a spell to conceal her power but occasionally it would slip. Her grandfather, Zeus, knew of her ability, but so far he hadn't shown any resentment or worry over it.

She nodded. "Okay."

"*Kori,*" Ares said, returning her gesture. The air around her shifted, a small breeze lifted inside the house and the god-of-war dematerialized.

Xen moved beside her. "I don't want you to leave again."

"You know I have to see this through." She turned to face him.

"We have yet to process the events of our last visit to Olympus, and this time I will not be able to be with you."

"Xen, I know you take my protection seriously, but you must trust Father."

"It's not your father that I don't trust, it's the other gods."

"Let's face it, we are never going to fully believe them." She contemplated everything for a moment. "I need a chance to see who is on my side, and we need to get closure on the whole Hal incident."

"What about our wedding preparations?"

"Oh no, don't get me started on that. You've purposely let Yiayia and Aunt Paula go crazy with that. It's going to be mental."

A small laugh escaped his lips.

She slapped his arm and it resembled hitting a hard stone column. There was nothing weak or soft about Xen. He and his men trained vigorously, and it showed.

"Would it put your mind at ease if I armed myself to the hilt before I stepped on Olympus."

"Now that would give me comfort," he said, pulling her to him. He wrapped his arms around her.

"Got any new fancy weapons I can take for a trial run?"

"Something tells me anything I give you won't work on any of the Greek Gods."

"It can slow them down, and that's all I need."

"Good point, *koukla.*" He tightened his grip, and she knew what was coming. His lips crashed to hers. When his tongue began a dance with hers, he moaned deeply.

She reciprocated with a small mewl of satisfaction.

He pulled back. "Careful. I might have to take you upstairs."

"You know I should pack and call my father back. The sooner I can resolve things on Olympus, the more time I will have to focus on us." She left the wedding out on purpose.

"Speaking of us... since it looks like Yiayia and Aunt Paula have the wedding arrangements in motion," he stuck his hand in his pocket and pulled out a little black box, "why don't we make things official?"

Her mouth dropped open. "Xen, we need to talk about the wedding. It's ballooning into something ridiculous. I want something small."

His lips turned up in amusement. "I think your *yiayia* and aunt said something about the Spoleto festival."

Her skin heated and blood rushed to her head. "You are kidding me?"

"No. They were serious, and I have already booked it."

"I am not having a reception at some football sized venue." She placed her hands on her hips. "I don't even know that many people."

"*Koukla*, why is this upsetting you so much?"

Small beads of sweat lined her forehead. No one was listening to her, not even Xen. All she wanted was something small with direct family and close friends. Not the whole crowd at some playoff in a final. "What is the matter with you all. It's just a wedding. There doesn't need to be any over the top fanfare. Is that what you really want, Xen?"

She thought he was a private person. He didn't do interviews, and people knew very little about his personal life. All anyone knew was that he was a billionaire who owned Phi Technologies. A company that also supplied everything his *Phi Athanatoi* warriors needed, and more. That he wanted a big wedding was baffling to her. Vampires were secretive. She watched him as he raised an eyebrow at her.

"You are making a big deal."

Her mouth dropped open. This was not her Xen—he didn't say stuff like that.

"I'm going to pretend you didn't just say that. I'm not making a big deal. You and my family are. I'd like a small deal. A very, very small deal."

He popped the box open and held out a diamond ring.

She looked at it. To call it gorgeous would have been an understatement, it was spectacular. A wide band with a huge, brilliant cut diamond at the center and smaller diamonds in a pavé design all the way around the band. Her mouth dropped open. Yes, she wanted this, but not unless they could both agree their wedding would not be some Ancient Greek comedy.

He pulled his hand back when she hesitated. "Maybe my timing is not right."

"Xen, I..." She dropped her head, needing a few seconds of clarity before raising it again to meet his sea green eyes. "...I can't do this right now."

By vampire law they were already married. They had bonded by exchanging blood. She wanted to be Mrs. Lyson in mortal terms too, but the fact that he could not see past his entertainment of a colossal wedding had dampened the whole idea of being hitched for her family's sake.

He closed the box and put it back in his pocket. "I want you to be happy, *koukla*. I will rein in Yiayia and Aunt Paula's wedding arrangements."

She had serious doubts he'd be able to control those two. Carissa had a sneaking suspicion their entertainment of the evening would involve clowns. A circus of epic proportions if someone didn't try to slow them down. She stepped toward him, and he pulled her in tight.

"Was that your way of saying no." His voice, low and husky, sent an ache in her heart.

"You know it's a yes but not until we can agree on the same thing."

"Noted, *koukla*. Can't say that I'm not affected by your rejection." He dropped his lip in a fake pout.

"That's not true and you know it, Xen."

He looked up to the ceiling. "You forget, *koukla*, that I'm a vampire, and I can read all your emotions as well as, occasionally, hear your thoughts."

"Was I projecting?"

"No, you weren't, and for once I couldn't pick up a thing. You are getting a handle on your power."

Her power had been erratic. She had slowly been coming to grips with it. "Good, stay out of my head."

"I can't help it if you sometimes think aloud."

She had an idea. She dropped her mental wall. *Vampire, kiss me.*

Are you teasing? he sent to her mind.

No, I want a hundred percent bona fide kiss before I go pack, she spoke back to him.

She hadn't time to register his next move. He dipped her and plundered her mouth with a deep bone melting kiss. She responded with the same fever pitch. He moaned deeper in her mouth. A light breeze whipped around them. A loud thud brought them out of their passionate haze.

Xen had her upright and his fangs were elongated. He was ready.

What I'd do for reflexes like that, she internalized. She looked to where the noise had come from and found a familiar god on the floor.

"Koal." She rushed forward to help him up. "What are you doing here?"

"Zeus wants you on Olympus pronto. He said something about seeing you before the court case."

Carissa looked back toward Xen. Displeasure danced across his features.

"Koal, what is the meaning of this?" he asked.

To his credit he puffed out his chest and stood to his height. Koal was as clumsy as they came, a minor god of stupidity and foolishness. In modern terms he was the court jester for the gods. Carissa flashed a smile at his bravado.

"Sorry Xen, but don't shoot the messenger. I'm just delivering the head kahuna's words."

Xen stepped forward. "Elaborate."

"He sent me to retrieve Carissa because he has something important to offer. He didn't say, and I wasn't going to question him."

"Koal, is there something else going on?" Carissa asked.

"Apart from your father's case. No. Nothing. That doesn't mean that it can't change in an instant with the gods."

"This unsettles me," Xen directed at Carissa.

"Does seem odd because Father was just here."

"Wait. What. Ares was here?"

"Yes, he came to collect me." She paused. "I asked him to give me some time."

"Then why would Zeus ask me to collect you if your father was already on the job?" Koal's face contorted.

Carissa raised an eyebrow. "I guess then there is more to it than just Father's court case."

"I think you should prepare before you go."

"Xen, apart from weapons, there is nothing more I can do in preparation, and to be honest, if any of them did want to do me harm they'd find a way, and you know it."

"And this is what makes me uneasy."

"You can't protect me every single minute of the day."

"That much is true, but when you are in the realm of the gods, I can't get to you."

Koal stepped forward. "She does have friends."

A smile tore across Carissa's face. Yes, she'd made a friend in Koal. "I know you've got my six," Carissa said.

He nodded several times. "You can count on me."

For whatever reason she had immediately liked Koal when she met him during her investigation on Olympus. Her father had also bound Koal to Carissa by a sacred *orkos*. Ares was the only one who could release him from the oath. As long as it remained in place, Koal could not betray Carissa. Not that she worried. Even before her father reacted, she had a bone deep connection to this clumsy minor god.

"*Koukla*, I would prefer that you didn't go as yet."

"Xen, you know that if my grandfather has requested my appearance this could mean something else."

"I know." He closed the distance and pulled her to him. "Take your sword at least."

"Done, and I'll do you one better. I'll take a gun too." Not a lot of use on the Olympian gods, but hey, it would slow down minor gods and goddesses if something went sideways.

"How about I supply the gun and bullets?"

He wasn't going to let it rest until she agreed. "Done."

He planted a searing kiss on her lips and was gone.

"Where did…" Koal didn't finish his sentence. His mouth hung open.

Xen appeared with a gun and her sword. "Now you're ready."

He planted a chaste kiss on her lips and stepped back.

"Koal, do your thing," she said.

He put a hand on her shoulder and they dematerialized. She landed in her father's rooms with no one in sight. She had been delivered like a parcel with no one to receive her. A definite leave the package without a signature moment. Unease washed through her.

SIX

"It will not always be summer: gather the harvest while you can." ~ Hesiod

Paula's house; Virginia
Morning, mortal realm – Day 3

"Hello."

"Yeah, hi ma'am. Am I speaking with Vetta Atheneous?"

"That's me."

"I've got that quote for a marquee, chairs, tables and a dance floor. I can email it across."

"Hang on a minute." She put the phone to her chest. "Paula," she shouted.

"I'm in the kitchen."

"Do you have an email?"

"Quit shouting." Paula appeared before her. "Here, let me." She held out her hand.

Vetta passed the phone to Paula.

"It's G r e e k c o u g e r at gmail dot com."

Vetta started laughing.

"Okay, right thanks," Paula said, then hung up. "Seriously, Vetta. It's just an email address."

Vetta couldn't help herself. She curled a hand into a claw. "Roar."

"Really, Vetta?"

"Well, you can't blame me, Paula."

"I have had that email address for years. My dear Alek was still alive."

Yiayia dropped her humor at the sound of Alek's name. He was a good man. "Okay Paula, just let me know when you get the quote. We need to start finalizing things. Do you think we should talk to Carissa?"

"Nonsense. We've got this covered," Paula assured her.

Vetta didn't think her granddaughter wanted the whole jumbo wedding, but she'd follow Paula's lead for now. It had been ages since they'd had a wedding, and she had to admit it made her heart swell to finally see Carissa wed. "What now?"

Paula clapped her hands together. "I forgot. We must start researching cakes. How large do you think the cake should be? Four tiers or five tiers?"

"Depends on how many guests."

"That's what I was thinking too. Otherwise we'd be forced to give everyone a little square."

"We wouldn't want that. Can you imagine the gossip about not enough cake on the plate?" Vetta rolled her eyes for emphasis.

"Okay, we'll get the biggest one we can." Paula tapped her head. "So what's on our agenda today?"

"I want to check something out."

"When you say you want to check something out, does this mean you want to go stick your nose where it doesn't belong."

"My nose is always where it belongs, on my face."

"Vetta. We can't go looking for trouble. After what happened in Charleston you should know better."

They'd been attacked by demons while snooping around in a bakery. Vetta had managed to taser one. Xen and his men had swooped in and saved them.

"Relax, Paula. We're doing things in daylight this time."

"And that's supposed to give me some comfort?"

"We'll be fine."

"Sure. That's what you said last time."

"This isn't like last time."

"Why, because it's daylight? Seriously Vetta, you must have a death wish."

She wasn't far from the truth there. For some reason Vetta had an invisible pull that had her wanting to live a little dangerously lately. Something ailed her, but she didn't want to think about it too much. She made her choices and she would live by them.

"Oh, come on Paula. We could sit on the porch and drink sweet tea all day, or we could get out a bit."

"Well, when you put it that way, there's only so much tea drinking we could do."

Vetta moved over to the table and picked up her handbag. "Ready when you are."

"Let me grab my purse and keys," Paula said as she dashed out of the kitchen.

Vetta made her way out the front and to the car parked in the driveway. Across the road was a black SUV.

Xen's men.

The vampire had promised her they would be close by. She'd have to speak to him. She didn't want him wasting his resources on her and Paula.

"Right, Vetta. Let's go."

Paula unlocked the car and Vetta opened the door, threw her walking stick in first then got in. They both fastened their seat belts at the same time. "Where to, Vetta?"

"I need to talk to Soteria."

Paula's mouth dropped open. "You haven't spoken to Soteria in twenty years. Why now?"

"The tide is shifting Paula, and we have to make sure Carissa is safe."

"What about our escorts across the road?"

"Just act normal. I have a plan on how to ditch them."

Paula turned and looked at her. "What harebrained idea are you cooking up now?"

"Head to Pembroke Mall. We're going to ditch these boys."

Paula reversed the car and navigated down the street slowly. Sure enough, Xen's men followed. If all went as Vetta had thought out, those boys would lose them in the throng of shoppers.

"What are you thinking, Vetta."

Vetta cleared her throat. "We will have to leave your car and catch a cab to Soteria's house."

"What?" Paula swerved.

"Relax."

"What if they smash my car?"

"Paula, no one is going to smash your car. We won't be gone that long. You spend longer looking for shoes."

"Well, that may be true. But you're forgetting Xen's men are not dummies."

"And you're forgetting my husband was Kekrops and the king of Athens. I can pull a good poker face if I have to tell a little white lie."

"Oh, I know that."

"Then trust me."

"I do, it's just you seem to attract a lot of trouble wherever you go."

"Like you don't?"

Paula pulled up her nose and twitched it. Then let out a laugh. "I must be crazy."

"Atta girl." Vetta cheered, swinging her arm with gusto.

A few minutes later Paula pulled into the parking lot of Pembroke. Their guards parked a few cars away.

"Let's not tarry, Paula. The faster we ditch them the better."

They both got out of the car and made their way into the shops. "I think we'll head for the ladies' lingerie."

"You need some underwear? I have plenty of new spares at home."

"No Paula, I don't need underwear."

"Then why are we heading toward underwear."

"Get your head into the here and now. Here, I'll spell it out for you—when we go sifting through the bras those boys will walk away. You wait and see."

Paula gave her one of her looks that said *you are bonkers*, but Vetta knew Paula thought she was crazy most of the time.

They moved through the throng of shoppers. Vetta didn't need to look back to know Xen's boys were not far behind. They were off like a herd of turtles—she could only move so fast with her walking stick. She navigated Paula toward Target. She didn't let Paula stop and look at anything along the way either.

"Won't they get suspicious. I mean we look like we're racing through."

"Oh please. We're slower than molasses running uphill in January."

"You're joking. I've raised a sweat."

They reached the underwear section. "Make like you're looking for bras. I'll do the same, and when you see them walk in the other direction, we make a run for it."

Paula walked a bit farther away, mumbling as she pretended to look at bras.

Vetta looked up to see Xen's men eyeing them. She pulled an over-the-shoulder bolder holder from the rack and put it up against her boobs. Trying the size. She glanced over at Xen's men, and they had a pained look on their faces. She suppressed the wicked smile threatening to explode, and it did when their guards turned in the other direction.

"Come on, Paula."

"I can't believe that, that stupid trick worked."

"Believe it. One thing I've picked up from Xen and his men, they might be bad ass and you might not want to meet them in a dark alley, but that's only if you are an enemy. They protect and respect innocent people."

"Hey, you rhymed."

"That's what you take away from what I said?"

"I heard what you said. I was merely pointing out that you rhymed."

Vetta huffed. They only had a small window, and they needed to giddy up. They wove through the center and came out at a different end. Paula was panting.

Vetta pulled her phone out and pressed a couple of numbers. She waited until the automated system asked where she was being collected from. "Pembroke Mall, Kohl's entrance." She paused as the auto system asked where to. "Thalia Road." She hung up.

"Why do I get a bad feeling about this."

"Paula, you get a bad feeling about everything."

"I must be psychic."

"I wouldn't call stressing over the trouble we will be in for ditching Xen men, psychic."

"Why do you need to see Soteria now? Couldn't you have just invited her over?"

"No, Paula. The sooner we see her the better."

"Why are you being so cryptic and secretive?"

"I'm not being secretive. We need to see her, and I don't want to talk out in the open."

"You could have told me in the car."

"No, this is something we have to discuss all together."

The cab arrived and they got in. Vetta hoped Soteria would not hold a grudge for twenty years. It wasn't her fault her husband had a falling out with Soteria's husband. Life consisted of ups and downs, and sometimes people got caught in the crossfire of what was going on in other people's lives.

"Vetta, we're here."

She hadn't realized she'd drifted into her own thoughts.

"I'll get this one," Paula said, pulling out her wallet to pay the cab fare.

She'd get the one on the way back. "Thanks."

They got out and the cab took off. "You looked like you were wool gathering."

"You could say that." Vetta made her way to the door. There were two ways this was going to go, and they were about to find out which way. She rang the doorbell and swallowed a gulp of air.

The door swung open and a woman with dark hair and a clear complexion answered.

"Hello Vetta and Paula. Please come in."

Not the welcome she was expecting. Soteria held the door and they stepped into the foyer.

"You're twenty years late," Soteria said, the door closing with a soft click.

Paula spoke first. "You were expecting us?"

"Not you, Paula. We haven't been as estranged."

Vetta mustered as much nerve as she could to talk to the goddess of protection. "I didn't think you would welcome me."

Soteria let out a laugh. "You should have come earlier, Vetta."

"You're not still mad?"

"Why would I be?"

"Kekrops, or rather Kerry, said I would not be greeted with a smile."

"Oh, for goddess' sake, Vetta. We exchanged words like most adults do when they don't agree. Kerry took it the wrong way."

"I had no idea."

"That's why you should have visited earlier. Let's sit down." Soteria ushered both women to the lounge.

"Do you want something to drink?"

Paula was about to open her mouth, but Vetta jumped in. "We're fine. We haven't much time."

"What brings you here?"

"It's my granddaughter, Carissa. I fear for her. I need you to protect her."

"I have seen your granddaughter and I don't think she needs it."

"Where?"

Soteria turned her head to the left and a man appeared where she was looking. One minute he was upright, the next flat on the floor.

He lifted his head and scanned the room. "Rough landing." He got to his feet. "Zeus has requested your presence, Soteria."

Paula gasped.

"Talk about bad timing," Vetta said.

"If you're here, Koal. That means Carissa is already on Olympus."

"She is."

49

"Why have you come for me in particular? Last time we were all sent a blanket request via Hermes."

"Well, you know Zeus, the all-seeing-all-knowing god." Koal shrugged his shoulders. "He said that whatever Carissa's *yiayia* asks for, you'd be wise to grant the request." He turned to look at Vetta.

Vetta's body started to tingle. A heavy rock settled in her stomach. Zeus had foreseen her intention. She knew right then there were things in motion, and everyone had a part to play, and hers was as simple as requesting, but asking any god or goddess came with a price. One she was now not afraid of.

"Soteria. I have come here today to ask to bestow your safety and protection on my granddaughter."

"Your granddaughter is the daughter of Ares. Why would she need anything more?"

"Let's just say I'm covering my bases, and your deliverance from any harm for my Carissa would soothe my aged mind."

Soteria eyed Vetta. "Granted."

"Good. Now we can get back to business on Olympus. If you are ready, Soteria."

"I don't need a bumbling fool to assist me. I can make my own way there."

She dematerialized, leaving Koal behind.

"I get that a lot," he said to Vetta and Paula.

Vetta got up and stepped forward. "Is my Carissa…" Her mouth felt dry.

"She's fine. Besides, she's got me looking out for her."

"Should we be worried?" Paula asked from where she sat.

"I am bound to her by the sacred *orkos*."

"What does that mean?" Vetta asked.

"That I cannot betray Carissa."

"You give her our regards," Vetta said.

"I will."

Wind whipped around the room before he too dematerialized.

Paula got to her feet. "I guess we can let ourselves out."

SEVEN

"We know nothing for sure: truth is hidden at the bottom of a well." ~ Diogenes Laertius

Ares' Chambers; Mount Olympus
Morning, realm of the gods – Day 1

Her father had yet to materialize. Her mouth felt dry and she wished he would hurry up. It would be unwise to use her compulsion to summon him on Olympus. Any power she used here the gods would scent like hounds. Carissa pulled the bottle of milk from the fridge and poured some in an ancient cup. "It would be good if they kept coffee up here," she whispered.

She put the milk away and took a sip from her cup. The familiar taste awoke her tastebuds. "Coffee." It all came back to her. The cups on Olympus were magical. One only had to speak their desire and the beverage would appear or alter. A perk she needed to remember. She took another savored drink then put the cup back on the bench.

Her fingers began to tingle, and warmth spread into her palm. It grew hot and looked like fire, but it disappeared the moment she recognized Koal's signature. He materialized all floppy right beside her. She lost balance and tipped sideways to the ground.

"So… sorry Carissa," he said. Bending to help her up.

She swatted his hand. "I'm fine."

"I didn't mean…"

She held her hands up to stop any further apology, and he sealed his lips shut in a manner that had her laughing.

"You know Koal, you really have to work on your zapping in and out abilities."

"Don't I know it."

"Is something wrong?"

"I came to warn you not to accept any gifts from any of the gods."

"Why?"

"Everything the gods bestow upon you comes at a price."

She turned his words over in her mind. "That is already known to me."

"I know but I wanted to make sure."

Koal knew something, but he wasn't sharing. His eyes widened in warning. And that was all the hint she needed. She knew he feared saying anything in case someone was listening in, and here on Olympus someone was always listening in.

"*Philaso.*" She spoke the spell to the room. "You can tell me now."

Koal's posture went from ridged to relaxed. He moved over to the dining table and sat down. "You might need a seat."

Carissa raised an eyebrow. "That bad, huh?"

"I wouldn't call it that but rather a word of caution."

She pushed a chair out and sat. "Well, out with it."

"I have heard that Zeus is going to grant you a boon."

"What kind?"

"Possibly the type you want to be wary of."

"You know we're talking in circles."

Koal rubbed the back of his neck. "What I mean to say is don't accept anything he gives you."

"How do you know he's going to give me something?"

"I overheard."

"Are you sure he didn't know you were there and just said it to test you? This is Zeus we're talking about. The all-knowing, all-seeing God."

Koal dropped his head and looked down at the table. "Right, I didn't think about that." Silence filled the room.

She was about to say something when Koal lifted his head and met her eyes. His lips curved upward in a grin. "He would not have known I was there because I was wearing Hades' cap. I was invisible."

"Surely he would have felt your presence, even if he couldn't see you."

"Not with the cap. It keeps my presence and power completely concealed."

"Okay, so let's say you heard him saying he wanted to grant me a favor… we still don't know what that could be, and I don't see how it could be any different from the necklace Athena gave me?"

"There will come a time Carissa when Athena will ask something of you. Nothing is given without something being returned."

Her fingers had automatically gone to the necklace. *Surely not.* This changed everything and not necessarily for good, but she didn't pick up that vibe. "Koal, what if you're wrong?"

"I hope for your sake that I am."

"It appears I'm just another pawn in their game." Her shoulders slumped. Oh, how she wanted to believe they would accept her as family and their usual frolicking and intervention in human lives didn't apply to her.

"Knowledge is power, Carissa."

Koal was right, but what benefit did he gain from this? "And what's your excuse? Will you come calling for favors because you helped me?"

He shot to his feet. "I am not like them. I don't play with human lives and certainly don't have the power to grant wishes."

She held up her hands to calm him down. It was uncalled for on her part. She wanted to be sure. "Koal, I'm sorry. I did not mean it like that. I was curious. How am I to know what can be granted and what cannot?"

He sat back down.

She reached over and put her hand on one of his. "I'm sorry.

You're a friend, and I accepted our friendship from the moment you tumbled into the interview room."

His face lit up at the memory. "That was some entrance, wasn't it?"

She let out a giggle. "My father didn't think so."

"No. He didn't."

She removed her hand and sat back. "So don't go accepting favors from gods unless I think about them."

"Yes."

"Got it and I am grateful for your warning."

"Think nothing of it. I'm on your side. The politics up here suck but that's a story for another time."

"Really, you guys get political?"

Koal rolled his eyes. "You have no idea."

A laugh bubbled in her chest. "I guess no one is free of mad men trying to dictate what's good for the people."

"Happens everywhere and we might have started the whole thing."

"The Olympian gods invented everything," she said, trying to lighten the mood.

His face turned serious. "They did."

It was her turn to roll her eyes. She had an uncle that would say the Greeks invented everything, now she was reliving the same thing, only here the Greek gods invented everything. She really did want to laugh but it would only serve to upset Koal, and she didn't want to do that again.

"So, what else has been happening up here whilst I've been in the mortal realm?"

"The same stuff."

"How are things with you and Eurynome?"

"We moved in together."

"That's wonderful." She truly was happy for him. Eurynome was the goddess of water, meadows and pasturelands and had been drained of her powers by Kronos and Iapetos. Her father Ares put her in a state of statis to keep her safe, but when the Titans kidnapped other gods and goddesses and drained their power everything had started to slowly die in the mortal realm. All gods, even minor ones, held various power in all the spheres of the mortal world. Carissa, Xen and some of the gods and goddesses won the fight against Kronos and Iapetos, and power was restored to those who had suffered.

"Well, speaking of Eurynome, I should be getting back to her." He got to his feet.

Carissa jumped up too. "Thanks, Koal." She stepped in and gave him a hug.

"Just remember, don't accept anything first up."

"I promise."

He dematerialized.

She hadn't had enough time to reflect on her conversation with Koal before she recognized her father's signature. He materialized before her.

"*Kori mou,*" he greeted and pulled her into his warm embrace.

He stepped back. His face grim.

"What's wrong?"

"This isn't going the way I had hoped."

"The court case?" she asked.

"Yes, it seems that my uncle Poseidon is hell-bent on trying to convince the other jurors to vote against me."

"How is that fair?"

"It's not but these are the gods and they bend the will of most."

"Well then tell your father."

"One thing you don't do is bring in the big guns until you need them."

"But if your uncle is not stopped then he will succeed in turning everyone against you."

"That is true. However my sister, Athena, is trying to undo the damage as we speak. She can be persuasive."

"Then why the long face?"

"My uncle is not the type of man that would have a plan A only. I'm sure he knows I would try to intercept, and he would therefore plan something else to ensure his outcome."

Carissa shook her head, trying to dislodge the craziness of it all. "Seriously, you gods need a hobby."

Ares let out a laugh. "Indeed, we do, *kori mou*." He raised an eyebrow. "What do you say we go block my uncle from pestering the other gods?"

"How do you propose we do that?"

"We have a gathering of sorts."

"You want to throw a party?"

"Something like that, *kori mou*. A big fat symposium should do the trick."

A smile tore across her face at the same time as her father's. "Let's get this party started."

He zapped them out of the room, and they landed in the middle of what looked like a Corinthia Hotel in London. She only knew of it because her cousin, Chloe, Aunt Paula's daughter, had sent her photos.

"Father, this room…"

"Resembles a popular hotel in London, only it's bigger in every way."

She faked a laugh. "Yes, but why?"

"Hestia thought it would be ideal to renovate when she was going through an *I love the UK* streak, so this…" he waved his arms around, "…is the result of that phase."

Carissa rolled her eyes. "So, let me get this straight. You guys go through phases?"

"Why wouldn't we? You were all created in our likeness, so yes, we have fetishes that don't last."

She filed that little nugget away. She'd bet her last dollar and the coins in her London bus shaped money box that even the gods' and goddesses' architectural fetishes probably extended to other parts of Olympus. "Where's the crowd?" she asked.

"Don't worry, they'll be here in a minute."

True to his word, gods and goddesses started to materialize all around the room. Waiters also started to circulate amongst the throng that had filled the room.

"How did they even know?" she asked.

"I sent a mental message to a few and then it just spread."

"Who needs social media when you have brain connectivity to the gods and goddesses?" she muttered under her breath.

Ares let out a laugh. "Indeed, *kori mou*."

"Yo, what's up, Ares?" An unfamiliar god clapped him on the back. Then turned to walk backwards. "Good to see you hosting one of your famous parties. It's been too long." He flipped around again and moved amongst the crowd growing by the second.

"How about you take that end and I'll take this one. Get conversation going and see what the feel is."

"You really think they'll give away which way they are going to vote?"

"Trust me, *kori mou*. Give these gods enough ambrosia and wine and their lips loosen."

"That easy, huh?"

"You have no idea."

She smiled at her father and then moved through the throng of gods. Some paid her no attention. Others gave her the good top to bottom once over and then looked away. Many of the faces were known to her. She had interviewed most of them when an attempt on Zeus' life was made during her father's first hearing. The reactions toward her were expected and interesting. This was going to be a tough crowd.

Someone tapped her on the shoulder.

She turned.

"Greetings, Carissa."

Two sets of eyes from familiar faces looked at her. The smiles were genuine.

"Phthonos, Nemesis. Nice to see you both."

"As it is to see you too," Nemesis said. They both gave a small nod of their heads.

"Your father hasn't thrown a party in ages," Phthonos said.

She raised an eyebrow. "I didn't know it was a regular thing for him."

"Are you kidding? He's the bad boy of Olympus. Parties are his signature."

"Come, let's get you a drink." Nemesis tugged at her arm, interlocking it with hers.

"I won't say no to that. Looks like it's going to be a long night."

They made their way to the bar with Phthonos right behind them. "You seem popular tonight, Carissa."

"If you take a closer look, Phthonos, it's not popularity. Some of these gods and goddesses look like they want to kill me," she shouted back.

"It's not murder, Carissa. It's curiosity and something a little more… envy."

She stopped walking with Nemesis and turned. "That's jealousy, isn't it?"

"Yes and no, and you need to be able to distinguish between the two because they are different. There is good envy, known as benign and also malicious which over time can lead to jealousy, my darker side."

"Wait. Are you saying you are like a Dr. Jekyll and Mr. Hyde god?"

Phthonos flashed her a smile. "You catch on quick, Carissa. I'm exactly that, although I prefer to swim in the waters of envious love."

"Sooo envy is your game?"

"And you are getting spades of that from all these gods." He waved an arm around him.

"Where do you fit in Nemesis?"

"You can say that I bring balance."

"Balance to any situation?" Carissa queried.

"Correct."

"Should I worry you might be against Father."

"I will listen to both sides of the story and make my judgment in the end."

A rock formed in Carissa's stomach. It could go either way. "Who do you think will be the one to tip the balance in my father's favor?"

"Themis," Phthonos and Nemesis said at the same time.

She looked between them. "Come on. Let's get a drink first. We have a goddess to find."

They continued through the throng of gods and goddesses and the looks she'd been getting before hadn't ebbed. The fish out of water saying applied one hundred percent to her situation right now. Hopefully any interest in her would die down as they consumed their ambrosia mixed wine. They shuffled closer to the bar.

"Two ambrosias and one regular wine," Phthonos yelled to the barman. Before Carissa could blink the drinks were on the bench waiting for them.

"Now that's what I call service," she whispered.

The barman winked. "Never keep a god or goddess waiting."

EIGHT

"As a matter of self-preservation, a man needs good friends or ardent enemies, for the former instruct him and the latter take him to task." ~ *Diogenes*

Xen's mansion; Charleston, SC
Evening, mortal realm – Day 3

"What do you mean you lost them?" Xen's voice vibrated down the receiver of the phone. He had been pulled out of his rejuvenation sleep early. Something had compelled him to rise earlier than usual. Now he knew why?

"They tricked us."

"How do two old ladies trick trained *Phi Athanatoi* warriors?" His fangs pulsed and anger ripped through his body. "Everyone under-estimates older women, including you two who are hundreds of years older."

"We're sorry, boss."

"Find them now." He pulled the phone from his ear and hung up.

The door to his study opened. "You're up early," Kane said before dropping in the chair in front of his desk.

Xen looked across to Kane.

"Whatever it is, it's not good," Kane filled in.

"Yiayia and Aunt Paula." Xen let out a frustrated breath.

Kane started to shake his head. "What kind of trouble are they in now?"

"They've ditched the men."

Kane's eyebrows rose to his hairline. "You're kidding?"

"I wish I were."

"You think they're in trouble."

"No, but I know they are up to something, and I intend to get to the bottom of it."

"Want Adam to do his I.T. thing?"

"Yes, see if he can find anything on the street cams."

"He will."

"Good, I'm counting on it."

"You need anything else?"

"No. I have a few things to do."

"Want company?"

"Not tonight."

"Is something eating you up?"

A ball formed in Xen's stomach. He reined it in and got control. Carissa's refusal of his engagement ring had wound him tight. It hurt more than he cared to admit. "I'm a big boy. I'll handle it."

Kane threw his hands up in surrender. "Here if you need an ear."

The lykos was a good friend and loyal, but right now Xen needed space to brood and think. "I know where to find you."

Kane got to his feet. "Talk when I have something on our escapees." Humor danced in his tone, and his lips quirked up in added amusement.

"You know this isn't funny."

"Lighten up boss. You knew both Yiayia and Aunt Paula would not have made surveillance detail boring."

"True."

"But to lose the detail entirely is another thing. Our men are slipping."

"Our men don't know how to look after old women. They are trained for tactical experiences."

"Point made. I guess this is way outside the parameters that is the norm for them. Adam will find them," Kane said.

"I'm counting on it." Xen got to his feet too, grabbed his keys and phone and raced out of the room at vampire speed without another word. The velocity from his Porsche would be the balm to soothing his brooding mood.

He revved the engine. The sound purred in his ears. He smiled to himself then put the car into gear and exited from his underground parking. The wheels ate up the road and for a split second it gave him a small reprieve, but that didn't last. An image of Carissa flooded his mind and his thoughts turned opaque.

The senseless driving had done little to soothe him. He headed for his Phi Technologies organization. Time to throw himself into some work. There were a few unresolved matters he wanted to finalize. Something was bothering him about the libation bowl he had recently tracked down. It was an item Carissa's grandfather had been trying to find before he was killed. Why? He had no idea. Despite that he intended to find out what mysteries the bowl held.

He parked the Porsche and made his way to the elevators. Inside he removed a card key and slotted it into the space below the keypad. Then hit the number to take him two floors beneath the underground carpark. When the doors opened to his testing floor, several staff greeted him.

"Mr. Lyson. Good to see you. Can I get you something?"

"No, thank you." He made his way toward his occasional office.

Small hushes of conversation circulated. His presence here was known to do that since he spent less time there these days.

On his desk sat the libation bowl in a special Perspex box designed to suppress any power emitting from the object. He had retrieved it from a black-market seller. Amazing what people would sell you for the right price. The man who sold it to him knew absolutely nothing about Greek pottery. He thought it nothing more than a fruit bowl.

He could feel it's ancient power. This bowl held a deep ritual history. What he did know about it was that it was Attic, Black and Red Figure, dating to 430 BC. The images of dancing women were not uncommon but in the center was Nike holding an *oinochoe*—jug and basket. What was unusual was it had an inscription written around it, however some parts were faded. He'd need to work those out. He tried reading the inscription internally again. *When gods and… are summoned… will be yours.* That was all he could make out. It was obviously a spell and one of the reasons he did not read it out loud. For to do so could trigger unwanted attention. He didn't want to paint more targets on his and his warriors' backs. They had their share of fighting off unearthly creatures that walked the earth at night.

A sudden urge to hunt said creatures punched him in the chest. He closed the door to his office and made his way back to the elevators. Once inside he used his key again to access the floor below and his new weapons and training area. The doors opened and he stepped out to an almost empty floor, save for his security guard.

"Mr. Lyson," the guard said with a nod.

"Evening," Xen replied and kept walking to the back toward a huge weapons room.

His team had developed a new gun with bullets that disintegrated demons on the spot. He hadn't armed himself when he'd left tonight, but that wasn't a problem here. He also carried a spare *xiphos*—sword—and other weapons in the boot of every car he drove. One could never be too prepared. The VA guns he had yet to integrate into the necessary arsenal he kept as back up.

He pressed the code on the door, and a whoosh of air hit his face. He entered and made quick work securing his gun holster and the new demon blaster guns he had been thinking about.

He finished gearing up and heard the ping of the elevator. He scented Adam before turning.

"Boss, what are you doing here?"

"I could ask you the same."

Adam entered the weapons room. "Going hunting, huh?"

"Something like that."

"Want company?"

Xen raised an eyebrow. Having Adam along meant conversation, and right now he needed to let off steam in some alone time. "No. I think it best to refrain from any interaction unless it's a fight."

"Roger that, and we've located Carissa's grandmother and aunt."

"Any details on how they managed to lose our men."

"Yeah, are you ready to hear it."

"Trust me, nothing will surprise me."

Adam had a smile on his face. "They went into the ladies' undergarments section and naturally our boys gave them space. They then took off."

Xen shook his head.

"You should see the footage," Adam said with a laugh.

"I'd rather not."

"Where are they now?"

"Back at Aunt Paula's house, and we have two teams watching them."

"Did you find out where they escaped to?"

"I have an address and it gets interesting."

Xen slid a knife in his vest pocket and tilted his head. "How so?"

"The occupant's name is Soteria Zeus."

Xen's mind spun in a hundred different directions. The goddess here and amongst them? That didn't make sense. Soteria was the goddess of safety and deliverance. What was she doing living in the human realm? The gods and goddesses were forbidden by Zeus to live amongst mortals. Something bigger was at play here. "Get the plane ready. We leave at midnight."

"Sure, Xen."

"I'll meet you at the airport." Xen headed to the elevator. Before stepping into the waiting car, he turned and watched Adam lift his cell phone to his ear. Tonight Xen needed to hunt. He hoped at least his endeavor to rid the earth of evil would prove lucrative.

Shell casings dropped to his feet. It hadn't taken Xen long to find a group of demons ready to pounce on a bunch of unsuspecting drunk young adults. They were staggering and laughing and oblivious to the demons following them. The first human girl to see one of the demons screamed and ran, then mayhem unfolded pretty fast. Some of the young group stumbled, but Xen had removed them from harm's way and told them to run by dropping his fangs in threat. He was thankful this was one of the times where their flight instincts kicked in. He'd had the pleasure of experiencing on more than one occasion humans struck dumb by what they saw. Their brains refused to trigger the flight response. Tonight was a better night.

Two demons had disappeared to nothing but goo. Thanks to the modified poisonous bullets. To the demons they were lethal, causing them to combust from the inside. The disintegration also helped in that it kept clean-up costs low.

The last demon came running toward Xen. With his vampiric speed he moved out of the way. The demon turned and came at him again, Xen moved again. He was toying with them. He dropped both guns into his holster and unsheathed his sword. This time he didn't move. He let the demon step into his space and with a swift movement his sword sliced through the air and through the flesh of the demon's neck. Blood spurted and rained down to the concrete along with the demon's body. Xen's hackles rose in those split seconds. He was not alone. His acute sense of smell told him it was not another demon.

He glanced down as the head of the demon rolled to stop at a pair of shiny black shoes. "Well done."

Xen's head snapped up to the face of the voice, and one thought ran through his mind. *Impossible.* The Titan before him was supposed to be locked in Tartarus. The very prison that Kronos and Iapetos were in now. The prison they had escaped from and wreaked havoc amongst the godly plain and human one. Until Carissa, along with Xen, Zeus and the other gods sent them back. It looked like his old foe had found a way out too.

"Why are you here, Damion?"

NINE

"Let us conduct ourselves so that all men want to be our friends and fear to be our enemies." ~ Alexander The Great

Streets of Charleston, SC
Midnight, mortal realm – Day 3

"Now is that a way to treat an old friend?"

Xen pointed a finger across to Damion and then to himself. "You and I are not friends."

Damion touched a hand to his chest. "Oh, how you wound me."

"Save the theatrics, Damion."

"Don't get me started on Greek theater. I'm sick of it. You have no idea how many times I have had to watch the same boring plays over and over in Tartarus."

"That's your problem and not mine."

Damion kicked the head of the demon in Xen's direction. "That's where you are wrong. It is very much your problem."

The head rolled and stopped near the body.

"I asked you a question. What are you doing here?"

"Oh that, that's not really important right now."

"I think it is." Xen sheathed his sword. Damion didn't scare him, but having him here certainly rattled him, and there wasn't much that could put a chink in his armor. Someone was playing them all.

"Let's just say I have unfinished business."

"Correction, you have no business here."

"You don't know everything, Xenocrates."

Xen tsked. The use of his full name meant nothing coming from someone who would no sooner become your friend and with the same breath leave you to the wolves. Xen didn't trust him and never would. "I know you don't belong here on the human plane, and if Zeus were to find out you are here…"

"*Zeus*? Zeus plays everyone, and you and all your minions are too stupid to see it."

"If you have a problem with the Olympian god then I suggest you take your problem to him directly." Xen knew that was impossible. Without an invitation he would not be allowed to step foot on Olympus.

"Maybe I want to bring Zeus here."

"You're wasting your time."

He snapped his fingers. "I don't think I am."

A horde of demons from behind Damion stepped around him.

Xen drew the guns and started to fire. Demons exploded into goo with each hit.

Tires screeched, and Kane, Adam and a few other men jumped out of two SUVs. They joined the fight. Demon bodies popped and others dropped. When Xen's path was clear to Damion, he holstered his guns and unsheathed his sword. This he wanted to enjoy. He wouldn't make the same mistake he had made a thousand years ago by letting Damion live. No, this time he'd finish him. He rushed to the spot where he had been. Only to find that he was not really there. It was a projection. He looked up and scanned the buildings to see where it was coming from. With his vampiric speed he found the room the projection was coming from. He looked around. It was empty. No projector even though it appeared that a beam came from the very spot he stood in. Trickery. Damion's voice had come from where the projection had been.

The curtain blew inward and Damion's scent lingered. He had been in this room. The question was, how long had he watched from up here? One thing was certain, Damion had used magic, the thing Zeus had thrown him in Tartarus for not long after Xen let him go. Although the trickery Damion had used was not dark magic, there was nothing to stop him from upping his game. It was, after all, what he was known for. Dark magic held many risks and dire outcomes. This was not good. Xen needed to find him and fast.

"Care to fill me in on who that guy is?" Kane asked, walking into the room and sliding his guns in their harness.

"Someone I thought was dead and buried."

"What does he want?"

"I don't know but whatever it is, nothing good will come of it. Zeus had banished him to Tartarus. He's a Titan."

"Not another one," Kane groaned out.

"My reaction exactly."

"What do we need to know about him?"

"That he is capable of dark magic and belongs to a group of *telkhines*."

"Not the same ones that created Poseidon's trident and the sickle of Kronos."

"The very same."

"Oh, fuck."

"Indeed."

Xen moved from the window and started a slow scan of the rooms. Kane followed behind. "Are you picking anything up?" Although his sense of smell was strong it didn't match Kane's. As a wolf his was far superior.

"No. It's as clear as it is empty."

They headed to the doorway and Xen stopped. "Are you picking that up."

"I am and it's coming from behind the door." He stepped around Xen and pushed the door closed.

Stapled to the back was a note. *The age of gods and heroes is coming to an end. A new administration will rise.*

"Sounds to me like he has a screw loose," Kane said.

"That and prepare for battle. He wants a war." Xen pulled the note from the door and slipped it in the pocket of his black cargo pants. He pulled the door open. Without a word they exited the building and crossed to where Xen's men were cleaning up any remaining demon bodies. The bodies would be burned at one of Xen's facilities out of town.

"Who and what?" Adam asked as he approached with Kane.

"A discussion we need to have, but not here."

"I take it he didn't want to dance with us a little longer."

"He's not the dancing type," Xen replied.

"Too bad. I've got some new moves." Adam tapped out a few steps.

"What, you're tap dancing now?" Kane asked.

"Mate, I'm always busting some moves."

"Mate?"

"What, you're an Aussie now too?" Kane shook his head.

"Nothing wrong with Aussies, mate, and knowing their lingo is handy. You never know who you're going to meet." He tapped the side of his head.

"Honestly Adam, sometimes I really think you are half a brick short of a full load."

"Cheer up, alpha. I'm just poking some fun at you."

"If you two have finished clowning around, I'll see you both at the airport." Xen took off toward his car. His anger had just crawled up a notch. He ran the message on the note over and over in this head. What was Damion planning, why here, why now and how in the gods' names did he escape Tartarus?

The gods had a mole amongst them, someone who was pulling the wool over their eyes, and that meant Carissa could be in trouble. He had to find a way to get a message to her, and that wouldn't be easy. Unearthly creatures like him did not get the privilege to dally or communicate with the gods unless it was by their own prerogative.

He pushed his foot farther down on the pedal. The speed didn't help, and that told him there wasn't a modicum of a chance he would be able to stem his anger on the flight to Virginia.

They landed on the tarmac with a thud, and it brought Xen out of the deep pensiveness that had not abated. He hated it when he couldn't control a situation. If his long life had taught him anything it was that there was no room for weakness, and right now, his encounter with the Titan had left him feeling nothing but powerless, and that did not bode well with him. Damion was not supposed to be in the human realm. He had been cast in Tartarus a long time ago. The fact that he was here rattled Xen more than he wanted to contemplate.

"Boss? You okay?" Kane asked while unbuckling his seat belt.

"I want answers."

"We'll get them."

"None of this is good."

"When has it been?"

Xen raised an eyebrow. "Point." He wasn't going to argue with his *lykos* friend.

"Come on, boys. Let's see what our favorite duo is up to," Adam shouted from the back.

Xen watched as Kane shook his head. "Reckon that wolf has a screw loose since his accident in the Kalypso's cave."

Xen let out a laugh for the first time that evening.

"He might have broken more than just a few bones." Kane shrugged his shoulders, but the laugh lines at the corner of his lips clearly showed he enjoyed taking jibes at Adam.

Xen thought back to the skirmish with the Titans. Adam's injuries were critical at the time, but luckily for him, he had a little celestial help to move things along. As a wolf he would have healed, but it would have taken him far longer. "I doubt that," Xen voiced.

"There, boss man, we don't agree." He pointed in Adam's direction. "That wolf is a few sandwiches short of a picnic."

"What's this about a picnic? I'm hungry," Adam said, tapping his stomach.

Kane pulled another bag from the overhead compartment and slapped it right into Adam's stomach. "I'm sure Yiayia and Aunt Paula will feed you."

"I'd kill for *pasticho*."

"You might get lucky, *lykos*," Xen said, making his way out of the plane and to the waiting vehicles.

One of the men got out of one of the vehicles and tossed Kane some keys. He caught them and popped the trunk. They made quick work of throwing their gear in before taking off.

"Where to first?" Kane asked.

"Given the time, let's head straight to my hotel at Virginia Beach. You both need some sleep if you're going to see Yiayia and Aunt Paula in the morning."

"Food first," Adam reminded them.

Xen pulled out his phone and typed a quick message. "Food will be ready for you."

He'd let them rest and then see the women on his own.

Xen sat in front of Yiayia and Paula.

"Why exactly did you think it was a good idea to ditch the security detail? You could have asked them to take you where you wanted to go."

They both sat tight-lipped, staring at each other.

"Do I have to repeat my question?"

"No, *paidi mou*," Yiayia said.

"Then why were you worried about asking for a ride?"

"Well, I didn't know how the goddess Soteria would react if I turned up with, well, you know, some of your boys."

"Why did you need to see her?"

"Our husbands were friends for years and then we had a falling out."

That was news to Xen. He hadn't realized they had a long-term staying goddess on the mortal plane. "What did she say?"

"Nothing much. Just that she'd been waiting a mighty long time for me to show up after our argument."

There was more. He could sense their emotions.

"There's something else."

"I can't tell you, vampire, but just know this. Everything I do and Paula does is for Carissa, and you…" she lifted a shaky finger "…should trust that."

He knew she was telling the truth. Her heartbeat stayed at a steady pace.

"I do trust your word but here's the deal. You do not ever pull something like that again. Do we understand each other?"

"Yes," Yiayia said.

"We didn't mean to upset anyone but yes, we understand."

He stood. "Kane and Adam will be by in the morning to help you with anything you need and to pack for an evening flight."

"We're not staying?" Yiayia asked

"No. I think it's best if you are home, and Paula, I would like you to come back to Charleston too."

TEN

"In anger we should refrain from speech and action." ~ Pythagoras

Areopagus Courtroom; Athens, Greece
Midmorning, realm of the gods – Day 1

"Lies, you had every intention of killing my son." Poseidon was on his feet and pointing an accusing finger to her father.

What didn't he get? Hal had been all shades of crazy. He had tried to rape and kill Carissa so he could somehow absorb her powers. He wanted to reside on Olympus. No children of mortal and godly parents got to live on Olympus. That was the domain of the gods and goddesses, and only they dictated who came and went.

"Your son committed a crime."

"And you killed him."

"In my daughter's defense."

Poseidon sat back down. His face had turned dark red, and there was no mistaking his anger. Anger that was being channeled at her and her father.

Ares stood. "If I may be permitted to speak," he asked in the direction of a panel of judges. Namely Zeus, Hera, Athena and Poseidon. Her gut told her there was no way Poseidon was going to change his thoughts on the whole case. As far as he was concerned the problem wasn't his demented demi-god son's actions but Ares' action to save her and her then unborn child.

Zeus waved a hand for her father to proceed.

"Father, you are all seeing, all knowing. Might you be able to share a part of your memory for the court so that everyone..." he swept his arm across the room... "might see what actually did take place?" He dropped his weight back into the chair.

A hush fell over the courtroom. Then little whispers started up. Carissa leaned closer to her father. "You think that's a good idea?"

"Just trust me on this."

"You know I do, yet what if the replay is from an unfavorable angle."

"I know what you are saying, Daughter, however Zeus' memories will be from every angle, and that's what I'm counting on."

In no time the room reached a maximum in buzzing conversation.

"*Silence*," Zeus shouted.

The room fell to a hush and then utter quiet.

"I have considered this, and we have spoken amongst ourselves here. I will for the first time ever allow it, but take note, there will be no precedence set here. This is a one-time thing, and the only reason I am allowing it is that we have never before had an Olympian god on trial for murder. It is as unique as it is unusual, therefore, I will allow only a moment from my memories."

The room erupted.

"Well, I'll be," Carissa whispered.

Her father sported a huge smirk. "We just might have a chance."

"I don't think I want to see the replay."

Ares' hand landed on hers and he squeezed. He turned his head. "*Kori mou*, you will be excused. I can't have you relive that."

He released her hand and got to his feet. "I would ask at this time that my daughter, Carissa, is not present for the viewing of events."

"She should be present," Poseidon shouted. "It involves her, and Hal's death is very much at her hands as it is yours."

"Not when it can cause serious mental and emotional harm."

Poseidon was ready to fire something back at her father, but fortunately Zeus raised his hand to silence him. "My granddaughter shall be excused as it was Ares who struck the final blow."

"Echion. Take her to her rooms."

"Sister."

Carissa got to her feet. Just the thought of having to relive that episode with Hal was enough to weaken her. She hated what he did to her, hated that he tore a shred of her being and made her weaker. Hated that he took something precious from her and Xen. Echion put his hand on her shoulder. "Father," he said with a nod. They dematerialized.

They landed in the lounge room. The coffee table had an array of food already waiting. It was at that moment her stomach let out a little growl. Echion laughed. "I guess then that was good timing."

"I'll say."

She sat down, grabbed a plate and started to serve herself the different appetizers. She had to hand it to the Greek gods, they did things just as well as the mortal Greeks.

"Stay," she said through a mouthful of food.

"I should probably get back to Father."

He was in fact right. "Yes, you probably should. Although your company would have been very welcomed."

"Thank you for your invitation, Sister. It means a great deal."

Before she could mouth anything else, he zapped out of the room, leaving her there with her thoughts and the delicious food.

In the courtroom Zeus prepared his thoughts in a libation bowl. Hera ran a hand over the swirling memories. Then all the lights went out and a beam of three-dimensional visuals occupied the empty space in front of the judges. Everyone watched the events as Zeus had seen them. On an altar lay Carissa. Chained. Helpless. Everyone was fixed to the unfurling drama.

Ares' anger magnified with each moment. He had no regrets in killing Poseidon's son. Any man who acted as he had deserved Ares' wrath and more. That he ended him swiftly should be considered a boon.

Everyone watched in detail as Xen and his men fought demons. Gasps filled the room as Hal knocked Carissa out and destroyed the life inside her. Collective whispers amplified. When it was all over, Ares stood. "Do you have any further need of me?"

Zeus looked him over, and it didn't escape him that his father knew exactly why he wanted to be excused.

"You may go. The rest of you. This court is adjourned until tomorrow."

Ares dematerialized to his daughter's rooms.

She had fallen asleep on the couch. He covered her, waved his hand over the table and the food vanished. He might have missed many years as she was growing up, but he decided he wasn't going to ever be absent again. He would find a way to bend every rule his father had created. If he had been able to protect her she would have learned to use her powers. Everything might have played out differently.

He felt his mother's presence before she apparated. "Don't be hard on yourself. Sometimes these things have to play out a certain way."

"To whose advantage?"

"We lost here."

"But so did your uncle."

"My uncle has been full of hate for the last five hundred years."

"Well, you know we gods tend to hold on to grudges."

He scoffed. "For what exactly?"

"The red paint."

"Because I played a joke on him after he filled my bedroom chamber with donkeys?" He started pacing. "You don't see me holding a grudge."

"Your uncle is difficult."

"My uncle is selfish and should have kept a closer watch on his son."

"Yes, he should have but he didn't."

"You know, Mother, more than anyone that my actions should

not have brought about a trial. My uncle is hell-bent on destroying me for reasons that are unfounded and ridiculous." He stopped pacing and now stood face to face with his mother.

She lifted a hand and placed it on his arm. "Trust that you will get the votes you need."

"It is in the lap of the gods." He let out a small chuckle at the irony of it all.

"Should I be concerned?" Carissa's croaky voice asked.

"Stay, *kori mou*, there is no need to get up."

"Granddaughter," Hera said, rushing over to her.

Ares watched their exchange.

"Have a seat."

"I can't stay, Carissa. I'll need to get back to Zeus. I'm sure this whole thing is going to be the talk of the evening till tomorrow."

"Do we have any idea whether it will go our way?"

"None." Ares let out a frustrated breath.

"Wouldn't you have picked up the feel of the place and the gods?"

"We can do a lot of things, Granddaughter, but guessing which way the gods will vote is not one of them."

"Zeus would know," Carissa said.

"Never ask because you will never get that insight. Believe me. I have tried."

"So we let it run its course then."

"Perhaps," Ares said.

"Ares, whatever hairbrained idea you're thinking of, forget it," Hera scolded.

"Mother, it never hurt to throw a few breadcrumbs here and there."

"Bread turns stale unless there is an alternative."

"You mean, what will Father give in exchange?"

"Yes."

His daughter got to her feet and so did Hera.

"Do not bribe them, Father, it could backfire."

"Then what would you have me do?"

"Your argument needs to pull some heartstrings. You need to

convince the gods and goddesses that your actions were to save me from harm. Yes, you killed Hal…"

Ares lifted a hand. He did not want her to speak that horrid child's name.

"…I have to finish, Father. You know you have to take some blame for killing Poseidon's son. In human law a crime is a crime and punishable. I know this is not the same, but maybe just try giving yourself a punishment for saving me."

His daughter was as smart as she was beautiful. "*Kori mou.*" He pulled her to him for a hug. "I think that's brilliant."

Hera clapped her hands together and let out a little squeak of excitement. "Son, you're right. She has more than just beauty on her side. She has brains, and I can tell you that some days half of those gods come up short in the intellect department." She stood, blew them both a kiss and dematerialized.

"What now?" Carissa asked.

"What do you want to do?"

She raised an eyebrow at him. "I think we should suss out some of the gods and get a feel of things, and we should keep an open mind. Sometimes in their babbling there might be a small piece of information." She mimicked her grandmother Hera by slapping her palms together. "Now where's the best place to be if we wanted some gossip."

A grin broke across his lips. "How much time do you need to get ready?"

"What, you can't zap me into something?"

"It's not zapping and no, you deserve to be pampered." He snapped his fingers and Delia appeared. "Help prepare my daughter for this evening's events."

"I can get myself ready."

"You will allow Delia to help. This is what she does."

"This is slavery."

He scrunched his eyebrows together. "She gets paid to do what she does."

"Oh."

His daughter had just turned a nice shade of red.

"I thought…"

"*Kori mou*, slavery went out a long time ago, and the gods have always been about equal opportunities and fair wages."

"Really?"

"You're mixing the gods up with the Ancient Greek mortals."

"So sorry, Father. I thought she was here just to serve you."

"Well technically she is, but that's her job and she gets paid and rewarded handsomely for being my PA, assistant and housekeeper.

"Okay. Well then I will just stay out of that."

It was then that Delia spoke. "Daughter of Ares. Let me help you get some clothing ready."

"No, no. I don't want to hear daughter of Ares. Just a simple Carissa will do fine."

Delia looked over to Ares. He nodded his head in approval. Delia was old school and believed she should address his daughter in a formal way. He was, after all, a god and Delia was just a fairy.

"Mistress Carissa, it is then."

"Good. I'll leave you both to it." Ares winked at his daughter then dematerialized.

"Come on Mistress Carissa. Let's see what your father has in your wardrobe."

Carissa scrunched her face. "He has stuff already in there?"

Delia turned her head as she walked and nodded. "Yes, yes, he was very particular about it all."

Carissa digested that for a moment. If her father had stocked her wardrobe, then he obviously thought she'd be spending more time on Olympus. That didn't feel right to her. She was only here for the case. She didn't want to admit a simple thing like that could rattle her.

Delia walked into her bedroom and into her walk-in wardrobe. Obviously her father had done some renovation. The room was huge, and there were clothes and shoes in every color and style.

"Whoa," she marveled.

"That's what I said when I saw it too."

"This is way too much."

"No, no. This is good."

Not from Carissa's perspective because it alluded to her spending more time on Olympus, and right now, she did not want to spend any more time here than necessary.

Delia flicked through the dresses with a squeal of excitement.

"How about blue?" She held a long blue dress against her small frame.

"Do I need to be that formal?"

"You can do what you like. You're the daughter of Ares."

She wasn't opposed to dolling herself up. It was more the point that dresses were limiting, and she'd taken a leaning toward jeans and trousers.

"What do we have in pants?"

Delia's eyes opened wide. "You are the daughter of a god. You do not dress in trousers. Those are for women working in lower stations."

Now it was her turn to be shocked. "Let me get this straight. A sensible piece of clothing is considered beneath the gods and goddesses?"

Delia dropped her eyes to the ground. "Yes."

Carissa let out a frustrated breath. "They need to get with the times. That's ridiculous."

Her biggest pet peeve was that women were not allowed to wear trousers to church. It had always irked her because it was okay to wear a mini skirt as long as it was a skirt. If this line of thinking up here on Olympus didn't have patriarch written all over it, she didn't know what did. She'd go as she pleased and to hell with their archaic ways of thinking.

"Delia, I'm wearing a pantsuit combo."

"But…"

Carissa raised a hand. "I won't let them dictate my station based on the clothes I wear. Now let's sift through all this…" she swept her arm across the walk-in wardrobe "…and find some trousers."

An hour and a half later she was all dressed and ready in a velvet green pantsuit with gold sequence camisole and a pair of gold sandals. Delia had done an amazing job with her hair and makeup. "Thank you, Delia."

She bowed and then handed Carissa a pair of long diamond earrings.

"Please don't bow." Carissa threaded the earrings through her earlobes and walked out of the bedroom. Her father sat waiting. "Father, I hadn't realized you were here." Why hadn't she picked up his presence? That irked her. She should have been able to recognize his presence as soon as he materialized.

"I snuck in."

She raised an eyebrow.

"I didn't materialize. I walked in through the door."

The little rock that had settled in her stomach over her doubt of her abilities dissipated. "I'm not sure whether I like it when you do that."

He winked at her. "I didn't want to rush you, which you probably would have done if I had materialized."

He had a point.

"By the way, you look stunning in that suit. I'm sure it's going to raise a few eyebrows above the hairline."

A smile broke on her face. "Should we go ruffle a few feathers?"

"I think that's a splendid idea."

"Wait," she said. "Thank you again."

Delia nodded and dematerialized.

Her father was at her side, holding out a hand. "Shall we?"

She placed her hand in his and they zapped out of the room.

ELEVEN

"The tongue's best treasure amongst men is when it is sparing, and its greatest charm is when it goes in measure." ~ Hesiod, Works and Days

Apollo's Temple; Mount Olympus
Evening, realm of the gods – Day 1

Ares materialized them to a large temple. There were gods and goddesses everywhere. Music was playing, and they were lying around in a symposium style.

"Where are we?"

He squeezed her hand. "Apollo's"

"But…"

"Don't overthink it. How we act and how we expect our worshippers to act is entirely different."

"Doesn't that go against the whole god and human belief institution?"

"Carissa, the gods do as they please when they please. They are not bound by the same rules."

"Partying in a temple is grounds for punishment. Even I know that."

"Not when the partying is done by the gods themselves."

She shook her head. "Really?"

He nodded his. "Why don't we go mingle."

They navigated through the crowd toward the front and the sacrificial table that was now the bar.

"Ares," a raspy female voice called.

He turned his head and so did Carissa.

"Aphrodite." He embraced her and gave her a kiss on each cheek.

The goddess was dressed in a pale pink dress. She looked stunning. Then again she was the goddess of love, and it was easy to see why men fell at their knees for her. Even her father had. They shared a daughter and Carissa was about to ask when from behind Aphrodite a woman who looked a lot like her mother stepped forward.

"Hello, Sister."

Carissa's mouth dropped open. This she hadn't expected. She coughed her greeting out. "He... llo."

She looked Carissa up and down. "Did Father not supply you with enough dresses?"

And that was all it took. With those words Carissa knew she would not like her new sibling.

"Our father is very generous, and I chose what I wanted to wear, not what should be dictated."

Her sister's face turned red. "Well that's entirely acceptable, although that's not the way we do things on Olympus."

"You forget, I'm not from Olympus so the protocol is not applicable."

Her sister huffed.

"Harmonia," Aphrodite scolded.

"What?"

"Be nice. This is your half sister."

"Exactly, half in all senses of the word." She turned and walked away.

"I'm sorry for that Carissa," Aphrodite apologized.

Her father let out a frustrated breath. "Stay here. I'll be back after I have a word with her." Ares took off after Harmonia.

Aphrodite stepped closer. "How about I get you a drink. It looks like we could both use one."

"I think that's a marvelous idea." After that exchange Carissa needed more than one drink. She had a feeling she'd need several. Her father had other children, and it would not surprise her if they all thought of her in the same manner. Half and possibly not good enough for them. She wasn't a goddess.

"Carissa." The sound of her name brought her out of her musings. It was her brother—Echion. And she didn't think of him in halves.

He had a big smile on his face, and she couldn't help but return it. Maybe she was wrong about her other siblings. At least this one liked her. He gave her a tight hug.

"I'm so glad you are here," she said.

"I sensed you needed me," he whispered.

She was grateful for whatever connection she had going on with Echion. "I do."

"How about I move you over to my crowd." He released her and looked into her eyes.

Her lips turned up in a smile. "I think that's a brilliant idea."

He turned to Aphrodite. "Do you mind if I steal Carissa to introduce her to a few friends. I seem to never get the opportunity."

Aphrodite's face fell, but she regained her composure when Hera stepped next to her.

"Granddaughter," she said, moving in to give Carissa a kiss on each cheek. "I love your look."

Carissa slid her hands down her jacket. "Thank you. It's very me."

"I've been saying for at least a millennium that we need to ditch the frocks for some trousers."

Aphrodite chimed in. "Of course we should."

"That can be our next discussion at the G.O.O. meeting."

"Do I even want to ask?" Echion said.

"No, Echion. This is for the goddesses only."

He snorted a laugh and looked at Carissa.

"Grandmother and Aphrodite, please excuse us. Echion is going to introduce me to some friends."

"Oh, of course, child. Go." Hera winked and fluttered her hands.

Carissa had a feeling her grandmother knew she needed some rescuing too. *I did, Granddaughter.* The words drifted into her mind. She was projecting, and on Olympus most of the gods and goddesses could read your thoughts.

She pulled it together and continued to follow Echion.

"*Rigos,*" she whispered in Greek. A steal door came down in her mind. If Xen were here he would cue her in telepathically, and she would have known and not been walking around projecting her thoughts for all to read. She hoped she had only dropped the ball when she saw Hera. Every time she got emotional her guard fell away. It was something she constantly struggled with.

Echion brought them to an area of the temple that now housed dining booths. Carissa pointed to them. "A bit out of place, aren't they?"

"Not at all, Sister. The gods and some of us lessors do have a leaning toward all things American. Don't worry, none of it is permanent. It will be gone when the event is over." He snapped his fingers.

"Just like that, eh?"

"Yep. From the big guy." He pointed in Zeus' direction. He looked busy working the crowd.

Echion motioned for the two men already sitting there to move. "Here, Sis. Have a seat."

She sat next to one of the men, and Echion sat on her opposite side.

"Carissa, this Dorus and Cadmus."

She stuck out her hand to shake. "Pleased to meet you."

"We're all part of your father's army."

"So, Father has his own minions," she joked.

"He sure does," Echion said with a half-smile.

"Do you all like working for Father?" A little info from the employees never hurt.

"He is fair and does have a good work ethic."

She raised an eyebrow. "This is Ares we're talking about? God of war."

"If you peel away the layers you'll find a different man underneath."

She knew all the stories about her father. She'd read them all in Homer's Greek literature. The Greeks didn't worship him as much as the Romans did, and the picture she always had in her head was of a lust filled god who wanted only retribution and blood.

"He has his moments," Dorus said.

"And never get him angry," Cadmus added.

"True, but he is fair and does reward us from time to time."

Her ears perked up. "Reward. How so?"

"One time he sent us on a mission. It was the usual gods against gods scenario. We were to pull the two gods apart and make sure they didn't cause any damage to Olympus. You don't ever want to see tempers flying around when the gods are having a little spat between themselves."

"I think I can guess how big the damage bill would be," she said, knowing firsthand from a similar experience when she fought with Zeus and the other gods against Kronos and Iapetos.

"Well, we managed to separate them and calm them enough to stop the whole of Olympus from shaking. We were sure the whole place was going to crumble." Dorus took a sip of his drink. "For that he gave us brand new quarters with all the comforts and new weapons."

"Wow. That is generous." She reflected on her career when she was in the police force. She shook her head. This was not the mortal realm, and the type of behavior here was not applicable to her own world.

"What is generous?" Her father's voice startled her.

She turned her head up to look at him and swept a hand around the table. "The boys here were just telling me stories."

"Anything I should know?"

"No, not really."

He leaned forward and pulled her hand in his. "Are you okay?"

She knew what he meant. That whole exchange with Harmonia

had not gone down too well. "Oh, you mean that peachy exchange back there." She flipped a thumb in the direction. "Yeah. I'm good." She looked across to Echion and winked.

He returned the gesture.

"I might steal Carissa from you all," Ares said to the table.

The men nodded their agreement but said nothing.

"It was nice to meet you, Dorus and Cadmus." She shimmed out of the booth and got to her feet.

"Call if you need anything, Sister," Echion said.

"I will and thanks."

"No problem."

Her father watched her closely. "Let's go chat with Nemesis and Phthonos."

The goddess of retribution and god of envy and jealousy. They were an unusual pair but always hung out together, and they seemed to be good friends with her father. "Oh, they're here too?"

"They wouldn't miss one of these, there's just too much temptation."

"What exactly would they be tempted with?"

"You know, Phthonos sprinkles a little envy here and there, and Nemesis looks for those who are full of hubris, just so she can extract some punishment. I wouldn't cross her." His tone had lowered.

"I have no intention of crossing her," she whispered, more to herself. All these gods and goddesses around her were capable of inflicting harm in more ways than one.

She spotted where they were sitting and surprisingly they were alone and not mingling. They both turned their heads at the same time when her father approached the table.

Nemesis had a huge smile on her face. "*Ares*," she sounded out in a sing song tune.

Phthonos stuck his fist out for a bump. They both obliged him. "Good to see you again, Carissa," he said.

"Love the suit," Nemesis greeted. "I'm sure that's raising eyebrows."

"I really don't care. There is a clear divide between me and everyone here."

Nemesis looked at Phthonos.

"I'm picking up jealousy and envy in every corner, and I didn't have to weave any of my own in this crowd. You might think you don't belong, however they have already made up their minds. You are part of them, and they are very curious about you." Phthonos pointed a finger to Carissa. "And this is why you need to be alert around them. That curiosity can change."

"How so?"

"It can very quickly turn from envy to jealousy to vengeance, and this is where someone may try to hurt you. Be on guard. *Always*," Phthonos warned.

Carissa sat down and so did Ares.

"Care to elaborate?" Carissa asked.

"Okay, Greek god and ancient Greek thinking 101." He sat up and put his elbows on the table, leaning closer. "I sprinkle envy about. That envy is benign, although just like it's passive counterpart there is malicious envy. Malicious envy induces someone to rid the target of their envy. This stage is the jealousy stage. Jealousy has two counterparts, but when envy moves into the sphere of jealousy it becomes Zelos' problem." He paused. "Are you following me?"

"Yes."

"Good. I will continue. When Zelos takes over the reins everything becomes malicious. There is no longer healthy envy or jealousy, only sheer motivation to divest the target of whatever is causing the emotion."

"So she might be in danger, even now," Ares added.

"Wait. I haven't done anything to warrant such behavior toward me."

"Carissa, you need not have acted or exchanged words with someone for that to happen. Someone might become envious or jealous by just hearing gossip, and since you are the topic of much discussion lately, we believe you will unsuspectedly receive attention from either some of the lesser or gods and goddesses," Nemesis said.

"Again. Why?"

"Because the gods and goddesses here are always vying for attention from Zeus, and right now Father is giving you a great deal of time," Ares pointed out.

She digested the information. "So how do I protect myself whilst I'm up here?"

Ares squeezed her hand. "I know just the spell, but not here."

She didn't want to contemplate it anymore. From what they were saying she was likely to make more enemies than friends. *Time to shift the topic of conversation.* "You know you still need to work this crowd to see how they will vote," she reminded him.

"I have not forgotten, *kori mou.*"

"I might call it a night if you are okay with that."

"That is more than fine." He raised his hand to zap her out of the room. She reached out and enclosed her fingers on his forearm. "No Father, let me walk."

He searched her eyes. "Fine, but only if Echion can accompany you."

"Okay."

"Sister." Echion held out his hand.

She looked at her father. "I take it you called via the mind mumbo jumbo thing." The gods could communicate telepathically like Xen did with her.

"Be on your guard," he said.

She opened her mouth to say something but he dematerialized along with Phthonos and Nemesis.

She took Echion's hand. "Let's get out of here."

"On that, I am very much in agreement."

TWELVE

"False words are not only evil themselves, but they infect the soul with evil." ~
Socrates

Outside Ares' Temple; Mount Olympus
Evening, realm of the gods – Day 1

"You've been awfully quiet, Sister."

Carissa stopped and faced her brother. "How do you deal with all of this and all of them?" She waved her arm around.

Echion let out a laugh. "Let's say I've had many millennia to adjust."

Her mouth dropped open. She regained her composure. "You're kidding me."

"One does not jest when talking about the gods and Olympus." Humor danced in his eyes.

She slapped him on the shoulder. "Don't joke. I'm serious as all get-out."

"Look, it's not easy but being a child of Ares has its own perks."

Carissa raised an eyebrow. "How so?"

"Well, for one they know he has anger issues so they assume all his children would be alike, so most gods and goddesses tend to avoid you."

"I truly hope that is the case."

"You have Father here and me. Don't let it trouble you."

"Something is definitely making me uneasy, and it's not Father's court case."

"Do you have your weapons with you?"

"I do."

"Then I suggest you start carrying them. It will give you a sense of ease."

"I think you're right, Brother."

She moved her feet toward her father's quarters. Her brother was right. Having her sword on her would give her a layer of confidence. All that talk with Phthonos had made her a little jumpy. Her preconscious couldn't fathom why anyone would be jealous of her but her subconscious—that dark recess of her mind where she threw and stored things for later—had been flashing snapshots of all the looks she got from the gods and goddesses. They didn't like her. She didn't belong.

"I wouldn't overthink it," Echion said.

"It's good to observe."

"That it is."

She hadn't realized they'd reached her father's quarters. "We're here. Thank you for walking with me." They walked up the steps and Carissa knocked on the door.

"Trust me, any excuse to get out of there."

"You're not a fan either?"

"Carissa, I have seen much in my years, and the less you cavort with the gods the better life is."

"You don't stay here?"

"Not if I can help it."

"Where do you go?"

"We have our ways of staying under the radar." He winked. "And the walls have ears up here. We will have to leave that conversation for another time."

"I know what you mean," she whispered back. Understanding punched her in the stomach. She was certain someone would be listening to their discussion while out in the open. Inside she could control it, but outside, she didn't have a spell for that.

"Well, this is me." She pointed to her father's domain.

"Indeed it is."

"Would you like to come inside for drink?"

"Tempting as it may be, I need to get back to Father."

A pang throbbed her in the chest at his words. "I shouldn't have left either. He needs help."

"Sister, there is nothing more that you can do."

The reality struck her in a way she hadn't expected. She wanted to help, and sitting idle had never been a habit of hers. "There must be something…"

Echion held up a hand. "If there were, you know that Father would already have you doing what he asked."

She bit her lip as uncertainty laced around her. "Okay, but shout out if you need me. I do have a sword or two." She winked, trying to make light of her inner gloom.

"I know you would have my back, Sister."

She nodded her head. "I best get inside."

"That would be the safest."

She leaned in and gave him a hug.

"Be on your guard. I'm sensing tension tonight." His low whisper sent a shiver through her. He was picking up the same vibes as she was.

"I will."

He released her and headed back from where they came.

She turned and put her hand against the large door. Power tingled between the door and her fingertips. A light click sounded and the door swung open. Delia stood there waiting.

"What are you doing up? You should be resting."

"I wanted to wait. I sensed you at the door."

"Wait. When I touched it?"

"Yes. That's how I know to answer or be here."

"Does it open for everyone?"

"No. Your father and now you."

Carissa's back stiffened. She had never thought to ask it before. "What about the whole zapping in and zapping out?"

"Ah, not everyone can do that. There needs to be some sort of agreement between the owner of the premises and those that visit him."

Her shoulders dropped and her eyes rolled heavenward. "Thank the gods and goddesses. I don't need anything, so you can get some…" Her words died on her lips at the loud banging on the door. "Get my sword."

Delia dematerialized.

The banging continued. Carissa braced herself. Whoever it was, they weren't happy.

She recognized Delia's presence and turned. "Thank you. When I say, pull the door open."

Unsheathing her sword from the leather harness, its power tingled around her fingers and up her arms. She nodded to Delia.

With wide eyes and nimble fingers, she latched on to the door handle and flung it open.

Carissa's feet were planted to the ground, and she wouldn't hesitate to cut down anyone who posed a threat.

"There you are," Harmonia said.

Carissa lowered her sword. "What brings you here?"

"I came to apologize for my behavior earlier." She stepped over the threshold.

A bolt of power hit Carissa in the gut. *Don't trust her.*

"There was no need. I understand you might have not taken the news to having another sister too well."

The thin line on Harmonia's face turned up into a smile with teeth. Yet it didn't reach her eyes. "No, no. I've been very excited. I don't know what got into me tonight." She took another step toward her. "Can we start over."

Carissa raised an eyebrow. There were two ways this could go, and she had already done the math. Her sister would end up being a pain in the ass and they would argue, or she'd be sweeter than a red velvet cupcake. "Sure. Come in." She reharnessed her sword.

Delia's eyes had narrowed. Clearly she didn't like Harmonia. She shot Carissa a look of warning. "I'll bring some refreshments," she said and dematerialized.

"Come and sit down."

"So, you're staying with Father?"

"Well, I don't really have anywhere else to go in this realm."

"True. Maybe you can stay with me and Mother next time."

A cramp of power hit her in the gut again. A warning, or had she drunk something that didn't agree with her?

Delia appeared with a tray of warm and cool drinks. Carissa reached for the tea. "Thank you."

Her sister took a glass of water. "How long will you be on Olympus?"

"That's hard to say. It depends on how long Father's case gets dragged out."

Harmonia took a sip of her water. "You think he will win?"

"I hope he does."

A sigh left Harmonia's lips. "I do too."

That did sound believable. The tension that had been riding hard into her shoulder blades eased, and she dropped her shoulders into a relaxed slouch. She raised her cup to her lips and took a small sip of the tea. An explosion of memories hit her. It was the same tea her grandmother often gave her as a child when she had been unwell. Mountain tea. It was her turn to sigh.

"I heard you fought off Kronos and Iapetos." Harmonia shivered.

Not something Carissa wanted to relive. "Yes, but it was a team effort."

"I think Grandfather favors you."

"I think Grandfather favors all his grandchildren in different ways."

"Possibly. It's hard to know sometimes as they are self-absorbed."

"Sometimes we have to make the first move toward change."

"I see why they like you. You are wise."

"I don't think that has anything to do with it. I think we were all thrown together for a common cause."

"Looks like you and Father have a common cause."

Carissa put her cup down. This conversation was steering down a hateful path, and she would not entertain any family squabbles her sister may have had with her father. The time to steer the conversation on another path was now. "What do you do to fill your time?"

Her sister looked at her. Blinked. Opened her mouth and stuttered. "Gods and goddesses do not work like mortals."

"I know that. What is it you pass your time with?" Judging by her sister's reaction, she didn't think anyone had ever asked that before.

"We entertain and sit around talking."

"Your days must seem long then?"

"Not really. We have our own hobbies to keep us busy."

Carissa had a good idea what those hobbies involved, but she wasn't going to bring that up. It was best to keep things cordial. "Like painting?"

"That and others. Weaving is popular amongst the goddesses and somewhat of a competition. We run a big weaving contest every year."

"What exactly do you weave."

"Tapestries of course."

"Is there a prize for the winner."

Harmonia scoffed. "The goddesses don't need prizes other than to just be the victor."

"Who won last year?"

"Athena."

That was interesting. "And the year before that?"

"Athena wins every year. We have yet to beat her unblemished work."

Carissa digested that information. "Quite skilled then?"

"One day someone will beat her, and that smug look on her face will disappear."

That was nasty. "I'd like to look at some of these tapestries if you have time?" She'd judge for herself.

Her sister's face lit up. "I could show you now. The night is still young."

"Sure." Carissa stood.

Delia, who had not left the room gave her a warning look.

She took her sword, put it in its harness and strapped it on.

"You won't need that."

"I might not but it's coming with me."

Her sister feigned a smile. "Okay, let's go." She held out her hand.

Carissa closed the distance between them and placed her hand in her sister's. A tingle of energy danced between them. Recognition. Family. Her sister's eyes widened to saucers. Another thing she hadn't expected. They dematerialized.

The temple of a room her sister took her to was beyond anything Carissa had ever seen. Tapestries of all sorts lined the walls, beneath them shiny plaques in gold indicating the name of the goddess who wove it. Carissa looked at the detail. They were nothing short of spectacular. "Wow, these are beautiful."

"Thank you, Sister."

Every goddess you could think of had her work up on display. Her feet moved slowly as she took in each tapestry. "How long have you been running this contest?"

"Since Arachne decided to boast that her work was as good as Athena's."

"That long, huh?" She couldn't say why she found it amusing. Having only known her aunt for a short period of time, she could only think the whole weaving thing wasn't so much about the contest itself.

"Over there are our Aunt Athena's winning tapestries." Harmonia pointed to the far wall.

Carissa walked over to where Athena's work was showcased. On closer inspection her work was far superior to what she had seen already. "Aunt Athena's work is…" The air in the room shifted and Carissa recognized the signature. "…amazing," she finished.

"Why thank you, Niece." Athena winked.

"What brings you here, Aunt?" Harmonia asked with a sour look on her face.

"I could ask you the same thing."

"I was just showing my cousin some of the outstanding work of the competition and yours too."

Athena let out a laugh. "Come now, Niece. I hear you have the winning tapestry this year."

Harmonia scoffed. "One day someone will beat you, Aunt."

"I look forward to that day."

"Carissa, you should join us."

Carissa shook her head. "Oh, no. I wouldn't know the first thing about tapestries." She looked to Athena for support, however the goddess was giving her a hard stare.

"I think that would be a marvelous idea."

"Oh, no."

"Yes." Harmonia jumped up down and clapped her hands.

"But…" The words died on her lips.

"Where can we start her?"

"Perhaps we should let her choose her own project and just teach her how to use the loom."

"Loom?"

"Yes, the loom, Sister."

Neither goddess was listening, and Carissa didn't have time for this. She dropped her mental shield. Her power tingled. "Listen."

They both turned their heads.

Carissa pulled her power back. *Rigos*, she mentally chanted before Athena and Harmonia realized what commanded their attention. Her father had warned more than once that her powers could be seen as a threat. Being able to compel a god or goddess would only paint a bigger target on her back, and from her earlier conversation with Phthonos and Nemesis, she already had one.

"I am here for Father's case. I do not have time for tapestries. Nor the time to be taught. Now if you will excuse me, I'd like to get back to my father's house."

"As you wish, Niece." Athena winked at her and dematerialized.

Harmonia stepped closer. "You really should consider it. We need some competition."

"I appreciate it, but no thanks. Let's head back."

Harmonia closed her fingers around Carissa's wrist and zapped them to familiar ground.

Her father must have recognized their signature before they appeared. His arms were crossed and his biceps bulged. A thin line marred his lips, and an eyebrow was raised. "Where have you been?"

"I left a message." Carissa mirrored his facial expression with the raised brow.

"But why did it take so long?"

"Do calm down, Father. We were only gone a short while, and besides, there's nothing wrong with two sisters spending time together," Harmonia said.

A sharp pain hit Carissa in the stomach. She stifled it but her father picked it up.

"Harmonia, I think it's time you got back to your mother. She'll be waiting."

She turned to Carissa. "Reconsider. Good night, Sister." She stepped in for a quick hug. "Father." She bowed then dematerialized.

Ares waved his hand across the room. "*Philaso.*" He spoke the spell to prevent any prying ears from listening in. "Care to tell me what that was about?"

Carissa pulled her harness away from her body. "Which bit?"

"Everything. Leave nothing out." He motioned for her to sit on the couch.

She dropped her sword in its harness on the coffee table and sat back. In the short time she had known her father, she'd learned he didn't trust too many gods or goddesses. A deep sigh bubbled up from her chest. She let it out and relaxed her shoulders.

"Echion walked me back, and after a few moments of being here, Harmonia banged on the door. I got Delia to get my sword, just in case."

Her father smiled. "Good thinking."

"Then she went on about some competition and wanted to show me the tapestry room. Pretty impressive I must say."

"It is."

"While there, Athena appeared, and they both tried to coax me into joining the competition."

Her father leaned forward. She could see his mind spinning.

"I'm sure it was all innocent."

He let out a laugh. "There is no such thing as an innocent god or goddess."

Okay, he had a point.

"The question you should ask, *kori mou,* is why either of them wanted you to join?"

"Fresh blood?"

"Yes, got that. Why though?"

"Healthy competition?"

"True, it is a bore when my sister wins year after year."

"Yeah, but her work blows the others right out of the water."

"It does, but for her to ask you to join there must be a reason. My sister never does anything without some story of strategy in play."

"I could never win against her. I have no weaving ability."

"Because you haven't been shown."

"Father, seriously, I have no time for this."

"And my sister has other motives."

"Really?"

"Trust no one, *kori mou.*"

"There is nothing she could gain by me being in that competition. I'd epically fail to produce anything of the quality and workmanship those goddesses have put into their work."

"Stay on your guard. Trust your gut and instinct."

Her gut and instincts were not working.

"Pay closer attention."

"You have my word that I will."

"Good. Then how about you get some rest."

But first she needed to know if her father had had any success with the other gods and goddesses. "Were you able to convince any of them to vote for you."

"I think they have already decided."

Carissa moved to sit right next to her father. She put her hand on his leg. "What's the worst that can happen."

"I lose it and kill everyone in the room."

She let out a laugh. "I'd join in."

He rested his hand on hers. "I have no doubt that you would. Ready?"

She nodded. Her father zapped her to her bed.

Her sword appeared next to her a second later. "I seriously have to learn how to do that."

THIRTEEN

"Know who is the judge." ~ *Delphi Maxim*

Ares' Chambers; Mount Olympus
Morning, realm of the gods – Day 2

A light caress brushed across Carissa's cheek. It startled her, but she was quick to pull the knife that was under her pillow.

"Easy, *kori mou.*" Ares stepped back.

"Father."

"I did not mean to frighten you."

"It's okay. Is it time?"

"Soon. I wanted you to have something to eat before the trial resumes."

"I'll be ready in a few minutes."

"Good. Delia has breakfast ready." He lifted his hand and snapped his fingers. With a grin he dematerialized.

She pulled back her heavily woven blankets and got out of the bed. Her feet hit the cold marble. A chill seeped from her toes up through her body. She shivered and it gave her all the motivation she needed to get dressed. Her steps were lethargic as she made her way over to a large dressing room. Her choices of clothing were mechanical. "Be ready for anything," she whispered to herself while stripping off her pajamas.

The last time she was on Olympus for her father's case a giant attacked and had she not had her sword she wouldn't have been able to block the giant's attempt to strike Zeus. She pulled out black cargo pants with a black t-shirt and slipped into them fast, finishing off with a pair of boots Xen had gifted her. She then proceeded to strap on two leather holsters, one for her knife on her leg and one for her sword. When her fingers closed around her sword, power vibrated all the way up her arm. *We are one.* She eyed the gun Xen had given her and thought it best to arm herself with that as well. "No such thing as being too armed around the gods," she whispered to herself.

Last night had been an eye-opener for her—the gods and goddesses of Olympus would never see her as part of their club. She was part human and that would always be a sticking point in regard to being an equal or respected ally. She sheathed the sword and made her way through the large rooms to the dining area.

Logically it didn't matter because her life belonged in the mortal realm. Not here. Still something squeezed in her chest. Perhaps being near her absent father was what caused her to yearn for a life she thought she was missing. She shook her head to dislodge the thoughts running a marathon in her mind. The smell of coffee enticed her tastebuds. She couldn't wait to get her first sip. When she rounded the corner her father was already seated at the long table. He raised an eyebrow. "You sure you have enough weapons?"

Delia stood nearby. "Mistress, I have coffee and it's ready for you."

"It's Carissa, Delia. Please."

"Okay, Mistress Carissa."

She rolled her eyes. This would take time.

Her father flashed her a smile.

Carissa's glance swept the table. "Gee Delia, you went all out," she said, unharnessing her sword and sliding it farther along the table before she sat down.

"No mistress, I didn't go out. I made everything."

Carissa withheld her laugh. "No, all out is an expression meaning you went to a lot of trouble to cook all this." She swept her arm across the table.

"Oh, well I wasn't sure what you would prefer." She bounced on her toes and back again, her eagerness to please more than evident.

"Why don't you sit with us."

"Sorry, Mistress Carissa, but it's not my place."

"Delia, I'm not going to have you make all this and not at least share it with us."

Delia backed away.

Carissa looked at her father.

He looked up from the *Olympus Times* newspaper he had been reading. "I think you might have asked Delia to break her vow of servitude."

"Seriously, Father?" Just because she got paid, it didn't mean she couldn't join them.

Delia shuffled forward. "Mistress Carissa, please, it's okay."

"Special circumstances are in the verbal request," her father said, eyeing her carefully.

The wheels in Carissa's head started to turn at her father's words. "Delia, please join us for this breakfast feast that you have provided. It would make me happy, and I would be honored and so would Father."

Delia looked over to Ares, who gave a little nod.

"Looks like you've found a loophole, *kori mou*." He winked with a half-smile tugging at his lips.

Delia poured Carissa a cup of coffee and then took a seat.

Carissa brought the cup to her lips. The flavor burst in her mouth, and she sighed before taking another sip. She put her cup down and loaded a plate with an array of both Greek and American foods, and then it hit her. "Wait a minute, you told me once that the gods cannot live on ambrosia alone. Why is that?"

Her father put the paper down. "The ambrosia and the nectar we drink are more than enough to sustain us and our immortality, but over the years we have come to enjoy some mortal foods. We don't need them, but having said that we do indulge. Think of it as a delicacy for us."

She nodded, filing the information away in some recess of her noggin.

"We best eat up. Court starts in half an hour," her father said.

And she was ready for it. She expected trouble. There was no way Poseidon would make any part of the case easy. He was holding a lot of anger. She scoffed to herself.

"What is it, Daughter?"

"They say your rage and anger surpass the other gods, but from what I have seen, your uncle seems to be repressing a lot more anger than you."

Ares let out a laugh. "You are not wrong there, and I am quite sure he is going to direct a lot of that toward me in court today."

"Should we be worried?"

"Always, *kori mou.*" He finished the last bite of food from his fork, wiped his mouth and got to his feet. Then he snapped his fingers, and bad boy god looked every bit as dangerous decked out in black combat gear.

"What, no weapons?" she asked.

He grinned. "No need till needed," he said.

"Man, I need some serious hocus pocus."

He let out a laugh. "I think you look way cooler with all your weapons harnessed and in place."

It was her turn to smile. "I guess we should get moving."

"Shall we?" He gestured for her to take his hand.

She stood and closed her fingers around her father's.

He dematerialized them to the Areopagus at Athens.

The godly Areopagus did not represent the large modern day rock outcropping northwest of the Acropolis. It was only visible to the gods of Olympus and only habitable by the gods as the court of the gods. The room was not yet full, and Carissa looked to the front where the long table sat vacant.

"I guess we have a few moments to collect ourselves before everyone starts popping in."

"We do not pop in. I've explained this before, *kori mou.* We materialize."

She rolled her eyes. *Same thing.*

No, it's not, her father sent back to her mind.

"I was thinking too loudly, wasn't I?"

"Yes, school your thoughts. Every god in here will be listening in."

The one problem with Olympus was that all the gods and goddesses could do the mind reading thing. She needed to block them, although her method was not foolproof.

"Concentrate and use the word *thereos*. It will drop the door or shield around your mind. It will be stronger than what you've been trying to do."

She focused and whispered, "*Thereos*." A mental door slammed shut in her mind. This time she felt the shift harder than before.

Her father had dropped his voice. "You're getting better."

She couldn't help but beam. Baby steps, that was what it had been from the moment her father had unbound her powers.

The room began to fill. "Looks like they've redecorated," she said.

"Well, it did need it after the last battle." His lips twitched.

They had fought Kronos and Iapetos in this room. They had tried to take over Olympus, but in a combined effort and with the help of the magical codex that now hung around her neck in the form of a shield pendant, Carissa had managed to send them back to Tartarus. The looks and stares from the other night had a lot to do with that, and she knew it. She'd saved Olympus, along with Zeus, her father Ares and the other gods and goddesses. Did she trust them? The answer to that was a big resounding *no*. "Wonder who will be on your side?"

"The gods are never predictable. They can turn on you in an instant. They will favor the one who has the best argument. This is how it is done."

It didn't sound too different from law practice in the mortal realm. The lawyer with the best argument was always instrumental in how the jury might vote. That and evidence, albeit lawyer theatrics had a lot to with it, or so she thought. She twisted in her seat to survey her surroundings. It was a very large semi-circular room that resembled a smaller style of an amphitheater with several rows of seating. There was standing space on the sides and at the front a long table sat up on a podium. "The seats of the gods," she whispered to herself.

A thunderbolt struck at the front seats, and Zeus appeared. Carissa looked over, and the god of thunder winked at her.

Ares rolled his eyes. "A bit dramatic."

"Nothing like a little show of power."

No, there isn't, Granddaughter. The words filtered to her mind. She let out a little laugh.

"Something funny, *kori mou?*" her father asked.

"No, Father."

She smiled at Zeus. Then clamped her mouth shut.

The air shifted around her, and she recognized the incoming signatures.

"Brother," she said when he appeared.

Echion half bowed. "Father, Sister."

"Here, take a seat," she said, shuffling closer to her father.

"Any whispers we should know about?" Ares asked.

"Nothing. This one is hard. Usually the gods and goddesses like to mouth off about who they will vote for so you can get a feel of which way you think it will go. This time I'm getting nothing, which is rather unusual. Something is not right."

"Someone has bought them," Carissa said.

"That's what I think, Sis."

Ares let out a sarcastic laugh. "That much was evident from last night."

"Why didn't you say so earlier?" Carissa asked.

"It would not have mattered."

Her father was right. All that insight would have achieved was to ramp up her anger. "Then if you won't receive a fair trial, why are we here?"

"To be heard."

She raised an eyebrow at the god of war. "Seriously?"

"Carissa, don't discount for one moment that just because they've been buttered up with bribes they won't change their minds," Echion said.

"Are you saying that whoever tried to buy them all for their vote wasted their time."

"They did, *kori mou*."

"Then why do it?"

"Why do the gods do anything they do?"

"You know that's cryptic and doesn't answer anything."

"*Kori mou*, the gods and goddesses that took the bribes only did so to give them the right to ask for a favor in return."

"That doesn't even make sense. They took a bribe. They were paid for their vote. Done deal."

"Not necessarily, Sis. They see that as a favor. The exchange of money, goods etcetera means nothing. It's all about the asking."

She shook her head. The gods were a confusing bunch. "You know that sounds demented?"

"Not necessarily. You see, the gods and goddesses should never have to ask for help. It should be given without thought. The fact that no one offered to help and that Poseidon resorted to buying them says a lot."

"Does this mean, we shouldn't even bother?"

"No, they need to hear our side of the story," her father said.

"But they've chosen."

"Not all of them, *kori mou*, and that's what we're counting on."

She shifted in her seat and glanced around the now full room.

"*Silence,*" the god of thunder yelled.

The room fell to a hushed murmur before going completely quiet.

Poseidon shot to his feet. "My nephew is guilty of murder."

All eyes turned to her father. Ares huffed under his breath. There wasn't a chink in his armor. He just stared at his uncle.

Poseidon stepped away from the other gods and came to stand in the middle of the room. "My argument today is about my nephew's intent to murder my son Halirrhothius."

"That's rubbish, Poseidon, and you know it," Ares shouted from where he was seated.

Carissa tensed and her fists turned to balls. Her brother's hand went to her shoulder. It sent her the strength to hold back any words she wanted to let loose. It was Poseidon's son who was the cause of everything. Had Poseidon checked in on his son maybe he wouldn't have been as demented as he was.

"My son did nothing wrong. Yet you didn't hesitate to lay waste to him."

Murmurs started to rise.

"*Silence,*" Zeus warned.

"Your son tried to rape my daughter." At Ares' words the room broke into louder chatter.

"*Order.*" This time it was a goddess who spoke.

Themis, Ares spoke to her mind.

The goddess of justice didn't look too impressed with Poseidon. "Please present your argument properly."

Poseidon looked around the room. "My son was a demi-god, much like Ares' daughter who is privileged enough to sit amongst you today at Zeus' request. Many of us gods have demi-god children, yet none are sitting with you all today. As you know we are not to intervene in the mortal world. However Ares thinks himself different. He chooses when he comes and goes without thought that we try to uphold the rules. If he wasn't messing in the mortal realm my son would still be alive."

Carissa swallowed hard. She did not like the way Poseidon was twisting everything to make her father sound like a villain. He wasn't in the wrong, Poseidon's son was, and Carissa had suffered at his hands.

This time her father stood and made his way down to where Poseidon was supposedly giving his version of the events.

"How do you make these accusations, Uncle, when you weren't there? You accuse me of breaking rules at the same time I am not the only god in the room to be guilty of ducking in and out of the mortal realm, and let's not forget that sometimes there is a need for me to do that since my *Phi Athanatoi* are tasked with protecting humans from evil that slips amongst mortals."

"Excuses."

"They might seem that way to you, though had you answered your son's pleas, you might have been able to save the life of my grandchild your son killed." Gasps sounded in the room. "When you talk of who has been wronged here, you should consider the actions of your son."

They had seen that yesterday through Zeus' memories. How could they even sit here and dispute it? Carissa popped to her feet. "If I can speak?"

Whispers started around the room.

"*Silence*. Carissa will have her say." Zeus' voice boomed across the room.

She made her way down to where her father was and stood side by side with him.

"Your son, Poseidon, wanted nothing more than to kill me to take any power, but that wasn't enough. He kidnapped me three times and he somehow managed to team up with demons and wasn't afraid to kill anyone in his path to gain what he wanted..." She swept her hand across the room. "...the demise of all the gods here."

The room erupted. The discussion between gods became more animated.

Poseidon's face changed to one of sheer anger. He stomped toward her father.

Themis stepped between them and held a hand up. "You will keep your distance till everyone has heard all there is to hear. You know how this works Poseidon."

He stepped back.

"If you could all quieten down," Themis shouted.

"How do we know that any of what you are saying is true?"

"I'm not here to lie. I'm here because you should be held responsible for your son's actions. If you had checked in on him maybe once or twice, he may not have become unhinged. He was my childhood friend, and in the end that was not the boy I grew up with. The crime here is your lack of interaction with your child, and you would not be the only god guilty of that. You have abandoned your children and many have lost hope. It is your duty to step in occasionally to ensure they at least understand their powers. My voice here today is not only to defend my father and his actions but also request that you make changes to rules to allow your demi-god children the chance to understand what is different about them and that they have someone watching over them."

Her father's fingers squeezed hers. *Well done, kori mou.*

"My daughter is right, and you all know it."

"This is rubbish," Poseidon spat out. "He is on trial for murder. This trial isn't about the gods. It's about Ares murdering my son."

Her father released her fingers. "What about your son's murder of a baby."

"My baby," Carissa added.

"*Enough,*" Zeus shouted. "We have heard both sides, and we will decide if Ares is guilty of murder."

The room once again burst into animated chatter.

"What now?" Carissa asked.

"We wait till they've made up their minds."

"You guys really need some structure up here. This isn't how a court is run."

"*Kori mou,* this is the very beginning of the court system."

"But where or who is the judge? And why aren't there lawyers to represent each party? You know the usual courtroom theatrics."

"We like to keep things original."

She let out laugh.

"At least we still have our humor, *kori mou.*"

"What are you smiling about?" Echion joined them.

"Just the whole set up," Carissa said. "It's like a circus. No structure."

"Well, we do have to keep things mental, don't we?" Echion shrugged.

Zeus rose from where he was sitting, and the room fell to a hush.

"All those in favor of a guilty plea."

Hands shot up around the room, and Carissa turned her head to see how many. "It looks like a lot, Father."

"Have faith, *kori mou.*"

"All those in favor of a not guilty plea."

More hands rose. Up and up.

"How do they even count this?"

"We're gods. We have ways to do all things."

"It looks like we are even."

Athena stood. "And I have not given my vote yet."

"How do you vote?" Zeus asked.

"Not guilty."

"*No,*" Poseidon shouted.

The room began to shake.

FOURTEEN

Areopagos courtroom; Athens, Greece
Midmorning, realm of the gods – Day 2

Carissa latched on to her father's arm. The ground continued to shake as hairline cracks appeared on the marble floor, and water began to spurt through the cracks. She looked across to Poseidon who pointed a finger at Ares and then dematerialized. The gods and goddesses disappeared one by one.

Zeus waved a hand, and everything stopped.

"Well, someone doesn't like to lose," Carissa said while squeezing water out of her ponytail.

"Not wrong there, Sis."

"My uncle doesn't like to lose. His behavior is childish," Ares said.

"He obviously wasn't happy with you. Do you think he would try to harm you?"

Ares let out a laugh. "He can't kill me, *kori mou*, if that's what you are worried about."

"Well yes, that and how do you know he can't snap you out of existence?"

"We've been fighting amongst each other for many millennia.

Nothing is going to change any time soon. We fight together and then we fight amongst each other."

"You know that you're all nuttier than a five-pound fruit cake." She scoffed.

"It's about power, *kori mou*. And about being a danger to one another when one grows more powerful than the other."

Zeus had stepped around the table and moved in their direction. "That went as expected."

Carissa's mouth opened then closed. "You knew it would pan out like this?"

He winked at her.

"You could have said something and saved us the stress."

"It doesn't work that way," her father added.

"Why?"

"Because if you knew, Granddaughter, and whispers escaped, and they do, everyone would have voted for Ares, and Poseidon's anger would have been much more of a problem."

She digested the information and looked her mighty grandfather in the eyes. "Do you often know?"

"Not all the time. Sometimes the fates choose to not reveal certain situations."

"Have you foreseen any backlash. Is Father in danger."

Zeus let out a laugh. "Your father will be safe, but you, I do not know."

She glanced at her father. A thin line was sewn across his face. "I don't like that."

"I agree," Echion said.

"You think someone might try to harm me?"

"That's exactly what we think."

"But Poseidon directed his anger at Father."

"You saw that we scraped through…"

"By my vote," Athena interrupted.

"Exactly," her father validated.

"I will stay with Carissa. Till you finalize anything that needs doing," Echion said.

"That's a good idea," Zeus said.

"What happens now?"

"We sign off on the court transcript, file it and this case is over with," Ares answered.

"You mean to say that was documented?"

"Yes, Granddaughter, regardless of our nuttier than fruitcake moments." He winked at her.

Carissa's mouth dropped open.

Ares put a finger under her chin.

She shook her head. "Grandfather, you need to stay out of my head."

"I wasn't in your head. I heard you." A grin spread across his face.

"Father, would you leave my niece alone," Athena said.

"I'd rather be listening in on my granddaughter than any of the other gods up here. I've heard all their inner monologues and voiced complaints for far too long."

"Great. I'm the fresh fodder."

"Well, I wouldn't quite use that terminology but…"

"Far more interesting than everyone else up here, Granddaughter."

Hera had just joined them too. It was becoming quite a gathering, but the group that had been standing closest to them had disappeared.

"We should move," Ares said.

"Let's." Zeus snapped his fingers and dematerialized along with her father, Hera and Athena.

"Okay. It's just us."

"Do you want to use the same exit or would you prefer a walk?"

"I think using my feet might be the better option."

Echion held out his elbow.

"A true gentleman, Brother."

He gave her a genuine megawatt smile. "Indeed, Sister."

They used the passage to their left and began a slow walk.

"Do you really think I'm in danger?"

"Let's just say there will be a number of gods and goddesses that don't think you should have had the privilege to speak at court today."

"Why? I only spoke the truth."

"And that is what probably bothers most of them."

"How so?"

"Some of them prefer to be ignorant of the children they've left behind."

Carissa's heart sank and her body stiffened. What if her father had felt the same?

"Before you start thinking silly things, Father would not have left you alone for so many years if Zeus hadn't decreed that the gods stay away from the mortal realm. You know they've caused enough grief there over many thousands of years."

"Was I projecting my thoughts?"

"No, I picked it up when you tensed."

"You're right. Just by Father's actions I know, and he has told me so too."

"You're half mortal, Sister, you will always have the emotions humans have, and sadly, doubt is something that seeps in."

She let out a small laugh. "Everything you said is true and logical." She paused. "I feel for those demi-gods out there who have been abandoned."

"Don't. Xen has a register as you know, and he will keep an eye out. It is only you and Hal who slipped from the radar and that was for different reasons."

He has right. She'd had her powers bound so she couldn't be detected, and Hal had used other means to mask his whereabouts and power.

"Walking with you, Brother, helps make sense of it all."

"I'm more than sure you would have worked it all out on your own sister. Yes, we are a bit peculiar."

"You think?"

He let out a laugh. "We're almost there." He pointed with his free hand.

Her sigh of relief dissipated when four gods appeared in front of them to block their path. Echion stopped in his tracks and so did she.

"How armed are you?" her brother asked.

"Well."

"Good. I hope we don't need it—they are only minor gods."

One of the minor gods stepped forward.

"What brings you boys here?" Echion asked.

"Thought we'd get an up-close look at the demi-god who thinks she can speak in a courtroom full of gods and goddesses."

The other three stepped closer too.

"I can assure you boys that there is nothing much to see. I'm just a silly mortal."

The minor god who had stepped forward first, *the ringleader*, Carissa thought, pointed a finger at her and nodded his head before taking a quick look at his cronies. "See boys, she gets that she's nobody."

"Well bless you heart. You came here to put me in my place."

"You got that right you good for nothing loudmouth who couldn't stay out of the gods' business. Had to make it all about you and your baby."

Echion pushed Carissa behind him. "You listen here. You take your friends and get out of here before I raise hell."

"Ha. You hear that boys, this guy thinks he can best us," the ringleader shouted back.

Carissa moved from behind her brother. "He doesn't think, he knows."

The group now manifested weapons.

She looked up at her brother.

He smiled at her. "Ready for some fun."

"You bet." She unsheathed her sword and it hummed in her hands.

The minor gods charged. Two for her and two for her brother.

They broke apart and Carissa's sword came down hard on the first assailant's weapon, splintering it to pieces. The minor god's face turned ashen and he dematerialized. That didn't seem to deter the second assailant.

He came at her with a wide opening. Her foot came up and she kicked him in the midsection, sending him backwards.

He stumbled but managed to regain his footing and came at her again with the same maneuver.

She rolled her eyes at his fighting skills, gave him another kick and again he came at her. "Really?" This was ridiculous.

He swung as he got close.

She blocked his strike and stepped out of the way. He turned and she took aim. He in turn brought his sword up to stop her blow, but his weapon fell from his hand from the force of her strike. He dematerialized.

She turned to help her brother, who was now fighting the ringleader. He at least knew how to fight, unlike the two who had set upon her. Her brother didn't look like he needed any help. She sheathed her sword.

Echion unarmed his assailant and had him pinned with one sword to the throat and one behind his back.

"This fight is over," Echion's voice boomed.

But the ringleader thought not. He dematerialized and zapped himself to where Carissa stood. He pulled a short knife from his vest.

The gears in Carissa's brain sprang to action. She pulled out a gun and aimed it at his foot. The shot rang out and echoed around them. The ringleader dropped to the ground with a howl

Zeus, Ares, Hera, and Athena appeared with a bevy of other gods.

Ares moved in front of her.

"It's fine, Father."

The minor god on the ground howled again. "She attacked me."

Carissa shook her head and replaced her gun in her holster.

The mighty god stepped forward. "You dare attack not only my granddaughter but my guest?"

The ringleader cowered.

Ares bent down near the ringleader and grabbed him by the

hair. With his strength he lifted him up. "Who sent you?" he yelled amidst the screams of the ringleader.

"No one."

"Maybe some time in a cell will restart your memory. Guards." Zeus stepped aside and a group of men seized the ringleader.

Echion slid some heavy cuffs around his wrist. When they locked into place a bright red light traveled down the seams welding them shut.

Carissa raised an eyebrow in question.

"So that he doesn't dematerialize," her brother answered.

The guards marched him away.

Zeus waved a hand and the rest of the gods and goddesses disappeared.

"Let's get inside." Ares scanned the area.

Zeus, Hera, Athena, and Echion followed Carissa and Ares into his domain. They walked through the large foyer to a sunken lounge area where everyone dispersed and took a seat. They broke out into loud chatter about what had happened. Echion gave them the run down. Carissa watched and listened to all their assumptions of why she might have been attacked. She had not sat down, nor had her father.

"It was a scare tactic. Whoever sent them, it was to scare me," she said.

They all turned and looked at her.

"The ringleader was not pleased with the voicing of my opinion in court today."

"He said as much," Echion added.

"I always knew that having your say would irk a few gods and goddesses."

"More like half of them, Brother," Athena drawled with a raised eyebrow.

"Does this mean they'd rather not know what their offspring in the mortal realm are doing?"

Hera rose from where she had been lounging next to Carissa and took her hands. "For many of them, as hard as it is to hear this, Granddaughter, the answer is yes."

She bit her lip. The realization the gods were no different than mortals who left their kids hit her hard. A heaviness settled in her chest. "I guess I'm fighting for only a select few." She glanced at her father.

"*Kori mou*, do not let what's happened change your views. You spoke the truth, and unfortunately some gods and goddesses do not want to face the responsibility."

She deliberated his words. In truth there was nothing she could do about the gods or goddesses who didn't care about their half mortal offspring. "Should I expect more of what happened out there earlier?"

"Yes," Athena answered. "You would be safest back home."

"My thoughts are the same," her father agreed

"How about we have lunch first and then you can send Carissa home," Hera suggested.

Zeus clapped his hands together. "That sounds like a marvelous idea. A victory lunch before we send my granddaughter home."

Delia appeared. "Lunch is served."

Carissa opened her mouth and then slammed it shut. "That was quick," she mouthed in Delia's direction.

She beamed.

"How?" she whispered.

"I rang ahead." Her father held out his arm for her.

She took it and he gave her a quick wink.

She walked in sync with her father as Delia led them all to the large dining area for their lunch.

Carissa looked at the plentiful display of red mullet, lentils, beans, chickpeas, cheese, cooked chicory leaves, fresh bread, olives, nuts and fruits. Her mouth watered. She caught Delia's eye and held her thumb up. She again beamed back.

Carissa had already done a quick list in her head of what she would have first and removed her sword.

Her father swept her into her seat next to him. "I thought you might have gone symposium style."

"No *kori mou*, that's for after the meal."

The symposium was a gathering or more a drinking party. Now

she knew it took place after the meal. There was music, recitals, dancing and more importantly conversation. "Learn something new every day," she mumbled.

"And I doubt anyone wants to sit and discuss Socratic dialogues and literary works after that court hearing."

"You're right. Food and wine and chill time."

"Definitely need some relaxation, Sister." Echion took a seat next to her.

Several other servants appeared once they were seated. Each helped serve the food, and nobody wasted any time diving in.

"So, Granddaughter, have you given much thought to what I have suggested," Zeus said.

The truth was she hadn't given it any more thought since he'd asked, and she had a sinking feeling he already knew that but asked anyway.

"Grandfather, you honor me, however I can't see any good coming from it. What happened earlier is a clear indication the gods and goddesses won't accept someone like me."

"It's not their decision," Zeus answered.

"No, but can you imagine what trouble I would bring with me if I popped up here whenever I felt like it?"

Zeus' lips turned up in a smile. "Nothing wrong with an occasional dust up."

She raised an eyebrow. *He seriously didn't just say that.*

He did, kori mou.

She used her power to push everyone out and closed her mind off.

"I think you'd end up with more than a fight. It could get ugly."

"She has a point, Father."

"Yes, but giving her access isn't just about coming to visit you, Son. It's for Hera and me." Zeus looked across to his wife.

"What if we said we would like to make amends and see more of you."

The hair on Carissa's neck rose. She recognized the energy of the incoming god. "Koal," she said as he landed right behind her chair on the floor with a loud bang.

He jumped to his feet and bowed. "Apologies for the intrusion, but I think you all need to come back to the tapestry room."

Zeus got to his feet. "Speak. What has happened?"

"It's been reduced to a mess."

Athena jumped up and dematerialized along with Zeus and Hera.

Carissa tried to process. Why would anyone do that?

"Echion, get some men and meet me at the tapestry room." Her father grabbed her hand, and she snatched her sword before they dematerialized to the room.

She surveyed the damage. Athena's winning tapestries had all been slashed, and on the marble floor there was a message. They walked toward Zeus, Hera and Athena who were already looking down at it.

Carissa and Koal followed her father. "Be on your guard."

"Always. What do you think this is about?"

"I think you're about to find out."

Painted in red on the pristine marble floors was—*Voting for half mortals has a price. She doesn't belong here.*

Carissa read the message twice. Someone had lashed out at the goddesses tapestries. Because of her.

"This is because of me?"

"No child," Zeus said.

"This is because there are many disloyal gods and goddesses on Olympus, and they will feel my daughter's wrath along with mine."

A shiver ran up Carissa's spine. "Someone is playing a dangerous game."

"They are," Koal answered beside her.

"How did you come across it?"

"I was tasked to light the oil lamps, and as soon as I lit a few this is what I saw." He waved his arm across the torn tapestries. "I came to summon you immediately."

"Granddaughter, I will need your help with this, and you will have to accept my offer."

Damn it, he was putting her on the spot. For a split second she thought maybe Zeus did this to get her to accept his "get in and out of Olympus when you want" card, but she dismissed the fleeting notion as quickly as it appeared. There was no way he would do this to Athena.

"Who has access to this room."

"Everyone."

"Well, that's going to make it difficult." She tapped her chin. It was a long shot, but she wanted to ask, "You don't have any video surveillance, do you?"

"No, but with the right spell one can pick up a signature or signatures of who has been in the room." A hint of excitement laced Koal's voice.

"What do we need for that?"

"Clear the room," Athena shouted. "I will stay with Carissa and Koal."

Her father stepped toward her. "I will be in my chambers. I want a full rundown of what you find here."

She nodded.

"Echion, place some men outside the entrance and exit."

He nodded and then they dematerialized.

Athena motioned for them to step back. Then waved her hand. *Paragignomai,* she said.

Small particles of light rained down on the room and then swirled, taking shapes and forms in blurred fashion. If this was the recording of the last few hours, then this room was increasingly busy and there were a great deal of visitors. They waited and watched and saw many gods and goddesses moving about the room admiring the tapestries. This went on for a few minutes and then Athena spoke another spell and everything sped up. More and more moving visitors to the room.

"This should show us who did it."

"One can only hope, Niece."

"If it's like a recording then it should show us."

"Yes, but we are dealing with gods and goddesses, and there's a good chance those responsible for this covered their tracks."

"Surely they can't tamper with that kind of surveillance."

"No, but they can disguise their signature so that it doesn't appear," Athena said.

"Then we're wasting our time," Koal said.

"Koal. Sometimes the smallest detail can be important. Don't forget those that commit crimes are often hasty with something in their plan."

"Well said, Niece." Athena took a few steps toward them and watched the blur of signatures.

Carissa turned her attention to where Athena's tapestries hung. One signature went near them for quite some time. Light particles danced around the main areas.

Koal had moved back a bit. Something had piqued his interest. "We should be getting close."

"Yes, but there doesn't seem to be any action close to the tapestries," Carissa said over her shoulder while zeroing in on one particular tapestry. It was a scene where all the gods were seated together. There was a slight signature there.

Athena moved closer and waved her hand at the light particles that danced there.

A familiar sense crawled up Carissa's arm, except she couldn't place it. "Here," she shouted.

Athena and Koal both moved closer. They too waved a hand through the light particles.

"I've got nothing," Koal said.

Carissa looked again. "There is something faint, but it's masked by something."

"Doesn't matter, Niece, it will come to you when needed."

They stood there and then a minute later the light and signature blurs all disappeared.

"Did either of you pick up anything else closer to the tapestries?" Carissa asked.

"Nothing apart from what you did," Athena answered.

It wasn't enough, but it was better than nothing. This was because of her. Carissa swallowed hard and looked down to her feet.

"Stop thinking it's because of you. I make my own decisions, and if those numbskull gods and goddesses don't like it then it's too bad because they've given me a good reason to be my targets for the next millennium."

"I'd hate to get you angry." Carissa laughed.

Athena winked. "I might turn green."

"Don't tell me you've been binge watching popular movies?"

"Guilty." She stuck her hand up. "Let's get you back to your father."

Athena placed a hand on Carissa's shoulder and they dematerialized to her father's chambers along with Koal.

But when they materialized in her father's chambers there were two gods fighting with him. Ares had just run his sword through one.

A spear appeared in Athena's hand. She took aim, and it zoomed across the room and pierced the god who fought with Ares. From the force it harpooned him to the wall.

Her father raised an eyebrow at his sister. "I had it all under control."

"I know, Brother, but why deprive me?"

He let out a laugh.

Koal's mouth hung open. Carissa leaned over, stuck a finger under his chin and closed his mouth for him.

"It's getting crazier, isn't it?"

"Yes, and that is why I have to send you home and now," Ares said.

She didn't get a chance for any goodbyes. Her father had thrown her in a vortex that propelled her back to the mortal realm.

FIFTEEN

"Misfortunes are less sharp when shared with others." ~ *Dion Chrysostom*

Xen's Office; Charleston, SC
Early evening, mortal realm – Day 6

Carissa landed in Xen's office. Wind whipped all over her and slowed to a flutter. Strong arms circled her torso. She was spun around until she met a pair of sea green eyes. "Xen."

"*Koukla.*" His devastating smile told her how happy he was to see her. He placed a soft kiss on her lips. "Welcome home."

She wrapped her arms around his neck and pulled him in for another kiss.

"What news do you bring?"

"Victory on the trial. Father won his case. He has been acquitted. Poseidon, however, was not happy about that nor were half the gods and goddesses present. Apparently there are many that don't agree with keeping tabs on their half mortal children."

She pulled out of his embrace and started to pace the room.

"Your father's acquittal is indeed good news, but what is bothering you?"

"Those that didn't agree attacked me and Echion."

A growl escaped Xen's lips. He pulled her into his arms again. "Tell me you weren't harmed."

"I wasn't. It was a feeble attack. Probably as a warning, but it didn't end there."

He pulled her in tighter.

"Someone slashed Athena's tapestries."

He raised an eyebrow.

"There exists on Olympus a museum sized tapestry room. Every year the goddesses have a competition to see who will create the best tapestry. Obviously Athena is undefeated and because she held the deciding vote and placed it in favor of Father, someone on team Poseidon didn't like it."

"How does that affect you?"

She thought back to Athena and her half sister and their plea for her to join the competition. To Zeus' request she accept his offer to enter Olympus at leisure and Koal's warning. "I'm not sure what to make of it all. There are some things that just don't add up."

"Where the gods are concerned there is always an ulterior motive. Trust your instincts."

"Where is everyone?"

"Asleep." He wiggled his eyebrows and started a slow dance with her.

Her body responded. "I think I know where this is going?"

"Where exactly?"

"Upstairs."

That was all she needed to say. Her vampire raced through the house and up to their room. He pulled the harness off her and tossed it on the dressing table. Then made quick work of her clothes and his.

When they'd both come down from their post-orgasmic bliss, Xen wanted the encyclopedia version of the events.

"Tell me everything and don't leave anything out."

SIXTEEN

"Many hands make light work." ~ *Homer*

Xen's mansion; Charleston, SC
Morning, mortal realm – Day 7

"Paula, don't just sit there."

"Why on earth are you wrapped in tulle?" Paula asked Yiayia.

Yiayia had entered the kitchen wrapped in white tulle. Somehow she had managed to tangle herself in it, walking stick included.

Paula raced to help her and tugged at the different ends to pry it loose. "Seriously Vetta, how did you manage this?"

"I was thinking about making some tulle bows for the church."

"That still doesn't explain the mess you created."

"I thought I'd pretend to be the pew."

Paula rolled her eyes.

"It was a good idea. Until I tied that knot too tight."

Paula undid said knot. "I think you should let the florist do all that."

"Have you seen how much they charge for a bow on a church pew? It's criminal."

"Vetta, the minute someone says wedding these days the price goes up."

"We can save some money if we do them ourselves."

"I think we should let the experts do the job."

"I can do them just as well as the florists."

"You just tied yourself in a bow. How will you manage the church pews?"

Yiayia gave it some thought. Paula had a point. "How about I use you as the church pew?"

"Seriously, you're losing your marbles." Paula bundled the tulle up and dumped it on the table. "I'm not going to be your church pew."

Yiayia let out a long-frustrated breath. "Back in our day we did everything ourselves."

"Well, we're no longer back in our day as you put it."

"We should be able to round up some of the younger girls to help us."

"Vetta, have you heard of outsourcing?"

"Out what? Saucing?"

"Not out saucing. *Outsourcing.* It's when you give certain projects to other people to complete because it's counterproductive for you to do it."

"So, we out sauce to the florist?"

"Not sauce. Source."

"That's what I said, out sauce."

"No, outsource."

"Out sauce, outsource. It's the same thing."

Paula slapped a hand to her forehead. "Vetta, there is no sauce in source."

Yiayia tapped her ear. "It sounds the same to me."

"We should check your ears."

"There is nothing wrong with my ears. I can hear fine." She walked over to the coffeemaker. She hadn't seen this type before.

Paula grabbed a cup from the cupboard. "Here, I'll do it for you."

"Is that a fancy Clooney machine?" Xen and his team had the latest in everything.

"It's a pod machine and not the popular one that features the actor."

"Still a Clooney machine."

Paula threw a pod in and a few seconds later handed Vetta a cup of coffee.

"Sure smells good."

"It is," Paula said.

Yiayia headed to the table. "So, after we out sauce the pew bows, what else do we need to organize?"

"There is still a lot to do. We have to decide on the food menu."

"Oh, that should be easy."

"I'm sure all these boys will want meat for their main meals."

"Got that right, they're giants."

"Who are giants?"

Yiayia and Paula both turned to the voice.

"*Carissa*," they squealed in unison.

The voices of her aunt and grandmother in the kitchen were animated, and she realized she had missed them. Xen had filled her in on what happened in Virginia and why he dragged them back home. She gave a kiss to her grandmother and aunt.

"We missed you, *paidi mou*," Yiayia said.

"I've missed you both too."

"What happened up there with the gods?" Paula pointed upward a few times.

"Father was acquitted, but not everyone was happy about it."

"Hmmm. That isn't any different to cases here."

"You're right, Yiayia, it isn't. Can't keep everyone happy. It makes me sad though that not all the gods care for their offspring."

"All that matters is that your father cares for you. You can't fix everyone," Paula said.

"I know you're right, Aunt Paula, but a part of me wishes that all the demi-god children at least had some acknowledgment from their divine parents." Carissa moved to the fancy coffee machine.

"That Clooney coffee gadget is pretty good," Yiayia said.

Clooney? It took her a moment to place the reference. She'd seen the ads. A laugh burst through her lips. She hadn't realized that was what she had needed.

With the cup in her hand she walked around the table. "I heard you ran into some trouble."

Yiayia took a sip of her coffee and put her cup on the table. "Well, I wouldn't call it trouble."

Paula threw her hands up, palms out. "Just so you know, Carissa, it was all her idea." She pointed to Yiayia who sported a cheeky look.

"Oh, come on Paula, you enjoyed it."

Carissa eyed her aunt.

"Well maybe just a little bit."

"Ha, I knew it," Yiayia said with victory in her voice.

Carissa shook her head. "You know you were supposed to go up to Virginia and just relax. Not go looking for trouble."

"Well technically we didn't go hunting for problems, we just needed to find an old friend."

"Yeah, one who happens to be a goddess."

"I had my reasons."

"I'm sure you did."

"What if it went the other way and she zapped you two into oblivion."

"They can do that?" Paula asked.

"They can do a great number of things, and they are also unpredictable because mortals are mere fodder for their games."

Yiayia and Paula both gulped.

"Listen, I love you both very much, but when Xen gives you protection, don't try to dodge it. Ring him and keep him in the loop. I'm sure he would have provided you with the transportation and muscle when you went to see Soteria."

They both nodded. "You're right. The vampire is a good man."

"What about vampires?" Adam asked as he walked in the kitchen.

"Adam." Carissa turned and greeted him with a hug.

"You ladies behaving?" he asked Yiayia and Paula as he walked to the coffee machine.

"We're busy with wedding plans," Yiayia said with a smile.

And just like that Carissa forgot everything else. They were all still planning a ridiculous oversized supernatural wedding. She rolled her eyes. Her day just went to hell in a handbasket. She didn't want any part of this madness.

"You can help us with the food options, Carissa." Yiayia beamed.

"That's a great idea." Paula cheered.

Adam had a shit-eating grin on his face. He'd picked up her emotions and knew she wasn't getting any enjoyment out of the wedding talk. "I agree," he added.

Her eyes turned to slits, and she wished she could send laser beams his way, much like Superman. "Watch yourself wolf."

Adam held up one hand. "I'm just saying your feedback might save them some time."

She bit her bottom lip. That was it, she was going to kill the lykos. "Adam," she spat out through gritted teeth. "Don't make me compel you to do something you wouldn't want to do." Her words got his attention. "Excuse us for a minute."

"Right. I might just get back to what I was doing."

"And what might that have been?"

"Training some of Lox's men to use phones and computers."

"How is that all going?"

"Let's just say it's a big adjustment for most of them."

"Do you see them as a problem down the road?"

"No, they're good men. They want only to settle down and have families. They've been fighting for a long time."

She understood that. "Is there something I can help with?"

"No. You've got a wedding to plan." He grinned.

Her hand landed on his arm. "About that. How crazy have they all gone while I was away?"

"In a huge way."

She slapped a hand to her forehead. It was bound to become more ridiculous, and there was the subject of the ring. She had not accepted it yet. Even though she was bonded to Xen by vampire law, and they were wedded in all ways that mattered in the supernatural world, it was the mortal formality that had become a circus.

"If it's not what you want, why don't you tell them?"

"Easier said than done."

"Find a way, Rissa."

A half smile broke on her lips. "Better not let Xen hear you calling me that."

He gave her a thumbs up. "I'll keep that for when your other half is in his beauty sleep."

"You sure I can't tag along? Something tells me if I stay here I'm going to get dragged into wedding drama, and I really don't need that now."

"You'll do anything to avoid it."

"Ah ha."

"Okay. I'm heading out in half."

"Good."

Carissa watched as Adam downed the rest of his coffee and made his way back to the sink. He rinsed it and put it in the dishwasher. "As much as I would love to spend time with you ladies, I have to get moving."

Yiayia and Paula broke out in disappointed chatter. "Stay, we're going to make some cookies."

He gave them a half hug where they sat. Their faces beamed. They really liked Adam. "I promise to eat all of them when I get back."

He headed back to Carissa. "You have a way with them."

"They just want conversation."

"Speaking of which, I need to have one with them."

"Don't rain too hard on their parade."

"That's exactly what the wedding will be if I don't try to stop it."

"Go easy, Rissa," he said before exiting from the kitchen.

She pulled out a chair. "About the wedding." Her grandmother and aunt sat up to attention. Yep, this was going to be hard. She'd have to rip the bandage off the arm, otherwise there would be no stopping them. "I love you both, however we are going to have to cut some numbers and possibly get a smaller venue."

"What?" Paula asked.

"But." Yiayia opened and closed her mouth.

Carissa held up a hand. "I know you want to invite everyone, but that's not what I want."

"What will people think?"

"Does it really matter what they think? Seriously, our world is not what it was before." And she didn't want to share some of her new world with people she only knew by name and had never met.

Yiayia put her hand on hers. "If you really want something small then that's what you'll have."

"I'd rather spend the time with a few loved ones than a whole horde of mortals and immortals I won't see again after the wedding."

Paula let out a long breath. "That is true, but if that's what you want then we are going to have to shrink everything."

Yiayia squeezed her hand. "How about you write a list and then we can discuss if you can add a few people."

Carissa nodded her head. "That sounds more like something I would like."

"What about dresses?" Paula asked.

"I promise we can start looking at those in the next day or so."

Paula clasped her hands together. Her aunt loved to shop, and it was going to be mental, but she owed them that.

"Okay. I'm going to head out with Adam for a bit. Can you please try to stay out of trouble?"

They both pulled a poker face. "We're not getting up to too much today. Just out saucing the pew bows," Yiayia said.

"It's outsourcing, Vetta."

Yiayia waved a hand at Paula. "Same thing."

Carissa let out a laugh. "You don't need to out sauce too many. Remember, keep it small." She winked then bent to kiss her grandmother.

"Hey, where's mine?"

"Don't worry, Aunt Paula. You'll get your sugar too." She grabbed her cell phone. "Give me updates."

"Oh, the vampire said you can track us now. He put some app thing on yours and ours."

Not that that would stop them from getting into mischief, but at least now they could see where they were. She'd thank Xen later.

SEVENTEEN

"Education is the kindling of a flame, not the filling of a vessel." ~ *Socrates*

Highland Park; Charleston, SC
Morning, mortal realm – Day 7

Carissa threaded her hand on the handle above the window when Adam swung the SUV in a hard turn before pulling over near a small apartment block in Highland Park. "You didn't need the theatrics of that turn."

"Gotta have some fun, Rissa." He twitched his eyebrows, which was a very Adam thing to do.

She unbuckled her seatbelt. "What exactly are you teaching the boys tonight?"

"Basically how to turn shit on and what buttons to press." Adam was already out of the car.

She opened her door "They've been on the mortal plane for a few hundred years, right?"

"Yes."

"Why didn't they take the initiative to bring themselves up to speed."

"Money, resources, lack of housing. They've been moving around a lot. Some of them have phones and can use a laptop, but not all."

"Like Lox?"

"Yeah."

"You think they'll be okay with it all?" She slid out of her seat and her feet hit gravel.

Adam was already around to her side. "One step at a time. I think bringing them up to speed with twenty-first century technology might even be rewarding for some."

"I think you're right." She shut the door. "What do you want me to do?"

"If we can break them up in groups then we can both tackle more at once."

They walked toward the apartment block entrance. A tall figure emerged from the side.

"Hello, Carissa."

"Phil?"

He had his arms open for a hug.

She stepped in. "Good to see you."

"And you."

"Are you helping out?"

"I'm just the eyes," he said with a laugh.

Adam lifted his chin and Phil did the same.

"Okay Rissa, let's get this show on the road." They stepped through the foyer, and Adam knocked on the first apartment door.

Lox pulled the door open. "Daughter of Ares," he greeted.

"Just Carissa. No need for that kind of formality."

Lox smiled for the first time. "We need to have a word."

"I'd be happy to. Now or later?"

"How about when you finish up."

"Sounds good." Carissa had a feeling it was going to be in relation to their last exchange, which you could say was tense.

"Adam." Lox held out his hand

He took it and swung a hand to clasp Lox on the shoulder. At least they were on warmer terms.

In the lounge area of the room there were at least thirty men.

"Okay, listen up. I want you to break up in groups of fifteen. I will give each group a basic rundown of how to use a laptop and Carissa will show y'all the basic stuff you need to know to use a cell phone. Then we swap groups so everyone gets training on both."

They all nodded in approval and arranged themselves into the necessary numbered groups.

"Right Rissa, you're up and we have four apartments to do."

"You're joking?"

"I wish I was."

She pulled her sleeves up. At least they had all opened the boxes holding their phones. She noted the laptops would be shared. She knew who was responsible for all of this—Xen.

"Okay boys, let's show you how to use these babies."

"I'm sure they are not babies," one of the men said.

"No, that's a figure of speech or slang."

"Oh."

The fellow who asked looked young. "What is your name?" she asked.

"Jason."

"Nice to meet you, Jason."

"My lady." He half bowed.

Her lips twitched. *How very eighteenth century*, she thought. "Okay, let's start. If you all pick up your phones…"

And that was how the next few hours went. When she finished off with one group she rotated with Adam. Young Jason absorbed everything fast and was able to help the others in the group who couldn't grasp some of it, and that had given her an idea.

"Jason, will you help train some of the others?"

"It would be a pleasure, my lady."

"Just call me Carissa."

"Okay, my lady Carissa."

"You don't need to use my lady. No one does that anymore."

Jason's eyebrows rose to his hairline. "That's not right."

Okay, that wasn't going to be easy to let go of. "How about we practice you calling me just Carissa for today and see how that goes."

"Yes, m… Carissa."

She smiled. "Much better."

Adam walked over to Carissa. "If you two have finished here, we need to get started with the group next door and then upstairs.

"I've inducted Jason. That will help us move a bit faster."

"Good. I've got one of the other men to help with the laptop side of things too."

Adam led the way, and they all filed into the corridor and into the next room. Lox tagged along behind them. The hours ticked by, and they managed to grab any talent along the way, which helped them chew through the teaching.

Carissa caught Adam's eye. He had just wrapped up his end and started to make his way over to her.

"I'm all talked out," she said.

"I feel the same, Rissa."

"I hope you can spare five minutes for a quick chat with me," Lox asked from behind her.

She spun around. "Sure."

Adam stuck out his hand.

Lox closed his fingers around Adam's and gave him a solid handshake. "Thanks man."

"No problem. I'll be in the car." Adam spun and made a quick exit.

"I wanted to say that we probably got off on the wrong foot."

"Listen Lox, there was a lot going on, and you have to understand we had been looking for Kelly for some time. When the news arrived that some demon had kidnapped her, we feared the worst. So when I met you, I met you with the knowledge that it would possibly not end well. I was already angry, even after I saw Kelly was fine and healthy."

He nodded his head. "I figured that might be the case."

She gave him her hand. "Friends?"

His large palm closed around hers and his lips turned up. "More than that, allies." Her palm tingled, and power coursed from her arm down to where their palms met. Light blue energy flowed around their handshake.

"You are both bound by an orkos," Jason said as he stepped closer.

"Looks like I have your back indefinitely."

"And I yours," she said.

When the blue energy died off, she pulled her hand away. She hadn't expected that and would have to ask Xen what this *orkos* with Lox meant, but that could wait.

"Say hi to Kelly."

"She asked about you earlier, but you were busy with the men."

"Tell her I will pop in soon." She really did need to set some time for friends. Lately her life had been one big supernatural drama.

"Thanks again, Carissa," Lox said.

"No problem."

She turned to Jason who was still standing there and looking at her with awe.

"My pleasure, Carissa." He bowed.

She raised two finger guns in his direction and winked. "See, you got it." They could work on the bowing thing down the track.

He stepped close and opened his arms for a hug. She gave him one. Then took her leave. On her way out she spotted Phil.

"How'd it go?"

She dropped her shoulders. "It was long but at least they are fast learners. It would have been far worse if they didn't catch on quickly."

"True." An engine started. "Guess you better move. Adam is ready to roll."

She gave him a hug and bounced down the stairs toward the car. She made quick work of getting in and buckling up.

"I really need to eat something. I don't think my stomach can hold out anymore."

"Now there we are aligned. Burgers okay?"

"They'd be magic right now." She looked at her watch. "But I think it might have to be takeaway. It's getting close to Xen waking up."

"Then burgers to go it is."

He made a call to order the burgers ahead, and she settled into the leather seat and zoned out, her thoughts drifting. Several times during the day she'd checked to see where her grandmother and aunt were. Nothing unusual. She saw they had gone to her grandmother's house, which was still being renovated by Xen. Then they had visited a few shops in town. Everything seemed above board. For now it looked like they'd had an ordinary day. She sure hoped that was the case.

"You okay?" Adam asked.

"Yeah, just thinking."

"About?"

"Family."

He let out a laugh. "Have to say that yours likes to keep everyone on their toes."

"They do. I told them about a smaller wedding."

"Good. Now you have to tell Xen."

"I do."

There was a little fixing to do there. She had left him in the lurch. She wanted this but not the big shabam everyone had in mind. She'd deal with that later.

"What do you make of Lox?" she asked, changing the subject.

"He's not a bad guy if that's what you're thinking?"

"No. I didn't get that vibe. I had a conflict of interest when I met him, but there are no hard feelings."

"They've been through years and years of battles with the other factions of demons. Their name stands for happiness and welfare. Why they were cast to Hades' realm is beyond anyone's understanding, but they were, and they fought all manner of bad spirits in Hades' realm. You'll find when they settle, they'll want to help. It's in their DNA."

She digested what he said. When she and Lox were bound in the blue light with their hands, she only received happiness from that connection. There was nothing in that moment that made her think she should be shouting, *Danger, danger Will Robinson.* "I don't think he's a bad guy. I just wanted to know a bit more. His men were pleasant, and no ill feelings bounced off any of them."

"They were grateful for the help, and there is a lot of adjusting to do."

"True, and that takes time."

"It does." Adam pulled over near a popular burger place in Charleston. "I'll only be a minute." He unbuckled himself and pulled on the door handle. He was out of the car before she could blink.

"Those guys really are fast."

"I reckon," she agreed, and her head swung around fast. "Koal, what are you doing here?" And then her gray matter kicked into action. "Wait, have you been following me around all day?"

"Not entirely, but pretty much."

"Why didn't anyone pick anything up?"

"Bonus of the cap is it not only gives me invisibility, as you know, it grants me the ability to not be detected."

"I don't know if I should be worried about not picking anything up."

"I'm really good with this."

She rolled her eyes. "Why are you here?"

"Your father and Zeus wanted me to keep an eye out for you. They think whatever happened on Olympus may follow you here."

"So, you're their tracking device."

"Yes, no." He shook his head. "More like, be on the lookout for suspicious activity."

"Well, if you're here with me then you're not looking for anything out of the ordinary."

"You have a point."

"Are you going to stick around."

"Only for the ride. Then I have to stake out your vampire's place."

Great, that was all she needed. "You can go back to Olympus and tell Father and Grandfather I'm okay. I have enough protection and surveillance."

"I don't think they'd be impressed if I did that."

"Listen, Koal. I don't know what they think will happen, but I'm sure we have more than enough men to take care of any attack. Trust me on this."

"I do. They just wanted to be sure."

"Okay. You can call it quits as soon as we reach Xen's mansion."

"Deal."

He stuck out his hand and she gave him a vigorous handshake. Power tingled between them.

"What was that?" she asked.

"That's a gentlemen's agreement. I will keep my word." Then he pulled the cap over his head and became invisible.

Adam pulled the door open and jumped in the car with several bags.

"You sure you have enough?"

"Well, I was hungry." He shrugged his shoulders and passed the bags to Carissa. She turned and placed them where Koal was sitting. "She saw the bags move. A grin spread across her face.

Adam started the car and moved into traffic. "What are you smiling about?"

"Nothing."

"Doesn't seem like nada. Who were you entertaining today?"

"What do you mean."

"There was a faint fragrance following you around all day. Then it disappeared for a while, and now it's back and stronger. I can smell it."

She whipped her head around. "Why didn't you say something earlier?"

"I wasn't sure. But now I am. Who or what is following you?"

"Okay, Koal, time to come clean. So much for total invisibility and hidden presence. That cap needs fixing," she scoffed.

Koal pushed his cap up and appeared.

Adam just looked in the rearview mirror. "Good to see you Koal."

"Likewise, Adam."

"I don't think that cap fully works on wolves." Carissa tossed the words over her shoulder to where Koal was sitting.

Adam wrinkled his nose. "Well, we do have a higher sense of smell."

She slapped his arm.

"Should I ask?" Adam queried.

"No, I think it's best to just let this one go."

"I won't intrude."

"Thank you Adam."

"Yeah, thanks Adam," Koal said. "You okay if I just remove myself visually. I'll be out of your hair soon."

"All good with me."

With that Koal once again pulled his cap down and disappeared right before they pulled up to Xen's mansion.

"Wait," Carissa said to Adam.

He stopped at the gate.

"I think this is where you get out Koal."

The back door opened and then closed.

Adam hit a button and the garage door opened. He drove the car into the underground parking.

Kane was waiting, feet planted firmly on the ground and arms across his chest.

A big smile broke over her face. When the car stopped, she released her seat belt and got out to greet Kane.

"Where have you been?" she said, stepping in to give him a hug.

"Catching up on some much-needed sleep."

"Is the boss man working you too hard? You know I can always have a word."

He let out a laugh. "It comes with the territory."

"What's up?" Adam said.

"Came to grab you and warn you before you head upstairs."

Carissa's eyes turned to saucers. "What have they done?"

He chuckled. "You know, the usual."

"They have a usual now? That's really not good for anyone." She mouthed the last bit to herself. *I'm too scared to ask.*

"Oh, come on." Adam headed to the stairs.

She took off after him and hoped with every fiber of her being her *yiayia* and aunt hadn't turned the whole place upside down. They really were a force to be reckoned with. Well, in her mind they were.

"Adam, I think you better let me through first."

"Relax, Rissa. I'm sure it's not that bad."

Kane laughed from behind her.

"Since Kane's not giving anything away, I'm fearing the worst."

She pushed Adam out of the way and took the stairs two at a time until she reached the door that led to the foyer.

Her feet took her to the familiar voices coming from the kitchen.

EIGHTEEN

"Life without feasts is like a long road without taverns." ~ *Democritus*

Xen's mansion; Charleston, SC
Evening, mortal realm – Day 7

"You don't put vinegar in tomato salad," Yiayia could be heard as Carissa approached the kitchen.

"Who said? I've had it many times."

She caught her grandmother shaking her head at her aunt.

Then she looked around the kitchen and her mouth dropped open. "What is all this?" She swept her arm around Xen's kitchen and dining area. It catered to many of the *Phi Athanatoi* at different times, so ample space had been included in the design.

Four giant cakes sat on trollies taking up most of the space, and wherever there had been any space was now filled with large urns and flowers of different color combos.

"Carissa. We've narrowed down the flowers and cakes."

"What does that mean?" she whispered.

"This is nothing. You should have been here two hours ago," Kane said, shaking his head.

It was her turn to do the same. "What part of small did you not understand?"

"This is small," Paula said.

"What's small?" Xen walked into the kitchen.

She turned and faced her fiancé. "This…" she pointed in the direction of the cakes and flowers "…is a disaster."

A bell went off somewhere and two of the large cakes burst open. Out of them two male strippers popped.

"What the actual…" She didn't say it, and it bugged her that she actually wanted to. "Seriously?"

"Okay, that's it. I'm going to cancel everything. Actually no." She turned to Xen who was laughing along with Kane and Adam. "You're going to *stop all of this. Otherwise there will be no wedding.*"

She walked out of the kitchen and through the front door.

"Koal," she whispered.

He materialized. "Yes, Carissa."

"Can you take me to Olympus."

"I don't think that's a good idea."

"Okay, how do I get you to materialize me somewhere."

"Just think it and I'll take you there."

"He put a hand on her."

Xen flung open the front door. "*No.*"

He dashed to Koal and Carissa, but before he could reach her they had dematerialized.

"Guess she's pissed," Kane said from beside him.

"Royally," Adam added.

Xen growled and his fangs elongated. He turned to go face the troublemakers inside.

"You might want to put a lid on your current wedding planners."

"Stay out of it," Kane said to Adam.

Adam put his hands up. "Just saying."

"Noted." He withdrew his fangs.

Carissa's reactions toward the wedding were baffling. He stomped back into the kitchen.

"Ladies, we are going to have a word about all this."

"We didn't mean to upset her, we just wanted to make it easy for her," Yiayia said.

"I know but it's obviously bothering her."

"Well, she said she wanted a small wedding, and we were trying to pick things for a smaller wedding with a little bit of entertainment."

His *koukla* didn't want the whole fanfare of what her grandmother just said. He looked around the room. It was over the top, and the strippers were out of their cakes. He walked over to where the men threw on some shirts. "Collect your showpiece. Your services will not be required."

The men looked at each other then scrambled to get out of there. With their cake props.

Xen then walked over to her grandmother and aunt. "As much as this pains me to say, I am hereby revoking your authority to plan anything more. If it results in my fiancée running away, then there's something we're all missing, and that is her wishes."

Yiayia and Aunt Paula both dropped their shoulders.

"We'll clean everything up in the morning," Yiayia said.

"Good. Just be clear. I'll be doing the organizing."

"Yes, Xen."

"Yes."

"Now, I'm going to go try to find where she ran off to." It wasn't how he wanted to spend his evening, and why was Koal here? That meant Ares had his suspicions about all that occurred on Olympus. What were the gods playing at now? The sooner he found Carissa, the better. He rushed to his office. Kane and Adam were already sitting in the lounge area eating burgers. He dropped into his chair.

"Relax boss, she'll be fine." Adam took another bite of his burger.

"I'd rather she was here."

"Koal has been following her around all day."

Xen shot to his feet and walked around the table in Adam's direction. "Spill it."

"I could scent him all day and then he revealed himself in the car. When we got here, he vamoosed, but it looks like he hung around."

"Why is he here?"

"Rissa didn't say."

Xen growled at the nickname.

"Sorry. I meant Carissa."

"She didn't share what he was doing here?"

"I asked and she said I didn't need to know. I trusted her judgment."

"Hers I trust, but the gods, not so much."

"Might not be wise to go after her. Let her cool off," Kane said.

"You're right." He knew it, but every thread of his genetic structure wanted to go find her and protect her. He clenched his jaw, tight. "I suppose you could fill me in on how today went with the training of Lox's men."

At least that would take his mind off his bonded for a while.

Carissa and Koal materialized outside of Kirke's house. She knocked on the door and footsteps could be heard approaching. She hoped Kirke didn't mind.

The door opened and there stood her witchy friend. She glanced at Carissa from head to toe. "What's wrong?"

"Nothing major. I just needed a little time out."

She looked both over. "Come in, and you too."

"I don't remember if you met Koal."

"No. I had not. It's a pleasure."

Koal bowed. "Thank you, but I will wait out here."

"Your choice," Kirke said and shut the door.

"What have they done. Should I change them into toads?"

Carissa let out a laugh. "No, no need for that."

"What's troubling you?"

"The whole wedding thing."

"You should be enjoying the planning."

"That's just it, I'm not organizing anything. My aunt and grandmother are, and it's become one big circus. Xen finds it all entertaining. It's not at all what I want."

"Then tell him."

"I was going to, but I got walled in and the strippers coming out of their cakes was the final straw. What in the gods' names were Aunt Paula and Yiayia thinking?"

Kirke let out a laugh and walked into her open plan kitchen. "Whoa, I would have loved to have seen that."

"It's a nightmare." Carissa rolled her shoulders and sat on the couch.

Kirke threw some tea bags in two cups and poured water into them. "Sit them all down and talk to them."

"I tried that with my aunt and *yiayia*, but it seems the messaging was all wrong."

"Maybe you're reading into it too much." Kirke handed her a cup of tea. "Drink it, it will help you relax."

Carissa made a gagging noise. "No coffee?"

"No. Drink the tea."

"What type of tea is it?"

"Witches' brew." Kirke snorted a laugh.

"I won't grow an extra ear or something?" She let out a giggle. She blew on the tea and took a sip and then another. It wasn't half bad. "Mmmm." She raised an eyebrow. "I'm shocked but this tastes great."

"I might know a thing or too."

"You know a lot and I am fortunate to know you."

"Oh, stop. You sound like we are heading for battle."

They both drank a bit of tea and Carissa admired the silence. "Do you hear that?" she asked.

"What?"

"That lovely dead silence."

Kirke cast an ear. "That's not good."

"What do you mean?"

"It's too quiet, even the night animals can't be heard."

A loud thump sounded at the door and then it blew in. Wooden shards scattered everywhere, and both Carissa and Kirke dived for cover.

"Well, there goes my quiet time," Carissa said from behind a couch.

Koal appeared beside her. "There are lots of demons out there."

"Not these guys again," Kirke said, standing and blasting a magic illusion at the door. "I won't be able to hold them for too long."

"Koal, you need to get Xen."

"But what about you? I can dematerialize us."

"If we don't kill them, they'll move on to humans. We can't leave them roaming in the forest."

He nodded in understanding.

"Go."

He dematerialized.

"What's your plan?"

"My guess is they have us surrounded. It's either full frontal or face them at the back. I'm guessing there's less around back."

"Back it is then," Kirke said.

Carissa unsheathed her swords and followed Kirke. "Stay close. I'm about to throw us in darkness." Kirke waved her hand, and all the lights went out. She opened the door and stepped out on the back porch.

They could hear movement to their right. Carissa tapped Kirke on the shoulder and indicated to the left, but two demons stepped in their path. Carissa pushed Kirke behind her and plunged her sword into the demon's chest. A loud growl split the air. She pulled it out and sliced it through the air toward his head, cutting through the neck and removing it in a clean cut.

Kirke started blasting fire balls at the demons to their right.

The other demon to their left was about to attack when a voice called, "Enough."

A man from behind the demons headed toward them.

Kirke blasted a few more fire balls, setting some of the demons alight. They ran back from where they had come.

The man started to clap. "Good show."

"What do you want?" Carissa yelled when he got close enough.

Kirke snapped her fingers and the lights came back on. Now they had a visual of the man.

He pointed at her. "*You.*"

"I'm flattered but I'm taken."

He took a few more steps then stopped two meters from her.

Carissa recognized an incoming signature. It was Koal. He landed beside her with Xen, Kane and Adam. Xen let out a growl in the direction of the mystery man.

"What do you want, Damion?"

She turned her head sideways to glance at her vampire. "You know this dude?"

"Hate to break up this introduction party, but yes, Xen and I go way back. We're very good friends."

Xen stepped forward and unsheathed his sword. "You. Are. No. Friend. Of. Mine." His enunciation was clear.

"I'm not leaving without your bride."

"Not this shit again." Kirke huffed. "Find another girl," she said.

"Really. You know there are plenty of single women out there and lots of dating sites too." Carissa wasn't going to go through the whole kidnap scenario again. She'd already covered that ground with Hal. He'd kidnapped her because he thought he could gain godly power if he sacrificed her to the gods. She wasn't going to be another psycho's steppingstone in gaining access to Olympus. Damion would die trying to take her.

Adam and Kane had moved to face some demons closing in.

"You say the word boss and I'll shift," Adam directed to Kane.

Carissa's temper was building. She stepped from behind Xen. The sword tingled in her hand. "Now you…" she pointed her sword toward Damion, and it tingled in her hand, "…will grab all your friends and leave. I'm not going anywhere with you, and any disagreement you think you might have with Xen, I'm not part of it."

Damion scoffed. "This isn't about any disagreement I might have with your intended. This is about power. And you have something I want."

She rolled her eyes. Where the hell did these guys pop up from? "If you think you can gain something through me then you are sadly mistaken."

He let out a shrill laugh.

"The cheese has definitely slipped off this boy's cracker," Carissa said.

"Not wrong there," Kirke said, raising her hands. "Let me blast him."

"Careful, witch. He has a few tricks of his own," Xen warned.

"Who is he?" Carissa asked.

Xen took a step forward. "A thorn in my side."

"On my word witch, give him a good dose of your power."

"Say when vampire." Kirke had stepped beside Carissa.

"Y'all sure about that?" Carissa asked.

Xen turned his head and nodded. "*Now.*"

Kirke released a big fire ball of power toward Damion.

He lifted his arm to protect himself, and the power dissipated before it hit him.

"How the hell…" The words died on Kirke's lips when the same power came charging back at them. Kirke lifted her arms, and the power dissipated on an invisible force field. "Someone is shielding him with magic."

"Then anything we do will be useless," Carissa said.

"Witch, find a loophole."

Xen charged toward Damion at the same time the demons decided to charge too. Loud growls sounded from behind Carissa and Kirke. She looked over at Xen whose sword had just clashed with Damion's.

"Can you materialize us farther behind him," Carissa asked.

Kirke placed a hand on her and they dematerialized.

"Well, this is a better view of things," Carissa said.

"Now let's see if we can bring this guy down." Kirke threw a small dose of power toward Damion's back knee, and he buckled.

That was all the motivation she needed. She raised her hands and threw a giant ball of power at Damion's back.

"This gives new meaning to shooting someone in the back." Carissa laughed.

"And in this case, it's totally worth it. I'm sick of all these power-hungry men."

"Why me?" Carissa asked.

"Hold that thought. We'll have that discussion later." Kirke prepared to strike.

"Sure." She sighed.

The power hit Damion square in the back.

Xen had seen it coming and had sidestepped at the last second. The strength of the power propelled Damion forward. Xen gave him a martial arts kick and sent him face down into the grass. With his speed he disarmed Damion, pulled his hands behind his back and slapped on some cuffs.

"Well, that was easy," Carissa said to Kirke, but she spoke to soon. Two demons growled. Kirke blasted power in one of the demon's eyes and he dropped to the ground.

Carissa ducked out of the way of the demon charging her and sliced his midsection. He turned, growled louder and lifted his weapon to swing at her, but a sword from behind sliced through the air and took his head.

"I had that."

"I'm sure you did, *koukla*," Xen said before speeding over to Kirke and finishing off the demon growling from the blasts of power Kirke threw.

The demons took that opportunity to surround Damion.

Kane and Adam were already onto them. They had shifted and with loud growls tore through some of the demons. One demon had pulled Damion to his feet and was trying to break the cuffs Xen had placed on him.

"Looks like the boys need some help." Carissa lifted her chin in their direction.

"I'm on it." Xen flashed to where his men fought.

Carissa watched as they all fought. Xen took down two more

demons to get to Damion. More demons ran toward them. "We better get in there."

Kirke slapped a hand to her wrist to materialize them closer. When Carissa landed, she stabbed the demon closest and then aimed for his head. "They really don't want us to get him," she shouted.

The demons protecting Damion kept shuffling backwards but more kept joining the fight.

"Witch, see if you can break the circle guarding Damion."

Kirke threw more power to blind some of the demons. A few dropped to the ground.

Damion made a break for it and ran toward the tree line and into the thickness of the forest.

"He's getting away," Carissa shouted over her shoulder as she cut down another demon.

Xen raced into the forest.

Carissa kept slashing through and Koal reappeared. "Where were you?" she asked.

"Around front. Fighting off more of these monsters." He took a demon's head. "Where do they keep coming from?"

"Damion obviously has a portal open somewhere," Carissa answered and took down another demon. One more charged but he didn't make it. A large wolf opened his jaws, sank his sharp teeth into the demon's throat and ripped it out.

"Thanks, Kane."

The wolf gave her a small growl.

Adam and Kane shifted back to human form.

Kirke snapped her fingers, and the men were clothed.

"That could come in handy," Adam said.

"This is not a regular thing," Kirke bit back.

Adam lifted his hands in surrender, but he was grinning. He did like to stir things up.

Xen returned. "He managed to dematerialize before I got to him."

"He's obviously got help," Carissa said.

"Yes, and the question as always is who?"

"I'd like to throw something at whoever is helping him." Kirke signaled with her head and walked toward the back door.

"I think you need to fill us in on who this guy is, Xen." Carissa followed her friend.

Koal was on her heels.

NINETEEN

"We are not separated from spirit, we are in it." ~ Plotinus

Kirke's Cottage, Francis Marion Forest; Charleston, SC
Evening, mortal realm – Day 7

They all crammed into Kirke's cabin.

"Nice digs." Adam did a small turn about the cabin.

"You do know I'm going to have to spell y'all. This location and my cabin are supposed to be off the grid."

"Well, no chance of that now the demons and Xen's old friend know," Adam threw in.

"That's a very big problem for me."

Carissa grabbed her hand. "We will sort this out later. I promise." She didn't know how they would, then again she'd sure help her friend regain an unknown location. Kirke didn't like unearthly creatures knowing where she lived. Mortals she didn't mind.

Kirke calmed down a little.

Carissa turned to Xen. "Okay, spill it."

"Damion is a Titan who has dark magic."

Carissa's mouth dropped open. She closed it then opened it again. "You mean to say he's from the same stock as Iapetos and Kronos?" They had fought both Titans and won, casting them back to Tartarus. Her mouth did the fish thing again, a million things racing through her head. "How is he here. Why is he here? I mean apart from wanting to use Hal's kidnap move." She shrugged her shoulders.

"Whatever his reasons, I can assure you there will be only one outcome—war."

"You mean with you…" she scanned her finger around the room to her friends "…us?" Her hand went to her forehead, and she rubbed it.

"No," Kane replied.

Xen widened his stance and crossed his arms. He didn't answer. It seemed to her he was thinking things through, and it was agitating him. She could see the tick in his jaw.

"He means an all-out war with supernatural creatures," Kane said.

"Why? What does he gain by doing that?"

"Apart from having the mortal realm as his stomping ground?"

"No *koukla*, he wants it all for himself. He'd eradicate everyone."

She lifted an eyebrow. "Well, that's demented and would be a bit lonely. Don't you think?" she joked.

"Doesn't matter what we think. He has one goal. Annihilate everyone and everything in his path."

That didn't sound good. "I don't understand. That doesn't serve a higher purpose."

"For Damion it does. He thinks reducing this planet to nothing will make him king. He wants to rule."

"Rule what, the trees?" She laughed then shook her head. Tartarus sure held some nut jobs in there, and all of them were hell-bent on destroying everything so they could claim the mortal realm.

"What is it with Titans and world domination?"

"They're caught in a vicious cycle since the dawn of time," Koal answered from where he stood near the kitchen island bench.

"Nothing will change there," Adam said, opening the pantry.

"Keep your hands out of my cupboards wolf," Kirke said.

"What now?" Carissa asked.

"You need protection, *koukla*. He will return."

"I can look after myself."

"I never said you couldn't."

"Why me?" she asked again.

"Very simple, *koukla*, you're the daughter of Ares."

Kirke threw her thumb toward Xen. "What he said."

"How is that different from any of the other demi-god children? There are others out there. Not that I want these crazy Titans to get their hands on one, but at the same time why should I be the one they are always hunting."

"You have a direct line to Zeus." Kane stepped closer.

His words ricocheted in her brain. Someone had heard Zeus' offer to her. If she had the ability to enter Olympus as she pleased then she, a demi-god, suddenly became more interesting to those that had their own revenge plots against the gods. She was sure now that was why Damion made an attempt. "He wants to get to Zeus or the other gods through me."

"You got that right." Koal clucked his tongue and winked.

Xen's hand snaked around her waist and he pulled her close. "He will not get to you."

"How do you know that? He found me here. He can find me anywhere."

"Don't worry, Carissa. You have me." Koal shifted his cap and disappeared then reappeared.

True. As clumsy as he was, he had his merits. Though she would never admit it, it did give her some relief he was tailing her. He had shown his loyalty, and that in her estimation made him a friend for life.

She looked around the kitchen island. This was her tribe. Her people. They had fought the two Titans, Kronos and Iapetos, at the same time and defeated them. Yeah, she had the Olympian gods and goddesses help, but they managed it and they would do the same with Damion. "Maybe we need to outfox your friend."

Xen growled. "He is not my friend."

"You know him, and he clearly knows you," Kirke joked.

Xen shifted and put his palms on the bench. "Let's get one thing straight. Damion and I have never been friends. He is nothing but a thorn in my side."

"Then you have a history, and if you have a history, you will know his weaknesses," Carissa pointed out.

"I do."

"So share them, vampire, so we can beat him," Kirke said. "My magic is powerful, but if you say he has dark magic and hasn't given us a taste yet, then we're going to need every trick in the book to outdo him."

Carissa threw a thumb in Kirke's direction. "What she said."

"We're going to need spells and whatever technology we have to suppress his magic." Xen turned his head toward Koal. "It might also be an idea to let Ares know that he is topside and no longer in Tartarus."

"I can do that but will wait till we have Carissa secured," Koal said.

Kirke shifted. "I'm going to need stronger wards. It's time to take out the big grimoire."

"Ooh, the big guns are coming out," Adam cooed.

Kane slapped him over the head.

"What?"

Carissa let out a laugh. The adrenaline had left her body. All she wanted was something to eat and a hot shower.

Consider it done, koukla, Xen sent to her mind.

You're listening in?

When your guard is down. Always.

She bumped him with her hip. They needed to talk.

"Kirke, I think we've overstayed our welcome, and I'm really sorry about your door and this mess."

"If you allow it, I will organize to have it repaired," Xen said.

Kirke nodded her approval.

"Koal, when you're ready can you dematerialize us back to Xen's mansion."

"I'll help. It will make it faster," Kirke offered.

Carissa watched as Kirke stepped between Adam and Kane, threaded her arm around each of theirs and then dematerialized.

Koal did the same and Carissa and Xen followed suit.

They landed in Xen's office where her other three friends were.

Kirke locked eyes with her. "Think about what we said." She snapped her fingers and zapped herself out of the room.

Carissa released Koal's arm and turned her head toward him. "Let Father know."

"On it." He vanished.

"I need food." She headed to the kitchen.

"I'm with you on that." Adam followed.

When she got to the threshold of the door, she said, "Do you two want anything?"

"I'll join you in a minute," Kane fired back.

Only you, Xen sent to her mind.

Later, she sent back and proceeded toward the kitchen.

The house was quiet. Her grandmother and aunt would be fast asleep. She had left so abruptly she was sure it would have worried them. She scolded herself for her reaction to their version of a wedding. It was nowhere near what she wanted, and she needed to make that clear to them.

In the kitchen they found a large platter of pistachio. The Greek version of a lasagna. There was a note on it. "Sorry. We were only trying to help."

Tears welled in her eyes. She sniffled.

"You all right, Rissa?"

"Yeah, I've been a bit of a drama queen."

"Not really. You didn't lash out. You just left."

"I know, but I've made them feel bad. I know they want to help, but they're a handful."

Adam let out a laugh. "Trust me, it's the most fun I've had in ages with those two."

She smiled.

"Come on, let's dig in."

She grabbed the cutlery and plates, pulled out one of the stools. She didn't waste time. Her first few bites were heaven. She'd been running on empty for most of the day. She polished off two pieces and was digging into her third. "What do you make of this Damion?"

"I don't have much on him other than what Xen has said. I

think we're in for a hell of a battle, and you…" he pointed his fork toward her "…need to start blasting some of that power of yours."

"My power is still erratic."

"Then practice."

He had a point. She should be trying to use her power of *anakge* more. Who knew what she'd be able to achieve if she could use that compulsion at a whim.

"You're right. I definitely need to step up in that department."

"You got power, Rissa," Adam said between mouthfuls.

"And a couple of swords."

"Atta girl."

"You know, Adam, you really are good for one's ego."

He smiled. "Listen, we all have a purpose and gifts. No matter how little or big. Use that which was given to you."

She didn't want these so-called gifts—from the moment her father had unbound her power she had tried to control it. It was erratic and the very hasty training she had received was not enough. Now she had to accept them as they were—spasmodic. She needed quiet time to think through everything. Her life resembled a merry-go-round and she wanted to get off and take a breather, but the more she submerged herself amongst the gods the deeper she got and the further they dragged her into their sphere.

The clatter of cutlery brought her back from her temporary thoughts. Kane walked into the kitchen. "Boss wants to see you."

Adam got to his feet, collected the plate and rinsed it before putting it in the dishwasher. "Think about what I said." He winked at her then left.

Kane plopped down in the seat where Adam had been sitting. He raised an eyebrow. "Dare I ask what that was about?"

"Just general chit chat about the use of my power."

"Yes, that would come in handy."

"It's unreliable and you know it."

"I do but unless you keep at it, you won't have control."

"It's not like I can go around using it."

"Yes, you can." His lips turned up in a smile.

"What, you mean day to day?"

He nodded. "You can start small."

The gears in her head started to turn and a grin formed. "I could use it in small doses."

"You probably already do and haven't picked up on it."

She'd done it with Athena and her sister Harmonia. Where else had she been using compulsion to make people do what she wanted? Kane was right.

"You think a dash here and there might help?"

"That way, you're in control."

"But what about the rest of my power?"

"Focus and see if you can use small bursts of it. Having some control is better than having none."

"You're right, of course."

"He is." Xen strolled into the kitchen with his hands in his pockets.

"You need anything else?" Kane asked.

"No."

"I need some shuteye." He got up and headed out.

"Not wrong there." Her tummy was full now.

Xen stepped closer to her.

She spun on her seat to face him.

He stepped into her space and placed his hands on her face. "You haven't been yourself. Care to share."

"Things aren't going the way I want."

"The wedding?"

"That and I feel I'm being dragged into more godly business."

"Hmm. Perhaps there's way more going on than Zeus and the other gods admit."

"What use could I possibly be?"

"*Koukla*, you have power. That's reason enough for them. You have to stop questioning and start accepting. This is your world now. You have to make adjustments that work for you."

He had a point. She could complain all she liked. The fact was she should try to embrace the person she had become. With the gods and Titans popping up every now and then there would always be danger. She had to learn to protect herself and those around her in the face of that, but she needed to deal with something else first.

"Xen, we need to talk." She raised her finger and pointed up. "Upstairs."

He lifted her in his arms and sped them to their room where her rear hit the softness of the bed.

He made quick work of locking the door. "Now what did you want to talk about?"

How do I say, I'm ready to accept your ring and proposal?

He walked over to the bedside table and opened the top draw, fished something out of it and dropped to his knees in front of her.

"Would you do me the honor of becoming my wife?"

Her mouth opened and then she realized she'd been projecting. He had just saved her asking. Her gaze crashed with his then she looked down at the black box with the sparkling engagement ring. "Yes."

Xen took the ring out of the box and slid it on her ring finger. He pulled her too him and fell backwards to the floor with her lying on top of him.

"I should have said yes when you showed me the ring the first time."

"*Koukla*, you were not ready, and I should have sensed your emotions at the time."

She wrinkled her nose. "How about a kiss?"

She didn't need to ask anything more. He drew her to him and gave her a hot passionate kiss. She moaned in his mouth and that was all it took. Before she could register what had happened she was on the bed, her clothes were stripped from her body, and so were his. He stood, staring down at her.

Her eyes roamed over his body, and she licked her lips. Xen naked was a sight to behold.

"How do you want this? he asked.

"Hard and fast."

He dropped on the bed and then lifted her on top of him. With one smooth move he entered her.

She moaned.

He palmed her breasts and thrust his hips upward in quick strokes.

It elicited another moan from her.

He lifted his head and his fangs elongated. He sank them into her neck and took a deep draw. It didn't take much. She splintered in ecstasy and his release followed with a few quick, frenzied strokes.

She collapsed on top of him. "I'll move in a minute."

"I'd rather you didn't because that was just an appetizer for tonight."

She could feel him hardening inside her.

He flipped her to her back.

"How about we go slow this time." His lips found hers in a deep and hungry kiss.

TWENTY

"Beneath every stone a scorpion sleeps." ~ *Anonymous*

Xen's Mansion; Charleston, SC
Morning, mortal realm – Day 8

When dawn's rosy rays tickled her eyes, she bolted upright. Her heart hammered in her chest. Sun meant danger to Xen. She looked beside her, and there was no trace of the man in question.

Something wasn't right. She pushed the covers back and got to her feet.

She grabbed a pair of jeans and a t-shirt and threw on some sneakers. Her eyes roved over the bedside table. There was no note there. Very un-Xen like. She took long strides to the door and flung it open, then bolted down the stairs. She opened her mind to reach out to him. *Xen*

Nothing. Her pulse spiked. She ran into his office.

"Kane."

He lifted a hand. "Don't stress. He's fine."

"How did…" She swallowed a breath "…know what I was going to ask?

"Super hearing and acute sense of emotions."

"Where is he?"

"He went to check if your grandmother's residence is finished.

165

He got stuck there so used one of the rooms for his rejuvenation. I have men stationed there."

Her shoulders dropped, and she let out a deep breath. The surge of adrenaline receded. "I thought the worst. It's very unlike him to not leave a note."

"He had every intention of making it back. The men told me when I checked in with them half an hour ago."

Still, something wasn't right. Light had bounced in the room, and Xen usually kept everything dark. "There was light in the room."

"He was probably keeping surveillance all night."

"Of Damion?"

"Knowing Xen. Yes."

"You think he would attack us here?"

"It's more than likely. He's on a mission, and if we know anything about the worlds of men, gods, or Titans then we know that nothing will stand in their way for a chance at world domination."

"We haven't had a break, have we?" she asked, raising an eyebrow.

"No, we haven't."

"Seems like it's all bleeding into each other."

Kane got to his feet. "That's it."

She raised an eyebrow. Clearly she had just lost the page they were both on. "What's it?"

"What you said."

"Bleeding into each other?" She rolled things around in her head. Hal, Iapetos, Kronos and now Damion.

He came around the desk. His lips turned up in half a smile.

"They're all connected. All part of the same elaborate plot," she said before he could say it.

He nodded his head. "Now you're seeing it."

"But then who is behind them?"

"That's the million-dollar question."

"Who wins the most out of all this."

"The gods. Although I can't see what they really gain by destroying humanity and everything else in between."

"You're right there. To you and me it doesn't make rational sense, but to someone who is out for control of everything then it's the perfect landscape."

"More like apocalyptic. Yet again." She landed on Xen's desk. "If it is a god then the only way to uncover that is if I talk to my father and Zeus."

"You're right there."

Only they had their own problems up on Olympus. "They've got dramas up there."

Kane crossed his arms. "That's common practice for them."

"You're not wrong. I'll clue them in." She focused and her mind opened. "Father," she whispered.

Air whipped around the office. The god of war stood in Xen's library.

"What is it, *kori mou*?"

"Have a seat," she offered.

His brow wrinkled and he dropped onto the couch. He raised his booted feet to the coffee table.

She moved over to where he sat. Kane stayed firmly in his spot near the desk. "Well?" her father asked.

"Everything that has been going on from the very beginning. Right from when Hal kidnapped me and everything in between with the Titans has all been connected. They aren't separate situations. They are all one in the same."

Kane started to pace around the office.

Her father moved his feet off the table and leaned forward. "You're saying that one person is behind it all?"

"Yes, and the question is who?"

"Do you have any suspicions?"

"We think it might be a god," Kane said.

Carissa could see the wheels turning in her father's head. He was racing through all possibilities. "It always pointed that way, and I'm sure Zeus will have some suspicions."

"You need to be prepared, Father."

"As do you, Daughter. I need to train you more."

She nodded. "But you know it's not kosher for you to be here." Zeus had decreed that the gods should not meddle on the mortal plain. But meddle they did, and Carissa knew when they could find a loophole they always would interfere. Everything was connected. The gods, mortals, immortals, belief in every religious institution and the planet itself. All part of one. One big fat ecosystem with all the extras.

"I will find a way but first I need to talk to Zeus." Ares clicked his fingers and dematerialized.

"I'd like that trick in my tool kit."

"Wouldn't we all," Kane said with a laugh.

"What now?" she asked. There was no way they'd be able to investigate which god because they didn't have access to them. Then the penny dropped. Zeus had granted her access to Olympus despite the fact she hadn't wanted it. Koal had warned her against it. It would come at a cost. Then again, everything in life came with a price tag. There was no such thing as free. It was an illusion that everyone thought they had freedom. Mortals belonged to a complex system of social stratification. There were layers, lots of layers, and people were bound to act and behave within those layers. The gods and other supernatural creatures had their own system as well.

"Let's get some breakfast first."

At the sound of that her stomach growled. "That sounds marvelous."

They made their way to the kitchen.

"What I don't understand is why now? Xen and you have been around a long time, why now?"

"Because the prophecy was long ago written," Koal answered and then appeared next to Carissa.

She jumped. "You scared the living daylights out of me."

"Sorry."

"I thought you were gone."

"Nope, I'm hanging around," he said with a smile.

"What about this prophecy?" Kane asked.

Carissa held a hand up to stop Koal. "My story and Xen's were forged when Father helped Xen." It was Ares who saved Xen from the Lamia many millennia ago and that was when it was foreseen by the *moirai*, Clotho, Lachesis and Atropos that a child of Ares would be bound to the vampire Xen.

"How so?"

"We're fated."

Kane let out a whistle. "Still doesn't explain the Titans wanting to annihilate everyone and everything."

"They'd have a clean slate to start."

"Koal is right. They precede the Olympian gods."

"So, you're saying this is revenge?"

"I could be wrong, but at the same time it sounds like it."

"So, whichever god is behind all this, then they are very much team Titans and not team Olympians," Carissa said.

"Koal, perhaps I will have to take Zeus' offer."

"You know that comes with a price. He will be able to zap you out of here without notice. You will be bound to Olympus."

"Let's not make that decision yet," Kane said.

"Yes, I'd have to run it by my fiancé."

"And you know he won't like it."

"Oh, I know that."

Kane had plonked a cup of coffee in front of her.

"Thanks." She lifted it to her lips and swallowed some of the hot beverage. "This is good." The first taste was always the best in her estimation.

She pulled over the covered plate of spinach pie and grabbed a piece. "You want some," she said to Koal while taking another bite.

He nodded and sat down.

"I thought the gods didn't eat," Kane said, taking a seat.

"We don't and we do."

"Care to explain," Kane asked.

"We drink ambrosia and that sustains us, but over many millennia we got bored and wanted to sample some of the foods mortals so fondly love."

"Well, that makes sense," Kane said.

Carissa nodded her head in agreement and shoved the last bite of spanakopita in her mouth. Then washed it down with coffee. "I mean, what's not to like about mortal food," she added.

Koal picked up a piece of the pie. "I don't know why we never thought of it sooner."

Carissa let out a sharp laugh.

Kane's phone buzzed. He fished it out of his black cargo pants pocket. "Yeah."

He nodded his head several times. "We'll make our way there." He ended the call. "We should get over to your grandmother's house."

Her shoulders tightened. "Has something happened?"

"Nothing that our men can't handle."

She jumped to her feet and made to grab the keys. Koal had moved just as fast and put a hand on hers. "You won't need those. I can get you there faster."

He held out his hand to Kane and dematerialized them.

They landed in the middle of what used to be the living room. Xen didn't kid when he said they'd be renovating the whole house. Her grandfather who was Kekrops—the king of Athens and immortal—had built an underground bunker filled with ancient artifacts. It appeared he was collecting items for a very long time. Xen was now fortifying the room further by putting up special walls that numbed any of the magical properties the artifacts gave off. These signals could be picked up by other immortals or supernaturals, and that was a problem she didn't want to have on her doorstep. "Talk about renovating."

Adam walked through from the kitchen. "Well, that was fast."

"Helps when you have the gods around." Kane threw a thumb in Koal's direction.

"What's happened?" Carissa's stomach tightened.

"There's been a report demons have been lurking in the surrounding streets."

"You need to get the wards back up on this place."

"The wards are up. It's why they are roaming and can't find it."

"Wait, what kind of wards do you have up?"

"Some illusion spells with the help of that redhead witch —Kirke."

The air in the room shifted. Kane let out a little growl and pulled Carissa behind him.

Carissa recognized her friend's signature before she appeared. She stepped from behind Kane.

"Did someone call?" Kirke said with a grin.

Kane pointed a finger at her. "That's either coincidence or you're listening in." "Chill, *lykos*. I've spelled this particular room for Xen, so that when my name is spoken it triggers an alarm of sorts."

Carissa's lips turned up. "You know that I can call you at all hours now." She could annoy her friend to no end. But the truth was she didn't need a spell to do it. She could use her power of *anagke* to compel her friend to appear.

"For you I wouldn't mind, but I wouldn't recommend it to everyone else, so keep it to yourself, wolf."

Kane held up a hand. "You have my word."

"Now what's the problem?"

"Demons' roaming close by. The illusion spell is keeping them away for now," Kane said.

Carissa contemplated the situation. Having them lurking was not a good thing. They could potentially find the house and Damion could show up too. "We need to lure them away from their current location. Then your men can do what they do best."

"I've already communicated that to my men."

"How can I help?" Kirke asked.

Carissa looked at Koal.

He raised his hands palms out. "I can only assist you. You know there's a fine line with what I can and can't help with. You're not in the thick of it so no can do."

She nodded and he zapped himself out of the room. She turned back to Kirke. "We need to lure them away. They are out there in broad daylight. We can't have unsuspecting humans cross their path."

"They'll kill them," Kane added before fishing out his smart phone from his pocket. He activated an app. "This is where they are currently roaming. My men are at the top of the street." He pointed to his phone. "You need to get them to this abandoned house."

"I know just the thing." Kirke's eyes sparkled before she disappeared.

"Xen?" Carissa questioned.

"Your room but we need to set you up first."

She raised an eyebrow in question.

"Come on, it's easier to show you."

She followed Kane up the stairs. Her old bedroom door had been replaced with a new door. On the wall there was an access security panel.

Kane tapped something on his phone. The panel lit up. "Stick your index finger on it."

She did as he asked.

"Lift it and again."

She repeated the process several times.

"Okay, now you're all set."

She stuck her finger on the access panel and the door clicked open. "Neat."

"When you're done, I'll see you in the kitchen." He turned to leave.

"Kane." What would she do without these guys? "Thanks."

"None needed." He winked and made his way to the stairs.

She pushed the door. It was heavy. She'd bet that behind the ordinary wooden look there was metal. She closed it behind her and made her way into the darkened room. The windows too had been treated with new material. She walked over for a closer look. They looked like ordinary shutters but knowing Xen they would be more than that. Everything appeared in order in the room. She glanced over at her fiancé who lay half naked in his deep rejuvenation sleep. She ran her fingers across his jaw then planted a soft kiss on his lips. He was hers and she would protect him as he did her.

She turned to leave. It was time to see what other changes he had made to the house. Particularly her grandfather's basement full of artifacts.

Kirke appeared at the bottom of the street where the demons scouted the area. She stuck her fingers in her mouth and blew hard so they would hear it.

They turned and ran in her direction. She needed to act fast. She closed her eyes and lifted her hands to form a ball of energy then she threw that up into the sky. She stepped back and an illusion of herself stood where she had been a moment before. The real her was invisible. The demons would see the illusion and that was what she wanted. She waved her hand and her illusion turned and ran. She'd lead them to where Kane had specified. Then it was up to them.

They took the bait. She moved from her location when they charged by her and after the illusion of herself. She had one more thing to do. She dematerialized and materialized near the abandoned house. Kane's men were already there.

"Phil," she said. "I'm leading them here to the house. I'm going to cast an illusion on the house. Then it's up to you and your men."

"We're ready."

She threw out a spell to make the house look like Carissa's grandmother's house. The house the demons were looking for. Her illusion worked. The demons turned the corner and were running straight for the dwelling while chasing her illusion-self. They were close on her heels. Kirke threw open the front gate and house door.

"Get your guys ready, Phil."

She caught movement from the corner of her eye and knew they would follow the demons in.

Her illusion-self charged through the front gate, up the porch and through the front door. Phil motioned to his team, and they moved to protect the perimeter then a second team moved into the entry point and prepared to breach.

"Talk about the element of surprise," she muttered to herself. There was only one last thing to do. She dropped the spell so her illusion-self would disappear. She heard a growl from inside the house. The demons were not impressed. She thanked the stars for whatever reason the streets were dead today, and there were no people milling about, and then she heard a car start.

Phil exited from the front. "Nice work." He winked.

"Pretty close."

She was about to remove the illusion spell on the house.

"You might want to leave this place looking like Carissa's grandmother's. Just in case."

"You have a point. There could be others."

"I'm sure there will be," Phil said. "Thanks for helping."

"None needed." She gave him a thumbs up. "Better get out of here before you draw too much attention."

"We're done here, and we'll use the side lane." He pointed to where there were two SUVs waiting.

She nodded then waved her hands and disappeared.

Carissa marveled at some of the inclusions and alterations that had been made to her grandmother's house. Xen had gone all out. She could never truly repay him for it. She did have some money tucked away, but nothing that would pay for the kind of sophistication he added. Apart from all the tech, he had installed shutters on the windows and doors that closed with a touch of a button. Kane had told her that when she met him and Adam in the kitchen. "Well, that's security," she said as they moved toward a door in the lounge that led to her grandfather's underground room. She started the decent with Kane close behind.

"A necessary evil," Kane said.

She thought about his comment for a second before answering over her shoulder, "I wish it wasn't though."

"Necessary?" Kane asked.

"Yes." She reached the bottom then took a few steps before turning to face Kane.

"Carissa. You need to come to terms with the fact that there isn't anything normal about your family."

"I know, but having said that, the human half of my brain recalls and romanticizes the days I was ignorant and didn't know any better."

"I understand where you're coming from. We all experience that same thing when we find out we are *lykoi*. Suddenly all that innocence is gone."

"How did you deal with it?"

"We accept it and move on, otherwise it will eat you up. That's the past. Look toward the future."

He was right and she knew it. She nodded again. Then turned to see what changes Xen had made to the room. They had to keep the items here. If they moved them, they risked alerting other supernatural creatures that they held them and that was a fight they didn't want. Each of these items in her grandfather's collection held magic and power, and in the wrong hands they could give someone like the *kakodaimones* leverage. A risk they were not willing to take.

The footprint was the same, but the display of the artifacts her grandfather had collected over many millennia was now encased in what appeared to be security display cabinets. It was like a museum but even better. "Wow."

"State of the art security."

"I'm sure it is."

She raised a hand to one of the cabinets.

"I wouldn't touch them if I were you."

She pulled her hand back as if it had been scalded by hot water. "I'll have to remember," she said before walking over to her grandfather's office. Xen had kept that the same. She raised an eyebrow in question toward Kane.

"Xen wanted to keep it as is so you could remember your grandfather."

Her vampire was thoughtful. Under all that hardened battled exterior was a man who would give her everything. Heat radiated in her chest. Inside the office her grandfather's desk was still scattered with papers. Nothing was disturbed. She took a seat. "I might just sit here for a while."

"Sure. I'll be upstairs if you need anything." Kane turned and disappeared.

She shuffled some of the papers around on the desk. *Research notes*, she thought. It appeared he was always looking for artifacts of some type. He certainly was a man on a mission. She sighed and swung her seat around. Her knee hit the side of the desk where the drawers were. With a loud clunk the side of the desk panel opened, and a pile of papers spilled onto the floor. She bent to collect them and then put them on the desk. There were a few photos of a gold libation bowl. "What is it with these bowls?" She shuffled through some more papers and found some names. It appeared her grandfather had spoken to some people but had been unable to find the bowl. Why hide this one? The one Xen located had been written into his journal. The only difference was this one was bronze and the previous one clay. She shuffled through more papers and found a name scrawled in the margin of some research papers discussing the significance of ancient *phialai*, as they were called.

"Who is Pheme?" she asked the pages, hunting for any clue, but nothing else was written on the document. Her grandfather had gone to great lengths to find ancient items that held power. That libation bowl, wherever it was, held magic, and if it did, she along with Xen would have to track it down and bring it back to this protective bunker.

She stacked the papers back in the file and left it on the desk. She needed to talk to Xen.

A loud thunk had her racing up the stairs.

TWENTY-ONE

"It is futile to pray to the gods for that which one has the power to obtain by himself." ~ Epicurus

Carissa's grandmother's house; Charleston, SC
Midmorning, mortal realm – Day 8

Carissa took the stairs two at a time. She reached the top and came to a complete halt at the scene before her. Yiayia and Aunt Paula were standing in the lounge area with two big bouquets of balloons with a *sorry* printed on several of them.

"*Paidi mou*," Yiayia took a step toward her, "we wanted to apologize for our meddling."

Carissa's heart tore in two. The look on her grandmother's face made her shrink to a meter tall. She had been a complete ass to the two women who only wanted the best for her.

"Will you forgive us," Aunt Paula asked, shaking the balloons around.

A thickness formed in her throat. How could she not? "There is nothing to forgive. You were only trying to help."

"See, I told you, Paula. Let's give our girl a hug."

They shuffled forward with the ridiculous number of balloons for a group hug.

"Y'all having a party?" Adam asked, walking in with Kane.

"No," Carissa snapped.

Her aunt and grandmother handed her the floating bouquets with weights attached. She dropped them in the corner of the room near the windows.

"Wow, look at these floors, Vetta."

"What else has the vampire done?" Yiayia asked.

Adam walked over and held out his arms. "I'd be glad to give you ladies a tour." He had a soft spot for them both.

They slid their arms around his.

"Let's start with the kitchen." He exchanged a knowing glance with Carissa. He was a lifesaver.

"Find anything interesting down there. You were gone a while." Kane stepped closer and crossed his arms over his chest.

"Funny you should ask. I did."

Kane raised an eyebrow. "Anything we should be worried about?"

"I don't know, but what I do know is that my grandfather was looking for another libation bowl and chances are it holds some sort of power, otherwise he wouldn't have kept a secret file."

"What? Where?"

"Let's just say that my *pappou* was good at hiding things."

Kane held up his hands in surrender. He wasn't going to push it and she was grateful. She thought about it for a moment. They could go looking for the person who her grandfather had penned in the margins of his research without Xen, or she could wait until later.

"He was looking for someone named Pheme."

"You're joking?"

"Nope, I'm pretty serious."

"Show me."

She turned to lead Kane back downstairs when Yiayia, Paula and Adam came walking through the lounge again. "That vampire of yours has done an extraordinary job with the renovations," Yiayia said.

"Did you get a look at that cooker and range hood?" Paula asked.

"I did and, yes, he does have exceptional taste."

"He does." Paula nodded her head.

"We were going to head back down to the basement. Did you two want to have a look?"

They looked at each other with wide eyes and gave each other the okay. "We might need some help down those stairs."

"We can help there." A cheeky grin had formed across Adam's face.

"Wait. You're not thinking of?"

"Ah ha."

He had Aunt Paula in his arms squealing with delight faster than she could blink.

Carissa looked over at Yiayia. "Come on boy toy, think you can give an old lady a hand."

Kane didn't waste any time either. He flashed her a wicked smile. Both men bolted down the stairs with their super *lykoi* speed. Carissa's feet hit the stairs with a quick tempo, but she wasn't as fast as the boys. Her aunt and *yiayia* could be heard giggling from below. It made her smile that something so simple could elicit quite a number of giggles from both. When she cleared the last step her aunt and grandmother were already looking at the flash displays.

"We'll be in *Pappou's* office."

"Vetta, your old goat was quite busy."

Carissa rolled her eyes and motioned for Kane and Adam to join her in the office.

"What are we looking for?" Adam asked.

"An artifact my grandfather had flagged to find, but it doesn't look like he got the chance." She opened the file and pointed to the name in the margin. "I think this may have been his lead."

"Carissa. Pheme is the goddess of gossip."

"You could have told me upstairs."

"I needed to see what he was looking for and why he might want the goddess."

"This is interesting," Adam said as he came around and squeezed in to look at the picture of the libation bowl in the file. "I bumped into Pheme at the Vrykos pub a few nights ago. Come to think of it she was really friendly too."

"I'm not going to ask what happened."

Adam moved back around the table and to one of the chairs. He dropped his weight into it. "Don't worry, Rissa, it was all cordial and above board."

"I'm sure it was."

"What did she have to say?" Kane asked.

"She mentioned something about whispers amongst immortals."

"What whispers?"

Adam shrugged his shoulders. "No idea. I just told her not to spread stories."

"So let me get this straight. Pheme is the goddess of gossip, so she listens to immortal whispers and spreads rumors."

Adam pierced her with a duh stare. "Well, yeah."

"She must have been looking for someone in particular," Kane said. "Who was there?"

"It was the usual crowd. A slower night."

"Something about that smells off."

"Where can we find her?"

"Not sure but will ask around. She's a regular at a few bars. There's likely to be some gossip on the goddess of gossip."

Carissa huffed. "Ya think?"

"Well, if you have all finished in here, we're done with looking at the museum pieces and would like to get back upstairs." Yiayia and Aunt Paula had done the rounds and looked at all the displays.

Adam shot to his feet. "At your service."

Yiayia and Aunt Paula giggled.

"Silly wolf," Carissa said under her breath.

"That's me, Rissa."

Her eyes widened. She'd have to remember to not verbalize her thoughts. These guys could hear everything.

Kane moved around the table to assist the women back upstairs. "Are you going to join us?"

"I might make a few calls. There are some numbers in this file that look like leads."

"Shout if you need anything," Kane said.

"Will do."

The air shifted in the room and Kane and Adam both growled. Yiayia and Aunt Paula raised their hands to their chests, startled at the sudden change in mood.

"Relax," Carissa said. She didn't budge. The signature belonged to Kirke. The witch appeared before them.

The women squealed and pushed the boys out of the way to give her witchy friend a hug.

After they all exchanged pleasantries, Kane ushered her family out. "Be back in a minute."

In a flash they had the women upstairs and Kane returned.

"Where's Adam?" Carissa asked.

"He's going to keep an eye on them."

"Good idea."

"Was it a success?" Kane asked Kirke.

"It was as you predicted. There were demons prowling and more than likely looking for this house. I've spelled an abandoned house several blocks over to look like this house in its previous state. Xen's renovation helped in changing the look of this house, add to that I've enhanced an illusion spell to make it a one-story house to demon eyes."

Carissa took it all in. The lengths they had to go to astounded her. "Might be safer for my family to stay at Xen's mansion until we can sort some of this out."

"Agreed," Kane said.

"Might no longer be safe for anyone." A pang hit her square in the chest. The comfort and safety she'd always experienced in her grandparents' house now seemed distant. Things had changed.

"Are the demons eliminated?" she asked her friend.

"I can say with great confidence that Xen's men have removed the demons that were lurking."

Kane shifted his stance. "It took longer than I thought."

"I had an errand to run before zapping back here."

"Thank you for your help, Kirke."

"No thanks needed. I've had a gut full of these guys since Hal decided to open up the portals and let the demons into the mortal plane." Kirke blew a stray lock of hair out of her eyes.

"I thought that was resolved," Kane said.

"So did I. Perhaps they are broken, not working as they should," Carissa suggested.

Kirke shook her head vehemently. "No, no. My mother would not allow it. I'm sure she is mega pissed that her portals in out are being compromised."

Kirke's mother was the goddess Hekate, and the portals were her gateways and her responsibility. She had been angered to learn they were being used without her permission.

The fragrance of something cooking hit Carissa's nose. She glanced at the time. Where had the day gone? She shook her random thoughts away. "What do we do to fix it?"

Kane crossed his arms over his chest. "I think Xen's nemesis has a lot to answer for."

The papers on the desk fluttered.

"Of that I'm in agreement." Xen's throaty response filled the room.

"Xen." Carissa lifted herself from her chair and sailed into his arms. She gave him a quick peck on the lips.

"You're up early, boss. It's not even dark yet."

"I sensed trouble."

"You're spot on, vampire." Kirke moved to sit in one of the vacant chairs.

Xen's rejuvenation sleep usually went until dusk, but today he'd dragged himself out of it. Carissa knew it would take him a while to feel fully rejuvenated.

"What news?" he asked as he let her go and looked at Kane and Kirke.

"A demon problem several streets back and in daylight," Kane filled in.

On cue Carissa added, "And another mysterious libation bowl that involves the goddess of gossip."

Xen let out a whistle. "Is the demon problem stifled?"

"*Yes*," both Kane and Kirke voiced.

Xen turned his head toward her. "That leaves the *phiale*."

Carissa nodded.

"Do you need further help?" Kirke asked.

"No. You should rest. I've asked a lot from you, witch," he said in a teasing way.

"Xen's right," Carissa said. "I think we might be stretching the friendship."

"Never," Kirke replied then waved her arms and disappeared from where she had been.

"Kane, have you checked our database to see if we have any resident gods or goddesses on the mortal plane?"

"That was my next plan of action." He turned to leave.

Carissa eyed the papers in front of her. "Should we hit the phone and see where these leads go?"

"Why don't we split them?"

"Sounds like a plan."

Carissa shuffled through her grandfather's notes and wrote down some names on a sticky note for Xen then circled the ones she would attack. "You ring these, and I'll call these." She pointed to the paperwork. "Let's see if they turn up anything." She dropped back in the chair.

"I'll be out here." Xen sped out of the office and into the large display area.

Carissa picked up the phone and made the first call. The line rang out. She scribbled a note next to it, to go back. The next number she dialed wasn't connected. "Great. I'm going nowhere fast." She huffed. There were two more numbers, and she hoped that at least one of them would still be an active line. She looked up through the window of her grandfather's office. Xen was having better luck. She could see him chatting and nodding.

Xen punched the numbers Carissa had given him, and they were all fruitless. The contacts they were looking for were no longer at those addresses and the phone numbers for two had been redistributed to other people. It occurred to him to call one of his own contacts. A wildcard.

"Hello Pierre, I was wondering if you could help me recover a libation bowl."

"I'll see what I can do, Mr. Lyson. Can you give me the date of the artifact you seek?"

"Circa sixth to fifth century BC, but as you know dates can sometimes be out of range."

"And the material of the *phiale*?"

"Bronze."

"I will call you back soon, Mr. Lyson."

"Thank you, Pierre."

"Always a pleasure, Mr. Lyson."

Xen ended the call then headed to see how Carissa faired. Judging from the look on her face, she'd hit a dead end. "No luck, huh?"

"None. It was worth a try." She got to her feet. "You?"

"Same, although I did make a call to one of my own contacts."

"I'm scared to ask what type of contact he is?"

"*Koukla*, let's get one thing straight. Everything out there, in the eyes of the law is illegal. It would have been bought through either the black-market or elsewhere. My connection, Pierre, is legal, but it wasn't always that way."

"Okay." She raised her hands, palms out toward him. "There are conversations that we just don't need to have right now."

"True, and this is best reserved for another day."

His phone rang and he fished it out of his pocket?

"What news, Pierre?"

"I think there's something in the lost ownership you need to see."

TWENTY-TWO

"Observe due measure, for right timing is in all things the most important factor."
~ Hesiod

Pierre's Auction House; Charleston, SC
Evening, mortal realm – Day 8

"Mr. Lyson, so good to see you."

Pierre hurried toward them and stuck out his hand in greeting.

Xen clasped it and gave the auctioneer a good shake. Then turned to introduce his beloved. "This is my fiancée, Carissa Alkippes."

"Oh my, you have been busy since I last saw you." Pierre took both of Carissa's hands in his. "The pleasure is all mine. You must be special to snag his heart."

"You could say that," Xen replied.

Pierre let out an excited bubble of giggles and then turned. "Follow me," he said over his shoulder.

Carissa glanced at Xen with a smile on her face.

What's so funny, koukla. He sent the message to her mind.

Nothing, just not what I was expecting.

Were you expecting someone with two heads?

What? No. I thought he'd be shorter, balder and nerdier.

Pierre was anything but that. Tall, slender and a man who looked after his health and appearance. He was a polished businessman and it showed. His shiny shoes tapped on the surface of the basement.

He led them to a room. Inside was a table already set up with the libation bowl.

"I don't know how this one was missed," Pierre said as he came around the table and handed them each a set of disposable latex gloves.

Xen slid his fingers in the fine plastic and Carissa did the same. They stepped closer to the table and eyed the *phiale*. Xen picked up its vibrations. He looked over to Carissa and she had too. She leaned in for closer inspection.

"What do you know of it?" Xen asked.

Pierre took in a deep breath. "It was discovered in the southwest corner during a disassembling of the temple's entablature. It lay inside a narrow cavity between the fourteenth triglyph and the block behind it. It was undisturbed due to a collection of marble chips and dirt that had accumulated over the years in the void. It is twenty-two centimeters in diameter."

"Impressive."

"I'd say it is," Carissa said from where she was still eyeing the *phiale*.

Pierre took in another breath. Longer than the last. "If you notice, the exterior decoration consists of hammered wreaths of lanceolate leaves around the central omphalos. The center of the bowl was raised, and this is what they call the navel."

"How is it in your possession?"

"I believe Mr. Lyson, that this artifact was stolen then hidden here."

"But isn't this your establishment?" Carissa stood straight and asked.

"No, miss. There are several owners of this establishment. I have rung them about this piece, and none know anything about it."

"Wouldn't you want to find out who brought it here?"

"Indeed, miss, I'd like that, but where would I start if the item was placed in the lack of ownership cage and no one knows who put it there?"

Koukla, why don't we worry about those details later. Xen turned his attention to Pierre. "Could we borrow it till you've worked things out?"

"My instructions from my superiors is to sell it if need be. They don't want it and given it's a mystery all the reason more."

"What's your price?"

"Three thousand dollars."

Xen didn't blink. If only they realized the real value of the bowl. "Consider it done."

"Very well, Mr. Lyson."

"We will wait upstairs."

"Oh, you wish to take it now?"

Xen gave Pierre a stern look, one that said he wasn't going anywhere without the *phiale* in his possession. He'd known him for many years, and Pierre always knew when he was interested. "If it isn't a problem, yes."

"I can assure you Mr. Lyson, it would be my pleasure to bundle this item up for you." Pierre gave a slight shiver. Like the item offended him to some degree.

Xen suppressed a laugh at his antics.

"Why don't you make your way upstairs. I'll be up momentarily."

Xen guided Carissa up the stairs to the waiting area. "Seriously?" she asked him.

He stepped close and wrapped his arms around her. "*Koukla,* you have to forget everything you know. There is no telling how your grandfather amassed the plethora of objects that he did."

"You have a point."

"You know that his work now befalls to you."

"I have been thinking that this whole time."

He tapped her on the nose and then placed a chaste kiss on her lips. He wanted more but it would have to wait. He released her before he got carried away.

"Thank you for doing all of this."

"No need for thanks, we are one."

Xen didn't need to turn around for Pierre as he had heard and picked up his scent before he turned the corner, and he wasn't alone.

Pierre cleared his throat. "Mr. Lyson, your parcel is ready. This way," he said to the gentleman who had a wooden crate on a trolley.

"Lucky you brought the SUV," Carissa said.

"Indeed."

They walked in silence, and Xen glanced to Carissa and watched as a shiver ran down her. *You okay, koukla?*

Yes, this bowl is tingling. Can you feel it?

I feel its power.

Well, I'm feeling a bit more than that. It's almost like it's trying to tell me something.

We will take a better look once it's secure.

He pulled the remote from his pocket and unlocked the car. Then pushed the seats down to ready for the crate. Pierre's assistant loaded the item then left.

"As always, Mr. Lyson, your swift approach is welcomed."

"A pleasure." Xen bowed and Pierre returned the gesture.

Pierre turned his attention to Carissa. "I trust I will be seeing more of you with Mr. Lyson."

"That goes without saying."

He smiled, then took his leave.

Carissa helped with the trunk, but as she took a step back she sensed the air shift. Xen was at her side in seconds.

A man and women stood before them.

Xen pulled Carissa closer to him. "What do we owe the pleasure to, Thanatos?"

"Easy, vampire. We didn't come for trouble."

"Then why are you here?" Xen asked again.

"A warning and promise that whatever battle is to come we will fight with you."

Carissa raised an eyebrow. "You could have told Father."

"There will be lots of death when the time comes, and you will need us on the field."

"Why the sudden support, Eris?" Xen asked.

"Let's just say that for some battles you have to pick your side early."

Carissa opened her mouth to ask a question but didn't get a chance before they dematerialized. "Well, if that's not weird, I don't know what is," she said to Xen.

"I don't know what to make of it, but I'm sure there is more going on on Olympus than they care to tell us."

They got into the car and buckled up.

"I'm sensing your emotions are erratic. Care to explain?"

"Several things and the realization that my grandfather was messing with who knows whom makes me very uneasy. It also increases the pool of people that may have wanted him dead." A rock formed in her stomach. Her grandfather had been found dead in the lounge room years ago. More questions and no answers. "We haven't even begun to look further into it."

"I have had several discussions with Jones. He's trying to rebuild what happened and find who handled the case at the time."

That reminded her, she was due to catch up with Jones and Lopez, her ex-partner. She was being a horrible friend to a lot of people. She needed to get her social life back. "I can't shake that I'm missing a significant piece of information about everything going on."

"That is at the forefront of my thoughts too, *koukla.*"

He pulled into the driveway of her home. He pressed a remote and the garage door opened.

"Will it ever be safe here again?"

"We may have issues at the moment, but it will be."

She trusted Xen and his words.

He popped the trunk and sped out of the car.

"Need a hand," Kane said from the doorway leading to the garage.

It was then that Carissa noticed the elevator next to the door. "You installed an elevator." Her octave had raised a few decibels.

"Do you like it, *koukla.*"

"Like? I totally missed it when I was looking around with Kane."

"If I'd known you'd be this thrilled I would have shown it to you sooner," Xen said with an impish grin.

She looked at it and looked at the buttons on the wall. "It goes upstairs?"

"Yes, it does."

"Wicked." She flashed her pearly whites to Xen and then Kane. "Wait, why did I completely miss it?"

"It's spelled by Kirke. You can only enter from this floor. On every other level it has been spelled to look like part of the wall."

"That witch just earned more brownie points."

"Did someone say my name?"

Kirke appeared before her, and Carissa just sailed into her arms.

"You know, vampire. I don't think having a spell that summons me every time someone says my name is a good idea."

Carissa released her friend and stepped back. "Well, I don't mind, but I can see how frustrating that would be for you."

"Just a wee bit." She gave a universal hand gesture by pinching her index finger and thumb together.

"We best get this downstairs."

"What do you have there?"

"A libation bowl."

"Maybe I'll hang around."

"Suit yourself witch," Xen said, pushing the crate into the elevator.

They piled in the elevator, and Kane inserted a key next to the keypad and turned. Then hit the down button.

She could feel a dull hum coming from the crate.

Xen and Kane made quick work of getting the crate out and cracking the lid off. When the bowl was exposed the vibrations increased. Carissa stepped closer. *Pick me up.* The words floated into her mind. She stepped closer.

"It wants me to pick it up."

Three sets of eyes all turned to her.

"Then do it, *koukla*."

"But what if…"

"For it to communicate with you, it must have picked up on your demi-god half," Xen said.

"But what if it explodes or something." She was being ridiculous. More to the point though she didn't know jack shit about the bowl.

Kane, Xen and Kirke let out a laugh.

"You're in the room with supernatural beings, and you're worried about a libation bowl? I think it's fine." Kirke pointed a finger and nodded her head for Carissa to proceed.

"True." There was enough strength in the room to handle a lil' ol' *phiale*. Besides, the bowls were used in ritual practice so any energy coming from it was due to its age and reverence to the gods.

Pick me up so I can reveal myself to you, Olympian. She leaned over the crate and reached in to pull it out. Power tingled around her fingers. The Phiale vibrated three times.

"Did you catch that?"

"I did," Xen said. "Bring it here." Xen indicated a museum worthy Frank showcase table.

She placed the bowl where Xen had indicated, but when she released the tighter than usual grip she hadn't realized she'd had around it, her fingertips were marred with bronze. She looked at them and rubbed them together. She picked it up again. "Can you get me a cleaning cloth?" she asked them all.

Kirke clicked her fingers and one appeared in her hands. "Here." She handed it to her.

Carissa rubbed all over the bowl with a fair bit of effort. When most of the bronze from the center of the bowl had been wiped, she looked up to Xen. "I don't know why, but someone had this bowl spelled with a different color than it's true color. It's probably why Pierre and everyone else thought it was rubbish."

She wiped the rest of the bowl and placed it back on the stand. The energy had doubled, and she could feel it through her.

"There's something else."

"I know, *koukla*."

"So do I. I can feel it," Kirke said.

"I'm getting a buzzing sound," Kane said.

"*Apolyo.*" Kirke spoke the spell.

It began to shake.

"I suggest we step back," Xen said.

None of them needed to be told twice. The bowl began to levitate then spin.

A bright light engulfed the room.

The *phiale* had transformed to a spear.

"It can't be," Xen said.

They all turned in his direction.

"What? You don't recognize this weapon?" He pointed at the object in question.

Carissa kept her eyes on the spear. "I don't know about anyone else in this room, but I haven't got a cotton picken' idea about whose it might be, let alone recognize it."

"It's called *astrape*, meaning lightening. It is the spear of Athena. I didn't even know it was missing." Xen gave them all the background information they required to understand the value and severity of the object.

"I don't think we should keep it," Carissa said.

"I agree," Kane and Kirke said in unison.

"I am wholeheartedly in favor with the collective," Xen stated.

"Since we all agree, there is only one thing to do, but first…" Carissa paused. There were a thousand things going through her mind. "…Father," she called.

The air in the room shifted, and she recognized his power before he appeared. "What is it, *kori mou?*"

She pointed.

His eyes widened and he cocked his head to one side. "Athena," he whispered.

Again she recognized the shift and the tingle of energy. The goddess materialized at Ares' side. "What is it, Brother?"

He lifted his chin toward the item they were all looking at.

"*Astrape.* My beloved spear."

She glanced around. "How is this here, and where did you find it?"

"Aunt Athena, my grandfather was looking for it, and Xen

helped me restart the search. It is through his connections that we were able to track it down. In the form of a libation bowl, I might add."

The gray-eyed goddess took a few steps closer to Carissa. "I meant no disrespect, and we all agreed that it should be given back."

Athena cast a quick look of contemplation at them. Then walked to the spear. It levitated and then snapped into her right hand. At the connection the spear glowed bright with light. "You have no idea how many gods and goddesses would have killed to get this in their slimy hands."

"I know firsthand how many," Carissa's father said. "And if they know you have it, they will try to seize it."

"Carissa, come here."

She moved toward the goddess.

"The power of this spear is what everyone seeks. I will not be taking it to Olympus with me. There has been enough quarreling over many millennia. I had the spear spelled and placed here on the mortal realm for safety, but it looks like it has had its own journey and was possibly not the smartest move. Your grandfather was right to seek it. Athens was and is my city. Your heritage through your grandfather and mother has strong ties and to that your father's union with your mother, Aglauros, gives you a few perks.

Xen let out a breath. "More than we know."

"And that is what makes you a threat to many."

A rock formed in Carissa's belly. She'd be a constant target. "I didn't ask for any of this, but it's what I have now. All I want is to protect my family and those around me."

"*Kori mou*, you will always have our protection."

"And mine," Xen said.

"And ours," Kane threw in for him and Kirke.

Carissa's heart swelled, knowing those around her would fight for her and with her, but she could not continue to jeopardize everyone. Her burdens were hers and hers alone.

"Masking your power is of key importance at all times, but I will grant you an extra layer of protection should you need it." The goddess reached for her wrist. She snapped her fingers. "*Kleio.*" The spear disappeared and a cuff appeared in her hand. She clipped it to Carissa's wrist.

Carissa looked down at the gold cuff. "I feel like Wonder Woman."

Athena let out a laugh. "Only stronger." Amusement laced her words.

"Sister, is this a wise move?" her father asked the goddess.

"Brother, it's always best to be prepared."

"The goddess turned her attention back to Carissa. When the time comes, release the spear and it will call me to your side."

Carissa nodded in understanding.

Xen had moved to her side.

"Now the rest of you, come forward and place your hand on mine."

They all did what she asked. "Will you do us the honor, Brother?"

Ares spoke the spell. "*Orkos.*"

Light and heat surrounded their hands. "If anyone betrays the knowledge of this spear now hidden and with my daughter, I will know, and I will come for you personally."

Kane and Kirke both gulped.

"No one wants my brother's wrath."

"Roger that," Kane said.

"The knowledge of what has transpired here is not mine to reveal," Kirke added.

"I would not endanger my bride."

They released their hands from one another, and the goddess and Ares dematerialized at the same time.

"Well, that was not what I was expecting."

"I don't think any of us did," Kirke threw back.

Carissa looked down at the cuff. "This thing stands out a mile." The gold cuff shifted, shrunk in size, and altered from a solid cuff to a thin one with the meander motif decorated all round.

"It's connected to you." Kirke took a few small steps toward Carissa.

"Should I be worried?"

"Not at all, *koukla*," Xen answered.

"I think it would be difficult for someone to take it from you. If I'm right you're protecting *Astrape* and vice versa," Kane said from where he stood.

Carissa filed that piece of information away. These gifts, along with their oaths, were starting to become a burden.

Her phone buzzed. She fished it out of her pocket.

"Girlfriend. How fast can you get here?"

The desperate tone from Ligi ricochet in her ear.

TWENTY-THREE

"The greatest gift in life is friendship, and I have received it." ~ *Greek Proverb*

Ligi's House; Charleston, SC
Evening, mortal realm – Day 8

Carissa turned to Xen. She didn't need to tell him.

"Witch, can you materialize us to Ligi's house?"

"All I need is Carissa to think of the location."

Kirke grabbed each of their hands.

"You need me, boss?" Kane asked.

"Get some rest."

They dematerialized and landed in the middle of Ligi's living room.

A woman sat in a chair with her hands on her head.

Ligi flew into Carissa's arms for a hug.

"Who is this, Ligi?"

"Pheme."

Carissa almost staggered at the coincidence. Xen cast the woman a suspicious look then looked back at Carissa.

This seems strategic, doesn't it? he said to her mind.

She nodded in agreement. "Why the emergency?" she asked Ligi.

"She's my neighbor and lives next door and the hounds of hell have been chasing her down."

Xen raised an eyebrow. "What does that have to do with us?"

Pheme raised her head. "Everything," she whispered.

"How so?" Xen asked.

"His hounds dragged my sorry ass down to the underworld. Hades wanted to know…"

she pointed at Xen "…if you had some libation bowl."

Bile made its way up Carissa's throat. Was Hades friend or foe? If he was after Athena's spear, she needed to warn her and her father. And then another thought punched her in the gut. Was he behind everything that had been going on?"

I'm thinking the same thing, koukla.

Pheme stood up. "All this is not good for me. They know where I live?"

"And this is a problem?" Xen asked.

"For years I have slipped under their radar. I've enjoyed living in the mortal realm without all the politics on Olympus. You have no idea what it's like to be the goddess of gossip. I'd have a line all the way down the street waiting to see me."

"Hmm. Tell me about it," Kirke said.

Carissa cast her friend a look.

Kirke gave her a *what* gesture.

"Pheme, I'm sorry that your privacy has been disrupted. If you were not supposed to stay here, then why did you break Grandfather's orders and stay?"

The goddess' eyes widened to saucers. Her mouth dropped open. She stuck a finger out to Carissa. "Who are you?"

"I'm Carissa Alkippes. Daughter of Ares."

Pheme took a few steps back.

"Stop it. She won't harm you," Ligi said.

"How do you know that? She's Zeus' granddaughter. She might be a spy for them."

Ligi moved toward her friend and put her hand on her arms. "Listen. You can trust her."

Pheme looked over at Carissa and nodded her head to Ligi.

"Why don't we all sit down." Ligi indicated the furniture around the living room. They all settled into their respective spots.

"What is troubling you most?" Xen asked.

"Other than it being a privacy thing, I don't want any unnecessary minor gods and goddesses turning up and using my place as a hotel or cover."

"Amen to that."

Carissa gave Kirke a look.

"What? I can relate."

She turned her head back to the troubled goddess. "Okay, so relocate." Carissa shrugged her shoulders. How difficult could that be?

"Easier said than done. Once they know I've been spending considerable amounts of time here they'll summon me. Just like Hades did."

"What exactly happened there?" Xen asked.

"Don't get me wrong, he was nice as pie. All he wanted was rumors about where some stupid bowl was."

"A *phiale*."

"Yes, yes, one of those libation bowls—a bronze one." She paused. "He wanted to make sure that the vampire over there had it."

"That vampire has a name, and it's Xen." Carissa's tone had sharpened. Goddess or not, where were her manners? "Apart from Xen getting the bowl, did he say anything else?"

"Nothing at all. He zapped me back here."

"Pheme, why is it you stay here?" Kirke asked.

"Olympus has changed. Here I get some rest. Rumors in the mortal realm are not like the Olympian one. Gossip there can turn nasty. The gods and goddesses of Olympus are dangerous, and y'all would be foolish to think otherwise. They would double and triple cross you to get their desired outcome."

"And what might that be?"

"Power."

"What kind of power are we talking about?" Xen asked.

"The type that can obliterate this whole world."

"But then they would cease to exist."

"Their rage doesn't let them see past that."

"Okay, we're talking in circles." Carissa shot to her feet. "Hades wanted you to make sure Xen had the bowl?"

"Yes."

Carissa's anger turned up a few degrees. "Just to bring you up to date, we do, and you have my full permission to tell him."

"I already have but I didn't say it was Xen, only that a vampire had it."

Carissa's mind spun.

"That's why I asked Ligi to ask you here. Just in case there is danger."

"Pheme told me what happened, and I thought it best to bring y'all up to speed," Ligi said.

"What does this information mean to Hades? Why does he need to know I have the bowl? Did his intentions show signs he was coming after it?"

Pheme dropped her shoulders and sat silently for a minute. "Nothing like that. He was friendly. He just wanted to make sure you had it. I don't know the reason why?" She fell into a deep contemplative state then added, "But he did say, 'we' need your help, and when I quizzed him as to who the 'we' were he made a reference that I should already know. That 'we' means Hades and Zeus, they're in it together."

The spear belonged to Athena. Carissa doubted Zeus would want to claim it. He had enough power and didn't need it. Hades though, she wasn't sure. She'd never had the pleasure of meeting him. Right now all the emotions going through her were telling her one thing—they were all chess pieces. This was part of something bigger and that was what she didn't like, the game the gods and goddesses were playing.

"I can relocate you," Xen said.

"I would be forever grateful and in your debt." Pheme stood. "You really need to take cover. I don't know what Hades or Zeus want, but maybe you should be wary. You know, just in case."

"Thank you for the warning," Xen said.

Carissa's mind spun like wool on a weaver's loom. With Xen's help she'd keep the spear safe. She looked at Pheme and realized the goddess had been trying to warn them. She'd been angry and short with her. "Thank you for giving us the heads up."

"Pleasure, daughter of Ares, and from the whispers that I hear, you are lucky to have good friends around you."

Carissa took the goddess' hands in hers. A tingle of energy danced between them. Recognition. One half deity to full deity. Pheme's eyes glittered with awareness. The old saying, "Never look a gift horse in the mouth" rang true. "I'm sorry for my abruptness. A friend to Ligi is a friend to me."

The goddess nodded in understanding.

"If I hear anything I'll let you know."

"We in turn would be grateful."

"I will send Adam to relocate you." Pheme's lips turned up at the mention of his name.

"I'll throw an illusion over your house to cover you for the time being. Trust me, I know what it's like to have your incognito residence thrown into the limelight of every supernatural and godly being," Kirke huffed out.

Lox's men had been moved out of the forest, but Carissa further exposed her friend when she turned up for a chat. She would have to find a way to make it up to her witchy friend.

"Ligi, can I have a word?" Carissa asked.

"Sure."

They stepped out of ear shot. "I never knew about Pheme? You never mentioned her."

Carissa hadn't known her friend Ligi was a siren. She'd only found out when she was thrown into Xen's world and her father's.

"I did tell you. I said I live next to the goddess of rumors."

"You could have been a tad bit more convincing."

"Seriously? Girlfriend you would have thought me nuttier than a five-pound fruitcake."

Carissa let out a laugh. She would have too. "Come on, give me some sugar."

"We need a proper catch up." Ligi gave her a hug and a kiss on the cheek.

"We do, and we will as soon as I get some things sorted. I'm still trying to come to terms with this godly business." And that was the solid truth. From the moment her ordinary world changed, she'd had to accept not only the enormity that everything she knew and held dear was a lie, but she also had powers.

"I know." Ligi turned her head to where Xen, Kirke and Pheme were talking.

"We best get out of your hair." Carissa made her way back to Xen.

He looked up and she saw a storm in his green eyes. "You okay, *koukla*?"

She nodded. She knew he had been listening in to her thoughts. It was the one thing she kept forgetting—to shield her thoughts when around gods and Xen. *We will work it out.* The words filtered to her mind.

I know we will, but I can't say that it doesn't have its moments, she sent back.

Kirke stepped closer to her and Xen, waved one hand and dematerialized them. She popped them back in the lounge room.

"I should get back to my own abode."

Carissa pulled Kirke in for a hug. "Thank you."

"It's not every day I meet a goddess of gossip."

"I guess not," she said.

"Vampire." She dipped her head slowly.

"Witch." His lips twitched into a half smile, and he returned her gesture.

She snapped her fingers and dematerialized.

"Gotta admit she does that so well."

Carissa turned to face Xen. He said, "I can do certain things well too." He lifted his eyebrows with a devious grin. Then stretched out his hand and pulled her to him. She crashed into his chest.

"How about you show me your skills."

That was all she needed to say. He picked her up and used his vampire speed to take them both upstairs. With her still in his arms he put his thumb to the access pad on the door and it clicked open. He stepped in then pushed the door closed.

He put her on her feet and started peeling off his clothes.

With desperate need she did the same. Then she remembered with his speed and strength he could do it all faster. "Use your skills."

"Your wish is my command."

He tore her clothes from her body and his. His fingers cupped her face and his lips found hers. He deepened the kiss. His thirst for her did not abate and small mews of pleasure drove his. He backed her to the bed. There was no question how urgently he desired her. His fangs elongated and he leaned down to take a long suck of one of her breasts. He did the same to the other and then bit down. She moaned with pleasure. His hand traveled down her abdomen and to the place where her sweet nectar had started to slowly seep. His fingers found the nub that needed pressure. With slow strokes he built the crescendo for her and just as she was about to find her release, he latched on to her breast and drew hard. Her scream filled the room.

"Spread your legs for me."

She did as he asked and with one smooth stroke, he entered her warm silky heat. He wouldn't last long. She drove him to near madness with desire. With a few thrusts he spilled his seed into her womb.

He pulled out and spooned her into his arms.

"I think we should talk about getting you more training."

"What were you thinking?"

"Tactical training."

"Oh, no."

"Yes. We need your father."

Her eyes widened. "Not like the last time with Father."

"Something like that, *koukla*."

She needed to stop him. "Xen, I know you take my protection seriously, but we might need to think about a different approach."

"Like?"

"I need to get a handle on my power and to do that I need someone who understands the inner workings of the power."

"Your father can do that."

"My father has other fires to put out."

"Come here."

She turned around and wiggled into a spooning embrace.

"Stop that, *koukla*."

Her eyes fluttered and closed.

TWENTY-FOUR

"The day will come…" ~ Homer

Kirke's cottage, Francis Marion National Forest; Charleston, SC
Late afternoon, mortal realm – Day 9

"Now focus," Kirke said as she threw a blast of power toward Carissa.

When Carissa had woken that the morning, she'd decided she'd take matters into her own hands. Xen's idea of training was not the same as hers.

The blue ball that came tumbling toward her knocked her back. She landed with a thud on the long uncut green grass. Her rump ached, that was the third time she'd failed to stop it. She got to her feet. There would only be one way to walk away from Kirke's fire flying magical energy balls. She'd have to stop them. She gave her legs and arms a shake and cracked her neck from side to side. "Again," she called to her witchy friend.

She took a deep breath and cleared her mind.

Kirke sneered before throwing another burst of magic. The ball of power came head on. Carissa focused on what she wanted to do, she had never thought to use *anagke*, her power of compulsion to push the blazing and charging magic out of the way. She lifted her hand and focused. *"Kineo,"* she spoke the Ancient Greek word. The blue energy shifted past her and hit a tree in the distance.

She did a fist pump.

"Very good," Kirke shouted. "Let's see if you can repeat it."

Kirke didn't give her time to prepare. Another blast of energy came charging at her faster than the last. This one was bigger. If it hit her, it would send her flying through the air. She cleared her mind and repeated her spell. She tried it again and in the nick of time it flew past.

"That was close. I think I'm done." Carissa started to walk toward Kirke.

"One more, just for fun." Kirke threw another magical energy ball at her.

She sidestepped to see if it would change direction, but no, it stayed on target. She had an idea. She picked up her pace into a light sprint, raised her hand and envisaged running through the energy. She used her compulsion internally without uttering any words. She flicked her hand to the left in a sweeping motion. The rush of blue magic changed direction.

Kirke smiled.

"No need to grin from ear to ear," Carissa said a bit out of breath.

"I'll do as I please. Now come inside for some tea."

Carissa made a gagging noise. "Seriously, tea? Where are you, in the English countryside?"

"I have your favorite poison too."

"Music to my ears." She followed her friend inside the cabin and to the small island bench in the kitchen. She popped herself on a stool.

"I think you'll be okay." Kirke pulled two mugs out of the cupboard.

"I have a feeling I just might."

"How did you move the magic."

"I'd never really thought about using my power of compulsion before. So, I used that."

Kirke's eyes widened. "You compelled the power to move?"

"Yes." Her friend's face showed signs she'd slipped into some vortex of deep contemplation. Her grip around the cups had turned white. "Kirke," Carissa whispered, not wanting to startle her.

The witch snapped out of it and put the crockery on the bench. She looked around the large cottage then flicked her hand. "Promise me you will never tell anyone you can move magic with your compulsion."

Carissa couldn't understand why that would be an issue, but her friend's reaction was enough to make her agree. "Okay, I swear. What's the deal?"

"Compulsion, to compel someone is one thing, but when that power extends beyond you being able to use it in regard to people it's going to raise some eyebrows. You should be able to stop or counterattack when I throw or cast magic. That said you shouldn't be able to control the magic a witch throws at you."

"Isn't blocking and repelling the same?"

"No. Because you're not altering the magic hurtled toward you when you defend."

Carissa nodded her head in understanding, but that was silly to her. "I should not be able to compel the magic?"

"Yes."

She was still confused. "Why?"

"Magic is metaphysical. We are either born with it or we learn it, but in both cases you must have the genes, if you will, to be able to harness it. We gather our magic from the earth around us. We use that which is available. My balls of energy are created from wind and light. To counter it you would use wind and fire or water."

"You know all that is as clear as mud?"

"Okay, you shouldn't be able to compel my magic, but rather counter it or make it dissipate, not control it to attack me. It's my power."

"You know you could have said that in the first place," Carissa deadpanned.

Kirke didn't share her humor. "I'm serious. If you told a witch you can compel their power, they'll all come after you. That's way too much control for anyone to hold."

"Is it?"

"Trust me on this. Even a god. Can you imagine if one of the Olympians realized you could take the core of their power and throw it back at them?"

"How is that different from throwing power at them to counter the blow?"

"When we don't control each other's power, we can defeat someone or counter an attack to escape. With your compulsion you can throw it right back at them and that makes you undefeatable —dangerous."

Targets, more targets on her back. Targets that were getting bigger than vast space. She'd never asked for this power. It came as a package. She'd inherited all this from her father and his side of the family—Zeus, Hera et al. "This should be a good thing, but I'm starting to see why this power is a burden more than anything else."

Kirke shook her head while placing a coffee pod in the machine. "No, no. This is a gift. One that you inherited.

"You mean one that comes with a huge bullseye on my back."

"You're looking at this all wrong. It's about how you control that power and knowing when and where to use it."

"But you said if anyone finds out about it then it would make things worse for me."

"Yes, but we need to teach you how to mask that, so instead of throwing that power back you can compel it to change."

"Is that even possible?"

"Yes, but it won't be easy. It's far more complicated to manipulate power at that level, but your gift of *anagke* is way more superior than what I've seen in other supernatural creatures." Kirke put Carissa's coffee in front of her. Then turned to pour some tea in a cup for herself. "It won't be easy, but I think you can do it. That last blast I threw at you—you ran right through it."

Carissa took a sip of coffee and contemplated what Kirke had said. "It felt like the right thing to do at the time." It hadn't seemed odd or extraordinary. "Surely others can do the same."

Kirke eyed her from the rim of her cup she had just brought to her lips. "I have never met a witch, warlock or other supernatural creature who can split power so they can walk through it. I assumed it might be a trick your father showed you."

"Trust me, there hasn't been enough time for Father to show me anything, and I am beginning to doubt there ever will be. Their time and issues move very differently from ours."

"Then we shouldn't waste the time we have together. There's no telling when someone else may turn up to snatch you away."

"Exactly." She tipped her cup back and downed the last of her coffee, then swung out of her seat and took the cup to the sink to rinse before stacking it in the dishwasher. "How about we give it another shot with some of your witchy juju help."

"Let's." Kirke finished her tea then motioned for Carissa to follow her. She headed to her bedroom. In the room she spoke a spell and a secret hatch appeared. Kirke flipped it up and lights and descending stairs manifested.

"You have a secret basement too?"

"Come on, you're telling me you didn't know secret basements were all the rage back in the day?"

Carissa rolled her eyes. "Honestly, you were all a bunch of copycats."

"And what has changed today?"

"I believe it's called trending."

"Nothing has changed. People are still behaving in the same way, chasing fashion and..." she air quoted "...trends."

There weren't as many stairs as at her grandfather's newly refurbished basement. The space here was much smaller. Kirke made her way to a bookshelf and pulled out a heavy looking leather bound tome. She flipped the pages.

"Here, I think we need to practice this."

Kirke pointed to the page and location.

"And what is this?" Carissa asked, not able to make out the writing.

"This will help you. It's a two in one spell."

"Meaning?"

"When you use your compulsion, it will mask your true power

and cause a metamorphosis of power, making it difficult to pinpoint what you just did."

"I have no idea how that works, but I'm going to assume somehow it all comes out in the wash."

Kirke put the big book back on the shelf. "Why don't we try it?"

"I'm in your capable hands."

They made their way back out of the basement and to the sunshine outside. "Resume your position, but when I throw power at you, rather than shoving it out of the way, use the spell *metavallo*."

Carissa nodded her head in understanding. She resumed her previous position and turned to wait for Kirke's assault. The witch had already sent a blue ball of magic hurtling in her direction. She didn't even have the chance to blink, let alone focus. It hit her in the solar plexus and tossed her a meter backwards.

Ouch, that hurt. Her friend was not going to go easy on her, and she understood why. Carissa really needed to get a handle on this. She got to her feet and walked back to her previous position.

Again, the witch fired. This time she saw Kirke prep for the next assault.

She focused and whispered, "*Metavallo,*" as Kirke had instructed. She conjured up an image of snowballs, and the charging magic adjusted its direction and turned to charging snowballs.

Kirke threw up her hands and dematerialized. Then reappeared. "Well played," she shouted in approval. "But we are not done yet."

Carissa managed three more and then her fuel gauge pointed to empty. Depleted and hungry she staggered into Kirke's cottage. "That's worse than training with my father."

Kirke smirked. "Magic has its limitations."

"Doesn't everything?"

Her friend sent her a silent nod in agreement.

What they had managed today had been in her estimation productive. "I should be getting home." It was late and she was hungry. Plus, she needed to check on things. "Sure," Kirke said. "You deserve a rest now." She put a hand on Carissa then snapped her fingers, and they landed in her kitchen.

Yiayia and Paula were sitting at the table with a pile of food in the middle. They both startled at the intrusion. Carissa's grandmother had the walking stick up and ready for action. Aunt Paula had a fork in her hand. Both would be reasonable weapons when in need. Carissa remembered when she had stabbed a rogue vampire in the eye with a fork. Lucky for her Xen had appeared, and she didn't have to reap the repercussions of that event.

"You're back. We cooked a little something." Paula swept her arm across the selection of food.

"I'm starving. Kirke, do you want to stay?"

"It looks tempting, though I'm going to have to decline. I have a date."

Paula sprang to her feet to grab the aluminum foil. She started putting things on a plate

"How are things with Odysseus?" Kirke's boyfriend had been through a lot. Much like Carissa, he'd been used as a pawn to bribe and coerce Kirke.

"He's getting better."

"That's good to hear."

"Here, take some food. You can heat it up tomorrow."

"Thank you."

Kirke took the plate and hugged and kissed Aunt Paula and Yiayia. Then turned and gave Carissa a good squeeze too. "Remember what I said, keep it to yourself," she said in a low whisper. She stepped back and dematerialized.

Carissa stared at the spot. This she would keep to herself. The less who knew the better. "So how has your day been so far?" she asked her aunt and grandmother while sliding into a chair. She began to scoop food onto the plate.

"We've had…"

The air shifted and her father appeared.

"Seriously? Not now." She had only managed a bit or two. She looked at her father's worried face. "Can it wait?"

"*Kori mou*, when have you known the gods to be patient?"

He had a point. "At least let me grab a few things." She grabbed the foil on the table and started to pack some spanakopita and tiropita pies on it. When she thought it would suffice, she scrunched up the top to enclose them. She looked at her father who was eating a piece of spinach pie.

"What?"

"You want me to pack more?"

"No, but it's very tasty," he said to Yiayia and Aunt Paula.

They both gave thanks.

"Swords," he commanded.

They appeared on her body, perfectly strapped in. "This must be serious."

"Believe me, it is."

TWENTY-FIVE

"The god of war is impartial; he hands out death to the man who hands out death." ~ Homer, The Iliad

Chambers of Ares; Mount Olympus
Late afternoon, realm of the gods – Day 3

Ares materialized them to his chambers.

"What's this all about, Father?"

"If you remember, Athena pinned one of the minor gods that I fought with to the wall just before I sent you home."

She nodded her head.

"I managed to question him in advance of him passing out."

Carissa held up a hand. "Hang on, does that mean gods can die?"

"Minor gods like the rest of the gods don't die. They can at times leave this realm by being cast to the skies or the depths of Tartarus. The two that I fought with will cast to Tartarus. They will never be the same though because their wounds will close but never fully restore, therefore they will remain forever crippled."

Always something new with the gods. She filed that nugget away.

"And what did you discover?"

"He didn't directly name a god behind this but said Tartarus and all prisoners entombed there will rise and very soon."

"You're saying someone is helping them get free."

"Yes, and Kronos and Iapetos were only the beginning."

"Not all this again."

"I hate to say it, *kori mou*, but yes, it's all this again and more. It's the more bit that I'm worried about. Think about how many I have cast down there over the millennia."

"I'm sure Zeus' tally is probably higher than yours."

"Got that right."

"How do we stop it?"

"That's the problem. This plan has been in motion for centuries. Trying to find the sole person who has been aiding and abetting the cream of nastiness in Tartarus is like looking for a needle in a haystack."

"You're basically telling me there is no way we can intercept and put a stop to it all before it all explodes."

His features turned dark. "None."

She let out a long sigh. "The... there must be some way."

Ares shook his head. "If there were, I would not be having this conversation. I'd be assembling my men and taking action."

"Then why am I here?"

"I needed to talk to you about it, to prepare you for what's coming. You will need to assemble your own army and your own allies. The war with the gods and all from Tartarus will not be fought here on Olympus but in the mortal plane."

Carissa's mouth dropped open, but she recovered in an instant. "So innocent humans will be harmed in the process."

Ares nodded. "Zeus and I have thought about how we can fight without touching the mortal realm, and we think if we isolate it to Francis Marion Forest, we might just save countless innocent mortals."

The enormity and realization of what lay ahead made her nauseous. "What if..."

The air in the room shifted and the mighty Zeus appeared. "There is no simple solution to this, Granddaughter."

"Grandfather." Carissa stepped closer to give her grandfather a kiss on the cheek and a hug. "I feel like we've already lost." She slumped her shoulders.

"Nothing is ever lost, and you can't know victory unless you've fought for it," Zeus said.

"We will be nothing but cannon fodder like the human First World War. Bullet absorbers is what they were."

"That is where you are wrong, Granddaughter. You have decent fighters next to you and don't forget you will also have at your aid no ordinary men and women but supernatural men and women."

"That's great, but it doesn't comfort me."

"For that I am sincerely sorry," Zeus said. "It is our understanding you have a very small window of time to gather your forces."

"How small are we talking?"

"Three days."

"That's impossible." She placed a hand to her chest. Images flashed through her mind. Her head swam with the severity of it.

"You will have to enlist everyone you can get your hands on," Ares said from where he stood. "Do not underestimate your vampire."

Right, he was right, Xen could gather all the *Phi*, however three days was ridiculous. She shoved her hands in her pockets and began to pace. "We would be outnumbered."

The air shifted, and she recognized the goddess before she appeared. "But not outsmarted."

She narrowed her eyes at the goddess. "How do you mean?"

"You have at your disposal Xen who is a brilliant tactician, but there is someone else who will heed the call when you ask?"

"Who do I need to ask?"

"Lox and Xen and word will get out. You'll be surprised how quickly they can gather."

"You seem confident, Aunt Athena."

The goddess pointed a finger at her. "And you need to trust."

Carissa deliberated what the goddess said. "It could all turn sideways."

"It won't. You won't have to fight the Titans," her father filled in.

"That's right, Granddaughter. There will be two separate fights, and the Titans will be the responsibility of the Olympians."

"What about Poseidon, will he fight? He didn't seem too pleased with Father's verdict."

"My brother will join."

She faked surprise. Her father smiled at her.

"Explain to me what exactly will happen?"

She recognized the second incoming signature, her Olympian grandmother. "Sorry I'm late. I was gathering our forces."

"To answer your question, *kori mou*, the Titans will be fought by us and when they have been re-prisoned you and your allies will fight what is left behind."

"How will you re-prison them?"

"We have Hephaestus working on it," Zeus said.

"How do we know they've broken free?"

"Our guards have reported it. It's only a matter of days before they unleash war on your mortal home." Zeus grimaced and a pained look crossed his features.

"There are gods who won't fight because they see me as a threat. Will that diminish your numbers?" she asked.

"Not in the slightest," Athena answered.

Carissa nodded her head in understanding. She needed to get back and now. "I think you all know what I'm going to say."

They dematerialized her.

She landed in Xen's office with Xen, Kane and Adam.

Xen dashed from where he was sitting to her. "What's news?"

She looked long and hard at Xen, her shoulders dropped as she turned to look at Kane and Adam. "We have three days to gather as many men and women as we can to fight with us. Tartarus has been breached. Titans and a bevy of creatures are going to assemble at Francis Marion Forest. I'm sorry." Her legs weakened, and the dizziness she'd been holding back came to the surface. Strong arms banded around her and held her up.

Kane was there in a flash too with some water. "Here."

"Thank you." Her voice shook. "I am indeed the bearer of bad news."

"Let's get you seated and tell us everything."

Adam was stunned into silence. It wasn't every day she could silence that wolf.

"The gods have stipulated there will be two battles."

"Two battles?" Adam found his voice.

"That's what I said."

"Can it, *lykos*. Let Carissa speak," Kane chided him.

"Go on," Xen coaxed softly.

"The first battle will be with the Titans and the Olympian gods, and then once the bad guys have been secured again, we will have to fight the remaining unearthly creatures and demons."

"How did they escape?" Adam asked.

"Father said they had more than one person aiding them and trying to find that person is like trying to sift through sand."

"We should focus on what we can and that's fighting," Xen said.

"They were certain you and Lox can amass allies, and they have Hephaestus working on how to secure it."

"Don't forget, Rissa. You have the use of several different packs around the globe."

She looked at Adam. "How soon can you get them here?"

"I'll make the necessary calls." He jumped to his feet.

"Adam, explain to them that if they don't come there won't be much left of the mortal realm and everything they enjoy."

"Noted," he said as he made his way out of Xen's office.

Kane got to his feet. "I should do the same." He moved with long steps, urgency evident with each one.

In the quietude of the room Carissa expelled a huge sigh from her lungs. It was just her and Xen now.

"How confident did they sound at beating the Titans for a second time?"

"On a scale from one to ten, I'd say a definite nine."

Xen let out a whistle. "Then we should trust they can also foresee what is to come."

"But say this time they don't?"

"We won't really know till it is upon us."

"True, and that's what makes me even more uneasy."

"If the gods and goddesses battle it out with the Titans, then I say we've got a fighting chance of getting a few solid punches in."

"Do you think we can get the numbers?"

"I will certainly try."

She fished the phone out of her back pocket and dialed Lox's number.

"Speak."

"Lox, it's Carissa."

"What can I do for you?"

"I need you to gather your men. War awaits us all."

"You have my arm and that of my men in battle."

"Thank you."

"It is I who gives thanks, and we will fight for what is here. This is our home now."

She ended the call.

"That wasn't so bad," Xen said.

"No, it wasn't, but they are only a few."

"Yes, but a few who have fought every day with the *kakodaimones* in the underworld for many thousands of years. You can't get any more battle hardened than those men."

"True. I never thought of it that way."

"How about you head on up for some rest, and I'll reach out to any other contacts."

"Do you mind if I just lie down here on the couch. Just to be with you."

"Not at all, *koukla*." He reached over and placed a soft kiss on her lips.

She moved to get herself comfortable. Then watched as Xen went to his desk.

He sat down and sifted through some numbers on his phone. "I need you to get all the *Phi Athanatoi* to Charleston. This is global."

Her eyes fluttered a few times as she pondered the severity in Xen's voice, but sleep pulled her under.

TWENTY-SIX

"My speech will not be aimed at stopping your urge to return home; as far as I am concerned you may go where you like." ~ Alexander the Great

Francis Marion Forest; Charleston, SC
Evening, mortal realm – Day 12

Carissa paced on the large tree stump base, back and forth, trying to find the words she desperately needed. The last three days had been a blur. Xen, Kane and Adam had exhausted all their contact base to amass enough of an army. An army she was priming herself to address. She took a deep breath, and the chattering sounds of the assembled fighters died down.

Tonight she would ask them for the biggest sacrifice. To either follow her onward with whatever battle lay ahead or to leave and go into hiding until some demon or Titan turned up to slay them.

"I have asked you all here not to fight for me but for yourselves and the freedom to live as you should. This is now your home. You fight for it and all that you so recently discovered and hold dear. Don't be disheartened by the numbers of the enemy. For the enemy does not fight with the urgency of having something to save. They fight with only greed and violence. Violence that will be spread like a cancer across every inch of this earth. This violence cannot be accepted, nor can it come to fruition. Fight with me to end the threat."

A wave a cheers boomed from where she stood. The sound hit her in her gut.

"Well done, *koukla*," Xen said from beside her.

"Then why do I feel terrible."

"Because you're asking them to risk their lives in order to obtain a decent life."

"And none of this pleases me."

"You're looking at it from your perspective, not theirs. These men know only war and hardship. They've been conditioned and reconditioned and then some. It's not the same. They've seen the ugliness of losing men over and over for many millennia in the vastness of Hades' realm. This battle for them is just another fight for survival."

"That doesn't make me feel better."

"I didn't say it would, only that you should consider that for these men to follow you and the gods is an honor. To die for what they want is also considered an honor."

She contemplated his words before allowing Xen to help her down from the large tree stump.

"You did good," Lox said.

"I don't know what the outcome will be or how many we will lose in the process."

"None of us ever do. It's the risk we always take with us when we go into battle. Xen's men are the same. He knows that every time he comes up against a demon group or other unearthly creatures there is a chance some of his team might not make it. All warriors know this. Stop feeling bad."

Carissa stepped in and gave Lox a hug. "Thank you."

"Just focus on how we can pull the wool over their eyes."

And that was what they needed more than anything. To try to trick these gods and enemies back into the depths of Tartarus and make sure it could no longer have any weaknesses of escape. Zeus had asked Hephaestus for help. He needed new fortifications and tougher restraints for some of the Titans. He was working around the clock to deliver the project. He would use the battle to slip in and make the changes, then when the Titans were cast back to their dreaded cells there would be no escape for them ever again.

She cast a glance across the forest where she knew the enemy lay in wait, building up their own reinforcements and making their own plans to obliterate them all. Movement caught her eye. In the dark she could see a shadow emerge. He took a few steps forward and lit up a cigarette. She caught a glimpse of his face—Damion.

A low growl sounded at her ear. Xen had caught sight of him too.

"I'd like a nice slice of him," Carissa said.

"Not before I get one first."

"Either way, I really don't like him."

"You're not alone in your distaste," Xen said.

"Why do some men go off the rails like that?"

"Damion always had issues. He just needed a shove in the right direction to show his true colors."

She shook her head. "Most of the time I think there is such a thing as redemption and believe it is possible, but for Damion I'd say that ship left port long ago and is lost at sea."

"It did, *koukla*, and there's no coming back from that now. He's picked his side and so have we. Let's make sure ours has what it needs to succeed."

Lox had been silent. "Let's go over our plans."

They moved to a nearby tent. On the table inside were maps laid out with various markings. The red dots were the enemy and the blue dots everywhere else were their assembled men and women who had heeded their call. Even her friends had said they would fight along with her, regardless of their partners arguing to dissuade them. Her friends were not feeble women. And just like that they both appeared at the entrance of the tent.

"Carissa, what can we do?" Ligi asked.

She pointed to Ligi. "You're a siren, your singing will come in handy, and I want you and Tithon at their rear with your team. You will lure their whole back line." Carissa grabbed a pair of headphones from the table and tossed them to Tithon. There was a box nearby for all the other men. "For you, gumbo. We can't have you going insane when your girl starts to sing."

He let out a laugh. "Good thinking."

"Don't thank me. It was Xen who realized they were necessary. Kelly, I'll need you up in the sky. You will need comms, so you can report back to Lox and Xen. They will know where to move their men as required."

Lots or roars erupted from outside the tent.

"Don't tell me it's started?" Kelly said.

"They wouldn't dare. They said they would honor the time-frame to allow us to prepare."

"They could have been toying with you," Lox grated out as he made a move toward the exit. He didn't have time. Somebody entered.

And everyone just looked at the newcomer. Carissa studied his face. He was a man who had seen a lot.

His gaze traveled around the room, and a shit eating grin broke on his face when it landed on Xen. Both took steps toward the other.

They banded their arms together then hugged.

"Good to see you, *Srategos*."

Xen's face beamed. "Pleased you found us, *Antistrategos*."

Carissa scanned her memory for the Ancient Greek military ranks. He called Xen General, and Xen called him Lieutenant General.

"*Yes, koukla. We go way back,*" he said to her mind.

"*But...*" she countered.

"*I'll explain later.*"

"Is this your bride?" Xen's *Antistrategos* asked.

"She is." Xen puffed out his chest.

The man stepped around Xen and came to greet her. He held out his hand. "I'm Davos, an old friend, and by old, I mean old." He chuckled.

Carissa took his hand and when her palm was firmly against his, a tingle of recognition danced between them. Carissa instantly liked him, and she couldn't really say why other than her power recognized a kindred spirit. She'd have to quiz Xen later.

He smiled at her. "I see my friend has chosen wisely."

"I don't know about that. I seem to bring him a lot of trouble."

"I sincerely doubt that."

"Your timing is well placed," Xen said from beside her.

"Well placed or well planned?" Davos grinned.

"Your skill set in this battle would be very welcomed."

"You have my arm and my men when it comes to Damion."

"So, you know that dude too?" Carissa asked.

"Know—biggest thorn in our side for I can't even remember how long," Davos said.

"Too long, and Tartarus was not strong enough to hold him."

Carissa contemplated that for a beat. "He obviously wants revenge."

"No. He wants total annihilation, and there's a difference in that," Davos added.

"He won't care how many innocent humans or others get injured. I'm afraid compassion left him a long time ago. It's all a game," Xen said.

"Then his motives and actions are aligned with the Titans and anyone else on their side," she huffed out.

"Food," someone called from the entrance of the tent.

"Care to join us?" Lox asked.

"Sorry, I'm Davos."

"Lox." He held out his hand.

"Some of my men would be pleased to join you."

"Right then. I'll see you outside."

Carissa's mind spun. "You're…"

"…a vampire," he finished for her.

"I turned him," Xen supplied

She digested the information with slight movement of her head in acknowledgment.

"We should get you something to eat, *koukla*."

"We should, but first tell me the story of Damion? We haven't much time, and I'd like to know what I'm up against." She looked from Xen to Davos.

"The short version is that Zeus cast him to Tartarus for using dark magic." Xen stepped back to rest on the desk behind him. "Long ago Damion, along with many others, were tasked to assist the Cyclopes and Hephaestus with all metallurgical projects for the gods. Their work was unparalleled, so intricate was their attention to detail, that it caused a rivalry amongst the Cyclopes and themselves. Naturally it spiraled into a full scale argument…"

"Or a punch up, to be precise," Davos interrupted.

"…and they split from Hephaestus and the Cyclopes' workshop and went their own way. Their skills were not only in metallurgy. That fine delicate work had a complete opposite—dark magic."

"More like destructive," Davos interjected.

"When you say dark magic, what kind are we talking about?" Carissa asked.

"Devastation. They poisoned all living things they came into contact with in retaliation for their work arrangements. They turned the water to Sulphur as an added measure. Let's just say, you wouldn't have wanted to cross their path."

"Zeus, your grandfather, was angered by all this," Xen added.

"Wait, did you just say grandfather?" Davos asked.

"Yes."

"Wow."

She curtsied. "Daughter of Ares, pleased to meet you."

Davos' mouth hung open. "You really don't do things by halves. Do you Xenocrates?"

Xen beamed from his position. "Let's finish the story, and then I'll fill you in on other matters."

Davos let out a whistle. "I've missed a damn fair bit by the sounds of it."

"You have." Xen brought himself to his full height. "Zeus, Poseidon and Apollo went after all the telkhines. All were killed except for Damion who was cast into Tartarus by Zeus' thunderbolt." Xen paused. "This is where it gets interesting. One of the slayed telkhines was Damion's daughter."

Carissa contemplated one small detail. "The advantage of having metallurgical skills is you can break out of the prison you helped build."

"He was not alone, trust me on this. Tartarus is one thousand times more complex than the best mortal maximum prison." Xen's features altered.

"It doesn't matter who helped him. He wants revenge for the loss of his daughter." A blow she hadn't seen coming hit her right in the chest. Wouldn't she or Xen do the same? Could he be redeemed? She pondered it some more.

"Don't even think about it?" Xen had read her mind.

"Carissa, what was done to all his friends and family was wrong, but Damion is a murderer. Don't try to justify his actions," Davos said.

"Agreed. And I won't hesitate to take his head." She put her hands up in surrender. "Hey, I'm sure he wouldn't spare any of us."

"No, he wouldn't, *koukla*."

"Okay, how about we go grab a bite." The smells of the cooked meat outside had wafted inside the tent, and her stomach started its hunger pains.

"Actually, I'll eat and you two can go source your usual form of nourishment." At her words Xen's eyes darkened.

She knew exactly what kind of nourishment he had in mind, but that would have to wait.

TWENTY-SEVEN

"War is sweet to those who never tried it." ~ Pindar

Francis Marion Forest; Charleston, SC
Evening, mortal realm – Day 12

Titans and all manner of unearthly beings lined the opposite end of the forest. Somewhere grotesque, ghastly and gigantic. The complete vision of nightmares. The noise had increased, and Kirke had thrown a spell to seal the noise in a dome that spanned from where they were located across to the enemy lines.

"Last thing we need is to bring attention and violence to mortals."

"You can say that again, witch." Xen was armed to the teeth with all manner of things.

"Is that the new explosive you've been working on?" Kane asked.

Xen grinned. "We're in trial phase, and I have to say this is the perfect opportunity to try them."

Carissa shook her head. "Do you believe these guys?"

"Oh, yeah," Kirke said.

"I think you've been hanging around them too much," Carissa said. "Not that there's anything wrong with that, plus I need someone to keep an eye on them when I'm not around."

"They managed not to get their heads blown up before you

came into the picture. I'm sure they're fine without either of us."
Kirke snorted.

"You have a point."

Xen handed Carissa two of his special demon killing guns.

"No clean-up costs." He winked.

Kirke waved her hand around. "Do you need all this."

"Have you looked at the guys at the other end?"

Kirke glanced across to their opponents. "You're right. Vampire, can I get one of those."

"I think I might have one spare."

Kane helped Kirke with the gun.

"What do you think our chances are, Rissa?"

Xen let out a growl at the shortened version of her name.

"They outnumber us. Although we do have some pretty bad ass fighters."

"We do, and I know we're going to kick them right back to where they came from."

"I certainly hope so."

"Any sign of the gods yet?"

"No, none."

"Father said they will appear when they are upon us."

"You don't think they'd let us go this alone?" Xen asked from a few feet over.

"No, they can't risk the Titans or any of those creatures running around topside."

"It gives me some comfort that this is one fight they will join," Kane said.

"Well, it is their prison they have escaped from," Carissa added.

"With the help of Damion." Xen let out a low growl to show his dissatisfaction.

"Face it, if it wasn't him, it would be someone else. There's more than one upset individual when it comes to the things the gods have said and done," Carissa said.

"She's right, you know. They have more than one enemy, and they've had many millennia to get those enemies."

"True that," Adam said.

Xen nodded his head in agreement. "I hope this ends most of the madness."

"I think we all hope this is it, and let there be peace, and may everyone leave my forest. You know a girl can only deal with so much."

They all burst out in rowdy laughter.

Carissa hoped that most of them would be protected and hoped that they didn't lose too many friends.

A loud horn brought them out of their discussion.

"What the hell was that?"

"That is them getting their lines ready for battle." Davos had joined them. He had just harnessed his swords.

Xen looked over in the enemy's direction. "It is upon us."

"Get word to Lox," Xen said to Adam.

"I'm on it." Adam turned in the direction of Lox's tent.

"Is everyone in place?" Carissa asked Xen.

"They are. The only thing remaining is a good dust up."

"I'd say this is more than that," she said, trying to keep humor in her voice and not show any fear. She wasn't going to lie. It did frighten her. She didn't want to see so many good men taken down by a bunch of violent and bat shit crazy Titans. Honestly, they'd had plenty of time in lock up to get over it. Plus, from what she was told, they didn't have it so bad. They had their own system with perks.

"What is it about Greek gods and holding grudges?" she whispered under her breath.

The air shifted and Zeus, Hera, Ares and Athena appeared. Everyone dropped down in a bow at the sight of the mighty gods.

"There will be time for veneration later. Rise."

They all got to their feet. "Resume your places. We will lead and when the last Titan has fallen this war will belong to you."

Murmurs of agreement sounded throughout the camp then died down.

Zeus turned to Carissa. "Remember to use everything you've got."

She nodded.

"We are with you, *kori mou*."

"I know, Father. Now go show them what you've got."

"It would be our pleasure." Athena sneered.

"It will be nice to throw a few fire balls at them," Hera added.

"Oh, there will be more than that, Mother," Ares said.

The line of Titans grew louder at the sight of the Olympian gods, and they broke the line in attack.

The gods took to the sky, showing their might, and strife herself led them across the forest in a war that would be incomprehensible to the human mind. From his high position, Zeus ruler of men and gods, directed his colossal thunder to the ranks of the Titans. The Titans returned the great gods' power with a stream of spears. Phoebus Apollo waved a hand and the spears turned to winged arrows and made their way back to those who released them. Titans and several creatures close by fell. This was only the beginning of the immense clash.

Ares, god of war and battle lust, and his blazing-eyed sister, Athena, swooped down fully armed and ruptured the lines of the Titans.

Even Poseidon had shown up, and any suspicion Carissa held that he might have been playing on both sides of the fence was thrown asunder. The mighty earth shaker sent a blast that shook the earth and split a deep gorge in the ground. It burst wide open and swallowed several Titans.

All around them opposing sides with mixed armies locked in battle.

Artemis with her golden arrows let stream after stream rain down on the Titans. The front line was breaking, and mayhem was breaking loose amongst the ranks.

The gods kept clear of the demons and other unearthly creatures, which would be the Phi's and Lox's problem along with all their other allies that came to fight at their request.

Athena let loose her war cry, and Ares joined with his own as they both pummeled Titan after Titan, forcing them backwards into the deep gorge Poseidon had torn into the earth. Down, down they fell into the deep dark depths where Hephaestus had worked tirelessly for three straight days to secure the many locks and rooms of

Tartarus. As soon as the Titans fell endlessly to very dark depths of the earth they would land in Tartarus, and this time there would be no escape.

The gods and goddesses were weaving through the ranks and lines of Titans with ease and efficiency. It would be their turn soon.

"Breathe, *koukla*."

She took in a gulp of air. "I can't say that watching all this unfold isn't scary as all get-out."

"The stuff of dreams and nightmares and ours is about to commence."

Zeus threw down multiple lightning bolts to the last remaining Titans. They disintegrated on the spot.

"Now that we could use."

"Yes, but he can't eliminate all the unearthly beings. That's our job."

"Would be too easy, wouldn't it?"

"Indeed, and we wouldn't have been needed in the first place," Xen said from beside her.

They watched the gods from their posts and when the last Titan was thrown into the open chasm the earth began to shake and rumble. Trees, rocks, and all manner of soil fell into the huge gorge Poseidon had created.

"He's trying to close it," Xen said.

Carissa looked over at Poseidon with his mighty trident stabbed into the earth and a mini tornado swirling around him. Then he cast his hand out and the deep crack in the earth he had created began to close. Some of the teams behind them began to fall. A few men scrambled to stop some equipment toppling over.

And then the loudest roar she'd ever heard reached her ears and whipped her hair back from the full force of it. Some of the men raised their hands to their ears to block it. It was loud for her, and she could imagine how loud it would have been for many of the *lykoi*, vampires and *eudemonia* with a heightened sense of hearing.

Out of the depths of the crack, fingers with snake heads squeezed out. An unfathomable creature pushed its way through the now closing earth. There were hundreds of heads on its body, but only one human head, the rest were bulls, serpents, lions and leopards. On its back the creature had wings. It flapped them and they extended.

"What the hell is that?" Carissa asked.

"That would be Typhon," Xen supplied.

"Shit just got nasty," Adam said, coming to stand next to them with Kane.

"I'd say your terminology is very apt for once, *lykos*."

Adam turned his head to Kane. "Apt..." He shook his head. "Seriously, there's something wrong with you," he huffed under his breath.

Kane looked at him. "What?"

"Guys, get a load of this," Carissa said.

Typhon had pulled free from the opening Poseidon had been trying to close. With several of its long serpent fingers it made a grab for the god. Then everything turned incredibly bright.

Everyone crouched down and covered their eyes. Carissa's eyes burned like fire when she tried to sneak a peek.

Keep your head down, kori mou. *We've taken our true form.* Her father sent the message telepathically.

Xen, she reached out in the same way.

I know, koukla. He then shouted, "Keep your heads down and let them do what they need to do."

Whispered and shouted acknowledgments from around Carissa told her they all got the message and were shouting it out to those farther away.

Xen shuffled closer to Carissa and threw his arm around her.

"How is it we haven't all caught fire?"

Because I have placed a shield over you all, but it is dangerous to look upon us right now. Athena had answered her question.

"I think you have your answer," Xen said after lifting the information from her mind.

Her father updated her with what was happening.

Typhon had tried to reach for as many gods as he could, but they all took their true form and fired their natural flares of fire at the Titan. He began to burn, and his loud screams could be heard.

He tried to throw anything he could scrape from the land at the gods, however the gods burned brighter and brighter. With loud whimpering and cries of pain he scurried back to the gorge and dove in.

The earth began to tremble and then a loud sonic boom sealed the wide split in the earth and the bright light dissipated and they were once again covered with the night sky.

Xen helped Carissa to her feet. Everyone did the same and readied themselves in their previous positions.

Zeus, Athena, Hera and her father all appeared near her.

"This is your battle now, Granddaughter." He dematerialized along with the two other goddesses.

Her father stayed behind. "Use every trick you have. They won't play fair. It's not in their game plan. Also, Damion is still out there." He pointed across the forest. "Zeus didn't throw him into Tartarus because he believes you all have a score to settle with him." He stepped close to her and pulled her in for a hug. "We might not be here with you when you go into battle, which is any minute now, but we will be with you when you need us, *kori mou*."

"Thank you, Father."

He released her and dematerialized.

TWENTY-EIGHT

"Beware the toils of war... the mesh of the huge dragnet sweeping up the world." ~ Homer

Francis Marion Forest; Charleston, SC
Evening, mortal realm – Day 12

Her father's signature of where he stood had faded, and the lines of their enemy broke. The pounding of feet from the enemy line propelled them into action. Xen and Lox's men unleashed row after row of arrows. Yes, this fight was going to be a mix of both old and new, and Carissa hoped Damion hadn't armed them with any modern weapons. At least if they could have the upper hand, they might come out of this fight unscathed.

Another volley of arrows went up in the night sky and hit demon after demon. They disintegrated on the spot. Xen had the arrows laced with the cocktail mix he used in the lethal bullets against the demons.

Xen turned to Carissa. "I would prefer if you would stay back a bit."

"I'm in this fight whether you want it or not."

"I know, and I'm not saying you're the damsel in distress, far from it. I have a suspicion Damion will be targeting you. I want a chance to spot him first. We don't know what surprises he might have in mind."

Davos moved over near them. "He's right, you know."

"What's the game plan then?" Carissa asked.

Xen considered the options for a moment. "Hold back till we have a lock on him."

"Okay, then I will join when you give me the clear. But know this, I will not let my friends be endangered if you have no solid location or eyes on him."

"Fair enough," Xen said.

"I'm in agreement," Davos said.

"*Adam*," Xen called.

He jogged over. "What's up?"

"I want you to be Carissa's backup."

"No problem, boss, I've got Rissa."

Xen growled. "Carissa."

"What? That's what I said." Adam grinned back at Xen.

Carissa flipped her arm out and hit Adam in his midsection. He faked that it hurt.

"Come on, wolf."

"Adam, give us a minute," Xen said.

"Sure."

Xen wrapped his arms around her waist and pulled her in. "Stay safe," he said then crushed his lips to hers. There was so much force and meaning behind that kiss. She understood it for what it was. A kiss to show how much she meant to him. She broke the kiss first because she needed air.

"That goes both ways."

He released her and turned to Davos. "Let's start moving some chess pieces."

She turned to Adam who was in discussion with Kane and her witchy friend.

"I've got the various wolf packs ready." Kane had called in as many wolves as he could then Adam reached out to his own pack and summoned them. There were other packs too, and to their astonishment no one had resisted the call. It confirmed these men would fight anyone who threatened their existence and the planet.

Carissa was pulled out of her musings by a barreling firebomb. Adam pushed her to the ground. "You, okay?" he asked.

She nodded. "We didn't see that one coming."

He lifted her to her feet. "No, we didn't."

"Best get ready. I'm sure there's more where that came from," Kane shouted.

And no sooner had he said it than all hell broke loose. Firebombs that Kirke and some of her friends were intercepting and turning around. Shouts broke out, and a demon and rogue vampire horde clashed with their front line.

The scrape and ting of metal against metal could be heard all around them.

"Rissa, we're going to move back."

She glanced in the distance to where Xen was with Davos and Lox. They were barking orders to men, and everyone was moving like a well-oiled machine. She was grateful for their experience. These men were born and bred to fight. It was what they knew, and it was evident they could do it with their eyes shut.

The wolves were something else altogether. Primal instinct on how to lure their enemy out and then surround them before diving in for the kill. They worked in packs and fought alongside each other without breaking the line. They were like a belcher chain. Each one of them was linked to the other.

Kirke appeared next to Carissa. "Remember to use what you've been taught."

"I'm getting a lot of reminders from everyone."

"I'm serious. This could go on for hours. It won't be as swift as what the gods had with the Titans."

"I had guessed as much. It's a different ball game altogether," Carissa said.

"It sure is, and if you find yourself alone out there, use your power of *anagke* to call me." Kirke gave Carissa a hug and vanished.

"*Advance,*" Xen shouted.

Their front-line steamrolled through the group trying to break through. They repeated the movement as they headed straight for the enemy line.

"Carissa."

Her ear communicator buzzed with a familiar voice. She tapped it. "Kelly."

"Can you get your team over to the left flank. They have no one there."

"Roger that."

"Kane, Adam!" Carissa shouted.

"We're on to it, Rissa. Let's move."

They had heard Kelly too. They barked some orders then moved with stealth and precision, and she moved with them. Some of the *lykoi* preferred to fight in their wolf form. The gap in the left flank gave them an advantage. They could intercept the enemy heading to their line. Until of course their own front line had advanced enough to break through.

"Carissa, watch out, behind you. There are demons coming your way," Kelly shouted in her ear.

It didn't matter. They were all armed to the nines and ready for it.

Carissa swiveled on her feet and unholstered her guns. The demons appeared and made a rush for them. She aimed her guns and fired. Shell casings dropped to the ground. Demon after demon dropped.

What she hadn't anticipated was the line of rogue vampires that appeared straight after. She holstered her guns then unsheathed her sword. Two came at her but one didn't make it because Adam intercepted.

Carissa's sword blocked the blow that was aimed at her shoulder. The rogue vamp had strength and speed on his side. He spun around her but thankfully her demi-god genes gifted her enough ability to see his movement in time to block another blow. She backed up, but her assailant came charging toward her. He lifted his sword, but the strike never came. His head was sliced off and landed on the forest ground. The body followed in slow motion and right there behind him stood her vampire with his fangs elongated. He nodded then disappeared back to the action.

Their line had advanced and was almost upon the enemy line.

Xen, Davos and Lox pushed at the demon and rogue vampire hoards relentlessly. With one final shove their opponents line broke. They were through and then it became a sea of one-on-one combat.

Carissa tapped her communicator. "Kelly, how's Ligi doing?"

"She's got the whole back line in a trance with her siren song. You need to move in."

Kane and Adam nodded, and their team began to move out on the far left so they could advance around to the back line. Carissa wasn't worried about the right flank because Davos had placed his men there, and they had instructions on where to hit to cripple the enemy.

When they were in position they attacked the demons and other unearthly creatures that had joined Damion's fight. Ligi stopped her siren song as soon as she spotted Carissa.

"Boy, am I glad to see you, girlfriend. My voice is hoarse."

"I'd imagine it would be."

"Pull back and get to safety," Carissa directed her friend.

Ligi was many things, that said, she was not a sword wielding lass.

Tithon had pulled off his protective headphones. "What can I do?"

"What you do best, go take some demon and unearthly heads."

Kane motioned for a few men to get Ligi out.

And then they went in for the kill. Some demons were coming out of their trance, so they put up a bit of a fight.

Carissa reloaded her guns and just emptied round after round.

Some of the wolves ripped into the demons.

Many dropped but her gut told her it was all too easy.

"Tsk, tsk, tsk. So many tricks from you all. I hadn't expected the siren. Good move," Damion said from behind them.

Carissa spun on the balls of her feet. The wizard was here, which meant he was never in with the throng. Like, Xen, Davos, and Lox.

"What do want, Damion?"

Adam and Kane were beside her in an instant. They pulled her behind them just as Damion let loose a ball of fire.

They dove out of the way. It landed behind them.

Damion threw out more balls of energy and everyone scrambled. Jumped out of the way and made some attempt to get close to him to attack. Some of the wolves had taken a lunge to get his jugular, but they hit an invisible wall and flew backwards. He had an energy field around him, protecting him, and this changed everything.

He threw out more magic and more of the team dispersed and then he changed his objective and started to fire at Carissa. She focused and shoved each blow out of the way just like she had trained with Kirke. She would not let this guy win.

This angered Damion, and his features contorted to something darker, more sinister.

"What is your problem?" she shouted.

She looked around and saw more demons and unearthly creatures joining the fight. Kane, Adam and Tithon fought off different groups.

"You are my problem. I can't have the spawn of Ares walking around on earth."

"Excuse me? You don't even know me."

"I don't need to know you to know that your kind can never be trusted."

"And what of your kind?"

"My kind was destroyed, and I want to give those gods a taste of their own medicine. Particularly your grandfather." He threw out more fire balls.

Carissa focused and then used her power of compulsion to compel the magic and throw it back at him.

Damion's eyes widened.

And that was when the game changed. He dematerialized from where he stood and materialized closer. He threw up a burst of power into the air and then manipulated it to head straight for her. She watched as it came hurtling at her.

She heard screams—Xen.

She focused and called forth all her power. The big ball of magic and energy hit her with the force of a meteor. It pushed her flat on her back into the earth, causing a crater. She focused and manipulated the energy to fire and pushed back to her feet. The flames engulfed the crater. Consuming her. She wouldn't survive this. She focused to compel the darkness intwined with the magic and used her force of *anagke* to manipulate the fire and disperse its darkness. But it was too much. It was sapping all her energy stores.

This was the end.

She dropped to the ground on her knees and all her breath left her. She was choking. Trying to find air. The flames licked higher.

Use your gifts, Niece. She heard the goddess Athena as if she were standing in those flames with her.

Carissa pulled the bracelet on her wrist. "*Emphanisi*," she coughed out. *Astrape* appeared in her hand.

The flames burned and the spear heated in her hand. Consuming a large radius around her.

And the other gift, Niece. Carissa tugged at the chain on her neck. And spoke the spell to release the shield that was gifted again from Athena. The codex was released too and floated around her. It burned bright and so did the shield. The flames licked higher and higher. The clothes she was wearing had burned off her body. Her skin began to blister.

The codex spun around her three times, squeezing her life's essence, becoming one with the fire, then snapped back into her necklace. She knew what she needed to do to end this. Her feet left the ground as she levitated up out of the crater. Naked with nothing but a spear and shield.

When she cleared the crater and stepped out, she wiggled her feet in the cool earth. She took in the scene around her.

Damion stood with his mouth open and so did Xen, Davos, Lox, Kane, Adam and all their friends. The fighting had ceased. All. Eyes. Were. On. Her.

The flames burned behind her.

She saw in slow motion as Damion raised his hands to throw more magic at her, but she was faster because she could calculate his moves. She released *astrape* and the spear harpooned Damion to a tree, then he disintegrated. She held out her hand and the spear returned to her awaiting fingers. It was a bittersweet moment. They'd have no more trouble from Damion, and his own line of Telkhines were dead. It filled her with sorrow, but there was no way to redeem him.

There was one more thing to do. She flung it like a discus. "Seek out thy enemy." It sped and spun with a blaze of fire behind it and sought out each demon and unearthly creature, decapitating them. When it was done, and cries and screams reduced, the shield returned to her.

She dropped to her knees. Hot tears gathered in her eyes.

Xen raced to her with a jacket.

"*Kalypto*," she said, and the spear and sword returned to their previous enchantments.

"I don't know what to say."

"I'll say it for you. We won," she said, whipping away the hot liquid from her cheeks as she sobbed happily.

TWENTY-NINE

"There is another sacred bird, too, whose name is Phoenix." ~ *Herodotus*

Francis Marion Forest; Charleston, SC
Evening, mortal realm – Day 12

"Was that?" Adam's mouth hung open.

"Yes," Kane answered.

"Like a phoenix."

"Yep."

"Never thought I'd see anything as remotely miraculous as that."

"Now you have."

"You know you've been hanging around Xen too much. Your sentences are starting to sound like his."

Kane grunted and the *lykos* beside him grunted back.

"I guess Rissa is more god than demi-god," Adam said.

"You guess right."

Adam cast him a look and raised his eyebrows.

"What?" Kane asked.

"I think you need to get out a bit more. You've been cooped up behind your desk."

Kane gave him a slap upside the head. "*Malaka*," he swore.

"What? You've been grouchy more than usual. What's really going on?"

"A few personal matters and I have it under control." He wasn't going to tell Adam that lately he'd been rejecting women left, right and center. His appetite for intimacy had hit rock-bottom. Maybe the *lykos* was right. He needed time away. Things had amped up, and he'd barely had enough time to scratch himself these days. Perhaps that was what he needed—sun, surf and ladies, but his last and favorite option was off the menu. For him, not them. His animalistic mesmerism ensured that he had plentiful invitations and a range of offers and that was where the problem lay. He didn't desire any of them. Not even the idea of a one-night stand and the no strings attachment.

"Earth to Kane, are you still with us?" Adam sang from beside him.

He shook himself out of his current introspection. "Whatever gave you the idea I wasn't?"

"Ah, that faraway look you were sporting."

Kane didn't want to get personal right now. He defused it the best way he knew how—diversion. "Wonder what Carissa's status…" he pointed toward her "…means now."

"That she's more supernatural than human."

"I'd have to agree."

"Let's get over there."

They made their way around the crater. The flames still burned bright. When they got there, Xen had already covered her up.

"Rissa, are you okay?" Adam asked.

Kane hit him on the back of the head. "What do you think? She just won this battle for us."

"We need to clean up. Use the fire," Xen commanded.

Kane nodded and so did Adam.

They had just witnessed an apotheosis.

"*Koukla*, let me get you some proper clothes." Xen picked her up and carried her to the tent they'd been using. He put her down once inside. He spun around the room and collected some clothes. Then handed her a t-shirt, jeans and underwear. She made quick work of throwing everything on.

He watched her carefully with mixed emotions, running a projector of images across his mind. She could read them all. Delight, confusion, elation, wariness and lastly love. It was a heady mix.

"Tell me what happened," he asked.

"That last bit of energy he threw at me was very dark and destructive magic. I used my power of compulsion to absorb the power and manipulate it into something else. Hence the flames.

"But why flames? How did you know you would survive it?"

A sharp pang hit her in the chest. "I didn't. It was a guess. I heard Athena's voice telling me to use the spear and shield, but when I released the shield…"

"You released the codex," he finished.

She nodded and twisted her fingers together. Her eyes glanced at her still bare feet. She walked over by one of the makeshift cots and slid her feet into a pair of sneakers.

"I was being consumed by the fire when the codex spun around me then somehow infused me with new oxygen."

"Apotheosis."

"Literally."

"What does this make you now?"

"No idea."

He fished out his phone and turned the camera on then flipped it around to show her.

She didn't recognize the woman. That woman was her? From the crown of her head and half way down she now sported red hair and the tips were golden. She looked up at Xen.

"Like a phoenix," he said.

"You think…" No, that couldn't be possible.

"I do."

"But…"

"There's no but, you came out of the flames naked as the day you were born with nothing but a shield and spear. If that isn't rebirth, I don't know what is." He stepped in and pulled her close. "I don't even want to contemplate if that had gone south."

"It didn't and that's what matters."

"You're more than right." He dropped a kiss on her lips.

They heard commotion outside the tent. Then Ligi and Kelly barged in, followed by Lox and Tithon. The girls' mouths hung open. Carissa stepped out of Xen's embrace.

They ran to her and hugged her.

"Girl, you could really start a trend with that hair," Ligi said.

"Guess I'm joining you in being a redhead."

"You chose well."

"Hey," Kelly said. "Nothing wrong with brunettes. Don't forget where you come from."

They all laughed, and Carissa was glad to have them here with her.

Adam and Kane joined everyone else in the tent.

"Boss," Kane spoke first. "Cleanup is almost done. We'll start clearing everything out.

"Good. The sooner everyone is gone, the sooner I get my quiet back," Kirke said from the entrance. She stepped inside and moved toward Carissa. "What set you aflame?"

"Myself."

"I don't understand," Ligi said.

"I tried to manipulate Damion's power and that was the best I could do."

"The best? Rissa, that was epic."

Xen growled, still not used to the nickname.

She doubted it was epic. If it weren't for the codex and the gifts Athena had given her then she would not have survived. She needed to make it up to the goddess and knew just how.

The air in the room shifted, and Carissa recognized the signature—Koal.

The gods were summoning her. She knew it before he even said it.

He looked at her. "Your…"

"I know, Koal."

"You do?"

She nodded her head.

"No, I want to come with you," Xen said.

"No can do, vampire, but I can tell you this, she won't be long."

Koal put a hand on her and dematerialized them.

They materialized in Zeus' chambers. Hera, Athena and her father all sat around the lounge area with wine cups in their hands.

Her father was the first to place his cup down and shoot to his feet. He moved with quick long strides and pulled her in for a hug. *"Kori mou,"* he said in her ear. He released her.

Zeus, Hera and Athena all stepped closer.

"A Phoenix." Zeus marveled.

That was what Xen had said. "What does this mean?" Carissa asked.

"Your cycle of life has changed," Hera answered.

"Quite remarkable," Zeus threw in.

Carissa raised an eyebrow.

"It means that you will live for five hundred years before being reborn again," her father added.

"You're as immortal as your vampire," Athena said with a wink.

Carissa opened her mouth. Then closed it again. Okay, she didn't need to be a vampire, but what about her demi-god status.

"Am I still…"

"Yes, Granddaughter, you are, with the added bonus of living a long time," Hera said.

Zeus held out his hand, and Carissa put hers in his. "And the offer I made still stands. You can come and go from Olympus."

"I still don't know if that's a good idea. There were a lot of angry gods."

"Don't worry about them. They'll eventually come around," he said.

She turned to Athena. "Any more news on who destroyed those tapestries?"

"Nothing more."

Carissa knew she would have to solve that for them in due course, but not now. Now she had to focus on other things. Like her wedding, but before she finished here, she needed to share something with Athena.

She blurted it out. "I would like to join you in the tapestry competition. If you would like to show me." Athena was the mistress of sewing and weaving, and Carissa knew this was the only way to repay the goddess for her gifts that had saved her. And that reminded her.

She unclasped the bracelet. "This belongs to you. You should reclaim it." She dropped it in the goddess' palm.

Athena looked at it. "I have more than one spear, Niece. I think it belongs with your collection of artifacts." The bracelet transformed back to a libation bowl. Then it vanished.

Carissa had a sneaking suspicion about where it would be—her grandmother's house and in that super secure basement Xen had built.

"Now we think we've taken up enough of your time."

Koal stepped forward and dematerialized them to her grandmother's house.

They landed in the kitchen. It looked like it was lunch time.

Kane, Adam, Yiayia and Aunt Paula were all sitting around the table.

The women's mouths dropped open.

Yiayia and Paula got to their feet.

"*Paidi mou*," Yiayia squealed, staring at her hair in awe.

Paula was no different. "You know that makes you look like one of those musicians."

Carissa didn't want to ask what musician because that would start a different trail of discussion.

"You know, Vetta, I've been saying we should do something rad to our hair for years."

"Paula, get real. We'd look like a couple of old shriveled up punks."

"It's good to see you both." Carissa hugged them.

"What can we get you?" Yiayia asked.

"Food of any type would be good." Carissa's stomach grumbled on cue.

"Well, you're just in time."

"I've got beef *stifado*. We were just about to eat."

Carissa eyed the full plates, and the smell of cinnamon hit her. She stepped around her family and went over to hug and drop a kiss on Adam and Kane's cheeks. Then she dropped her weight into a chair to join them at the table.

Her aunt put a plate in front of her, and her grandmother sat next to her, still watching her closely.

"Let's eat."

Carissa dug in with gusto.

"Rissa, I guess we should say thanks for kicking Damion's butt and winning the war for us."

Aunt Paula shuddered at the mention of war.

"I don't know what all this means, but I know that at least we will be okay for a while."

"Thank heavens," Paula said. She did her cross.

"Do you get a sinking feeling that it's not quite over?" Kane asked.

Carissa read his features. He was worried and tired. "I do, but for now we're okay. How long is anyone's guess."

"I don't know about you all, but I could do with a few days off," Kane said.

"Then take the time you need. Trust me, Kane, I don't need anyone to babysit. I can more than look after myself."

"I'm comforted that you can."

"Roger that," Adam said.

Yiayia let out a deep sigh. "I'm glad too."

"Me too," Paula said

Carissa decided to take the focus off herself. "Yiayia and Aunt Paula, this stew is delicious.

They both smiled. "There's plenty more." Her grandmother indicated the big pot on the stove. Greeks never cooked in small batches.

Adam reached over. "I'm definitely having seconds," he said with a lopsided grin.

They ate in silence for a while, and Carissa picked up the energy in the room. It altered from curious to happy to curious to happy. She helped clean up, as did the boys, and then excused herself.

"If you don't all mind, I think I need sleep."

"Go rest, *paidi mou*."

Carissa made her way upstairs, punched the code on the keypad to her door and slipped inside the darkened room. She shrugged her shoes off and climbed into bed where Xen was in his rejuvenation sleep.

Her eyes fluttered closed.

A dream started. Hera was with her. She touched her and said, "A gift awaits you soon."

THIRTY

"Once made equal to man, women become superior." ~ *Socrates*

Carissa's grandmother's house; Charleston, SC
Evening, mortal realm – Day 13

Her eyes fluttered open, and a pair of sea green eyes looked down at her.

"I thought you might be out for a bit longer."

"No. I was only napping."

"What was the urgency."

"Believe it or not, nothing. They just wanted to tell me I will now have the luxury of living for 500 years, and then will be reborn every 500 years."

"Phoenix."

"Yes, pretty much. I guess you don't have to turn me into a bloodsucker then."

He sat on the bed. "I had suspected but what exactly does the rebirth involve?"

"They didn't elaborate, and I didn't ask further. Athena said I'm as immortal as you."

He flashed her a slaying smile. "Stay in bed. You could use the sleep."

"Sleeping is overrated," she joked.

"Not if you have bags under your eyes."

"Okay, maybe for a little while."

"What did you have planned for tomorrow?"

"Wedding and bridesmaid dress hunting."

"Good luck with that," he said as he got to his feet.

"Shoot me now."

He let out a laugh and it was rich like honey.

"You know, you should laugh more."

"I promise to laugh more. Now get some rest, *koukla*." He leaned over and gave her a scorching kiss. "I'd rather stay but have a few things to wrap up with Lox and his men this evening."

She understood after everything that had gone on. There'd be aftershocks.

"I understand." She waved a hand at him. "Scoot, go do what you need to do."

She lay her head back on the soft pillow. She'd just rest a bit more.

Dawn's rosy rays tickled her nose and eyelids. She opened her eyes, and her head was like a heavy load of soil. Dense. Xen was right. She'd needed the sleep. Speaking of which, he wasn't in bed rejuvenating. He must have gone back to his mansion. She'd pop in there later. With a degree of lethargy, she forced her lazy bones out of bed and into the shower.

She dressed in her usual jeans, shirt and flats. It was going to be a long day, and she wanted to ensure comfort. She looked in the mirror and found her bright hair would stand out a mile away. She grabbed a hair clip and pulled it all up. That helped hide the bright golden ends. She wasn't ashamed, but it did attract too much attention. She headed downstairs to collect her aunt and grandmother.

"Coffee is ready." Her aunt had just put a hot steaming cup on the table.

Carissa gave her aunt a kiss and did the same to Yiayia. "Are you both ready for today?"

"We are," her aunt replied for both of them.

Carissa looked at her watch. They had to meet Ligi and Kelly at the first appointment in half an hour. She had asked Ligi to be her maid of honor, and she enthusiastically accepted. Raising the cup to her lips, Carissa took a sip. She mulled over everything that had happened while drinking her coffee. When she reached the halfway mark, she decided it was best to get their day started. "I think we should get moving." They all stood. Her *yiayia* and aunt already had their bags hanging on the back of their chairs.

In the garage Xen had left an SUV for them. She buckled up her grandmother, and they made quick time to the first appointment.

When they walked in, Ligi and Kelly were already picking out styles of dresses to try. Carissa didn't mind because she hadn't given it much thought. She'd choose a color based on what looked good on the girls.

Ten minutes later Kelly emerged with something she thought would look good. "What do you think?"

"There is no way that I'm tryin' that on." Ligi pointed a finger up and down and looked downright disgusted.

"What's wrong with it?" Kelly asked.

Carissa watched the whole exchange.

"That is something out of an eighties horror movie."

Kelly scrunched up her face. "There is nothing wrong with this dress aside from the color."

"Uhm, sweetie, you're forgetting those plum puff shoulder pads that look like they belong on shoulders of a linebacker."

"I found the perfect dresses for you," Yiayia said from behind Aunt Paula. She stepped around her trying to hold up the dress. It was pale blue and flowed to the floor in an A-line design.

"Now that's what I'm talking about," Ligi said.

Kelly scrunched up her face.

Carissa watched them all, huddled together in deep discussion. This wedding wasn't about the union of her and Xen, that was already solid, it was about the joy and participation these women contributed to the ritual of that union.

"How many shops are we booked for?" Aunt Paula said.

Carissa shrugged. She'd let Ligi and Kelly organize it.

"Three," Ligi chimed in.

"We best shake a leg if we're going to make all the appointments." She looked down at her watch. "We've got to be out of here in fifty minutes if we're going to make the next one."

"Okay girls, try the blue on first." Yiayia threw Ligi and Kelly a dress each. Carissa had picked up that she'd been listening when they'd rattled off their sizes at home.

She gave Carissa a wink. "How about you go look for yours, my child.

Carissa removed herself to sift through some of the gowns. Nothing really called to her, and she would have preferred to be anywhere but here. She picked up her grandmother's shuffled steps. She had heightened senses now. She shifted her body and turned toward her. Yiayia's beaming smile filled her heart.

"What?" Yiayia's questioned.

"Nothing. I was just thinking we should upgrade that walking stick to something a little fancier."

"There's nothing wrong with this walking stick. It does the job."

"I know that, but you need a new back up. Your current one is looking kind of worn out."

Yiayia looked down at it. "A bit like me."

"That's not what I meant, and you know it."

Yiayia's lips tipped up. "Find anything you like?"

"No, nothing is really calling to me."

"You'll know the one when you see it, but it also helps to try one on."

Just then a sales assistant stepped forward. "I'm so sorry it's taken me ages to get to you. What style were you looking for?"

Carissa scrunched up her nose. Wedding dresses looked all the same to her. They were for one specific purpose with lots of frou-frou. "I hadn't given it much thought."

The assistant looked her up and down. "The A-line style would look great on you, but then again so would a full skirt."

The woman zoomed around the room, pulling dresses out and

showing her. Carissa hated to say it, but she didn't like any of them. She shook her head and the woman started to get flustered.

"How do we look?" Kelly shouted from the dressing rooms.

"I like the color, just not sure about the style," Paula said.

The sales assistant headed toward the chatter of the other women. "But it's a lovely style, and it shows off the bountiful cleavage line." And she didn't stop there. She kept at it for a full three minutes without taking a breath, trying to convince them all that these dresses were the holy grail on these women.

Carissa rolled her eyes. "If you can give us a minute, please." She wanted this woman out of earshot. "What do you girls think?"

"I'm with you, the color is great, but the style does nothing for us." Kelly turned her nose up in distaste.

"We could get more wolf whistles wrapping ourselves in brown paper." Ligi pulled at the straps of the dress. "And I doubt these have any staying power. My boobs will fall out."

They all let out a laugh and the sales assistant turned to look at them. Red crept up her neck. No doubt she thought they were talking about her.

"What about you, Carissa? It's more about you than us," Ligi said.

"Nothing is really calling out."

"Try something."

"I'll have another look."

She shuffled through the styles the assistant had pulled out for her and nothing made her want to try any of these. She walked back to where the women were all huddled together. "I think I'll give it a miss and see what the next boutique has."

No one argued and she found that odd. To be honest she realized they were all acting a tad strange around her, like they were walking on eggshells. She'd let it ride a bit more before confronting them.

They piled into their cars for the next appointment. This boutique was slightly larger than the last.

No sooner had they walked into the shop than the sales assistant swooped down on them. "Can I get you all something to drink?" she asked."

There were a few squeals of excitement because champagne was on the menu. The assistant then eyed Carissa. "And for you?"

"I'll have coffee, thank you. Black, no sugar."

The woman scrunched up her face.

"Seriously, girlfriend, you don't want bubbles?"

"I'd rather wait till lunch."

Ligi didn't pester her anymore, and Kelly had been quieter than usual.

Everyone scattered to find dresses. Ligi and Kelly highjacked the sales assistant, and her *yiayia* and aunt went looking for a toilet.

That left Carissa standing there staring out the window. People were walking up and down the shopping strip. Then she spotted a vehicle that looked like one of Xen's men. She pulled out her phone.

"Kane?"

"Yeah."

"I don't need babysitters. Call them off."

"Xen wanted to make sure."

Her anger rose a few notches. "I'm only going to say it once, call them off, or I'll walk out there and blast their car."

"You can do that?"

"I can."

"Okay. Noted. I'll tell them to leave."

"Thank you."

She ended the call and slid the phone back in her pocket. A minute later she saw the car leave.

Yiayia and Paula came back from the toilet. "What's wrong, *paidi mou?*"

"Nothing to worry about."

Yiayia laced her hand around Carissa's, and Paula did the same from the other side. "How about we go look for something." How could she refuse.

They shuffled through a few dresses, and she had to admit she liked the style of a few but not enough to expend energy trying one on.

Ligi and Kelly came out of the dressing room in a similar powder blue dress.

She had to admit the A-line, V-neck style looked amazing on them. "You both look beautiful."

"They do," Paula and Yiayia agreed simultaneously.

"We'll take those," Carissa decided without further thought.

"How about you? Anything?" Kelly asked.

"There were a few but again I'm not feeling it."

"Why don't you try something on?" the sales assistant asked.

"Thank you, but I'd rather not waste your time or mine."

Everyone looked at her and a heavy silence filled the room.

She broke it by saying, "What color shoes do you think would go better, silver or gold?"

That started a whole heap of conversation and took the emphasis off her. Maybe her behavior was off. Truth be told, she was no longer the same person. Nonetheless she'd try to enjoy the day without making her friends and family think she was some monster ready to explode. Far from it. She had finally accepted there was no going back, that she should look forward to the future and she knew it would be a long one now with Xen, but she would also lose people along the way that she loved. Deep down this was what niggled at her. She would lose her human family.

Yiayia slid her hand in hers. "Why don't we let them take care of things, and we can go to the car."

"I need to pay."

"You don't need to do anything. Your vampire has organized everything."

Carissa rolled her eyes. "Of course, he has. I have money."

"You're already his wife by his vampire laws, so it's your money."

They exited the shop and walked toward the car.

Another hard realization. With everything that had gone down with the gods, Titans and everything else she'd given next to no thought about what her relationship meant and who she was.

"You're right, Yiayia, but every now and then I'd like to do things myself."

"I'm sure you will have plenty of time for that."

She wasn't wrong.

"Now help me get the seat belt on."

Carissa jumped to action and did as she was asked then moved around to the driver's side and jumped in.

Aunt Paula, Ligi and Kelly came out of the store with their garment bags. The girls helped Paula get in.

Ligi leaned in at the driver's side. "Lucky last, girlfriend." She winked.

"I hope so."

Ligi dangled her keys. Her car was parked in front.

"I'll wait for you," Carissa said.

They veered away and made their way to the last boutique appointment.

The last shop was not anything like the first two. This shop presented like an older style establishment that had been renovated and had kept the original features. Inside it looked new but still had the grand ornate ceilings. Carissa liked it and hoped it was a sign.

An older sales assistant came forward to greet them. She too offered refreshments.

"Come with me," she indicated to Carissa. "You ladies can sit here."

Carissa rose her eyebrows to her friends and family. They too looked on wide-eyed.

She followed the lady in silence. When they cleared the room to another section that housed only wedding dresses, the saleslady looked at Carissa.

"I think you need something elegant and timeless."

"I have no idea what that might look like. All I see is dresses and nothing is popping out."

"I know."

"How do you know?"

"Your aunt called me."

Carissa smiled at her aunt's intervention.

"I asked her a few questions about you. Some of what you like, etcetera." She waved a hand. "And I think I have just the dress."

She pulled out a strapless wedding dress with a corseted bodice. The skirt was layered in two types of material. "This is French tulle and Italian silk organza. The beading on the bodice is hand loomed. I think this is for you."

Carissa's throat clogged. The dress was exquisite.

"Now, come. You can try it on here."

Carissa followed and made quick work of stripping and getting into the dress. As if being able to read her mind, the saleslady helped her button up.

"Follow me." She took Carissa to a corner that housed three full-length mirrors and a podium for her to stand on. Carissa's mouth dropped at the elegance of the dress, and it fit her like a glove. Like it was made for her and her alone.

"Now wait till I call your family and friends in." She scampered away, leaving Carissa staring at the dress.

All Carissa heard were gasps, sobs and tears from Yiayia and Aunt Paula.

Ligi inched near her. "Girlfriend, that dress is all you."

"It is beautiful," Kelly marveled.

Yiayia and Aunt Paula had yet to recover from their tears.

"And it needs no adjustment," the saleslady added.

Carissa finally found her voice and croaked out, "I'll take it."

The saleslady clapped her hands together. "Splendid. Now let's get you down from there."

Kelly and Ligi stepped forward to help Carissa down. When their fingers touched a spark of power danced through them. Ligi and Kelly took in a sharp breath.

"What does that mean?" Kelly asked.

"Recognition of supernatural beings," Carissa supplied.

"You're one of us now."

"I am." They hugged each other. She'd been on the outside before and hadn't known her friends were supernatural. Truthfully, she never would have believed them prior to meeting Xen.

She headed for the changing room. The sales assistant helped her unbutton the back of the gown. She slid out of it and handed it through the curtains.

Dressed and ready she made her way to the front where she contemplated her day today. She needed a good meal and a drink.

"I don't know about y'all, but I've worked up an appetite," Ligi said.

All the ladies agreed.

"Food is definitely on the agenda," Carissa agreed.

The saleslady came around from the counter. "Your dress will be delivered later tonight."

"But…"

She lifted her hands to stop her. "It's been taken care of."

"Let me guess. The groom."

The sales assistant grinned. "You're one lucky lady."

They exited the boutique, and Carissa took a deep whiff of some cool air that whipped by. A concrete ball formed in her gut. She looked up and down the street and couldn't shake the unease that had settled in her bones.

Something was coming, but what?

THIRTY-ONE

"Every heart sings a song incomplete until the other heart whispers back." ~
Plato

Greek Orthodox Church, Race Street; Charleston, SC
Early evening, mortal realm – One month later, Day 45

Several guests, including Yiayia and Aunt Paula, waited outside.
The limo pulled up and the driver instructed them to wait. He
dashed around and opened the door. One photographer and video-
grapher waited, poised and ready to snap and roll. The priest
dressed in his recognizable vestments stood ready to receive the
bride.

The door sprung open and Ligi and Kelly got out first. Carissa
gathered the plume of material and made her way from the limo.
The camera lens was on her, and she could hear the multiple click,
click of the camera.

"Look this way," the man behind the lens called.

Carissa did her best to smile and do as she was told. She turned
to her grandmother and her aunt and watched as they held their
hands to their chests and smiled with pride and joy. This, she said to
herself, was for them. For everything they had done for her. The
traditional customs made no difference as far as she was concerned,
she was already Xen's wife, and there wasn't a supernatural creature

who didn't know that now. They had all fought together and beat the enemy.

"Here," Aunt Paula called too, and Carissa looked up to her aunt and smiled. Her aunt snapped a few photos with her phone.

They proceeded to the top of the stairs. Her father had just popped in and held his arm out. He would be walking her down the aisle, and she beamed with joy. Her father had advised her that the other gods would pop in at the back once the ceremony started and would dematerialize before it finished. The clash of the pagan belief system and the Christian one went through her mind too, but she'd let that rest. For now she just wanted to be a girl being walked down the aisle by her father to her groom and soon to be husband. The priest walked down the aisle first. When he reached the altar he motioned for the bridesmaids to come forward. Then for Carissa and her father to proceed.

They started the slow walk toward the front. The groom and groomsmen turned to look, and when her eyes locked with Xen's through her veil, there was no mistaking how much this union meant to him. In that moment his eyes gave away all the emotions he kept bottled up in his tight and stern vampire exterior.

They came to a stop, and Ares handed her to Xen. He gave Xen a hug. "Look after my daughter," he whispered.

Carissa heard her father's words to her husband to be. Then it all hit her. *Ironic*, she thought. *Two distinct religions, polytheism and monotheism.*

But intertwined, her father answered in her head. She'd have to have that discussion.

Xen nodded at her father and reached for the lacy material of her veil. Carefully he lifted it. "You've taken my breath away." His voice was low and husky.

She beamed at him. "So have you." Her vampire with his zip code of a smile looked delectable in his suit. His best man, Kane, and his groomsman Adam looked handsome. She was sure there'd be a few girls chasing them down by the night's end.

The priest commenced the presentation of the sacrament. The first part was the Betrothal Service.

The priest blessed the rings. He touched the bride's and groom's heads with the rings and made the sign of the cross then instructed Kane to move out of line and take the rings. He crossed them over three times before sliding both Carissa's and Xen's rings on their right hand ring fingers. The priest then pushed them into place. He took the crowns from a tray full of sugared almonds and did the same as he had with the rings. After the third blessing he placed the crowns over their heads and motioned for Kane to stand behind them. Then motioned Kane to lift the crowns from their heads and crisscross them three times. The symbolism of the crowns signified that the male and female were king and queen of their house and family. As Kane executed his task the priest said, "Crown them with honor and glory." Once that was done he read from St. Paul about love and respect and how a husband should protect his wife and protect her with his life.

I always will, Xen said to her mind.

The priest continued that she, the wife, should respect her husband. The next reading was from the gospel of St. John that talked about Jesus' miracle at the wedding in Cana. Reflecting on the change of water to wine. Carissa and Xen drank from a shared goblet. It was to symbolize the sharing that life brings after marriage.

Lastly the priest led the couple around the table, followed by Kane who held on to the ribbon of the crown. They circled the table three times, taking their first steps as husband and wife. When they resumed their positions, the priest gave one final blessing and asked the groom to kiss the bride, although it was not customary to do so.

Xen planted a chaste kiss on her lips, but when she looked into those sea green eyes they told her of his joy. She'd loved him with all heart even before she'd met him. His chest swelled.

"Ahem," the priest interrupted. He pulled them away to sign the relevant paperwork in front of the witnesses, the best man and maid of honor.

The priest then positioned them and the bridal party facing toward the crowd so each guest could come up and give their

1

tnnglé

ää

congratulations.

Yiayia shuffled forward first. "*Na zisete*." Her words of *May you live*, which implied that they have a long life as husband and wife, punched Carissa in the stomach because she and Xen would live a long married life together. She was a Phoenix now, however she knew her grandmother didn't mean it that way.

"Thank you, Yiayia."

"I can't tell you how happy I am to finally see you as a bride."

She hugged her grandmother and held on for some time before letting go. A thick hot tear slid down her cheek.

Aunt Paula was next. "You're in good hands, Carissa."

"I think it's the other way around Aunt Paula," Xen said.

"He just called me, aunt." Her aunt moved along with a big wide smile and happy tears.

The ritual went on for some time until the last guest gave them all their congratulations.

"Now bridal party, I want you out on the front steps," the photographer shouted.

And then it hit her. "Wait a minute. Xen, your reflection…"

"No, *koukla*, those are old wives' tales."

They all followed the photographer to the front of the church. Lucky the church had some strong stadium lights. He gathered everyone in to take a traditional everyone photo. Then they made their way to the limo as husband and wife.

"After you, Mrs. Lyson." Xen beamed.

"Why thank, Mr. Lyson." Carissa winked playfully.

Once seated inside, Xen tapped the driver on the shoulder, and he put the privacy window up. Xen didn't waste time. He grabbed Carissa and put her in his lap.

"Have I told you how beautiful you look?"

"Not really but you can tell me now."

"You've made me the luckiest immortal on this earth."

"I'd say the feeling is mutual."

"Let me kiss you the way I really want."

"Permission granted."

His head moved in close, and he took her lips with fever pitch abandon.

You're mine, he sent to her mind as his tongue danced with hers.

The vehicle slowed and she broke the kiss. "I best tidy myself up. That photographer is likely to bite my head off if a hair is out of place."

"The only person doing any biting will be me." Xen let his fangs elongate.

Carissa whacked him on the arm and the door opened.

The venue was in downtown Charleston at one of the waterfront plantations. The plantation itself dated back to 1786.

They exited the car and the photographer got busy. Carissa's mouth was sore from smiling.

Xen motioned for the photographer to come over. "How about you take more natural shots for the rest of the evening."

The photographer nodded. "Yeah, sure Mr. Lyson."

Xen held out his arm to Carissa. "Let's go drink and celebrate as husband and wife."

"I guess some of our guests need the official version." Her mortal family needed this and deep down she did too.

"They do, *koukla,* and I can't say that I'm not enjoying this either."

She spotted the rest of the bridal party already making their way up to the old house.

"Who chose the venue?" Carissa asked.

"Your grandmother."

"Nice pick."

"Well, I think they have done well regardless of all the drama."

All the memories of her grandmother and aunt trying to organize the wedding came crashing back. Lucky for her they didn't have a stadium filled wedding. Yiayia and Aunt Paula had finally conceded and cut their numbers to what Carissa thought was sensible.

"I don't know what planet you're on but my recollection is a bit scary." Humor laced her words.

"They were only trying to please you."

"Seriously? You don't remember that cake episode?"

They stepped into the glass portico, and the guests were already drinking a variety of cocktails and champagne. Carissa had specifically asked that there be less formalities. She wanted to just blend.

A waiter came to them with a tray of champagne. "Would you like champagne or something else?"

"Champagne is fine, thank you." Carissa took a glass and Xen did the same.

She raised her glass and was joined by their bridal party. "Cheers."

Everyone responded in the same way and voiced their congratulations.

"Thank you," she repeated several times and Xen did too.

"Rissa, you look amazing," Adam said.

A low growl escaped from Xen's lips.

Carissa had a sneaking suspicion he was only toying with the lykos.

The MC made an announcement for the guests and the bridal party to be seated. They all made their way to their specific tables.

The guests were seated first and the bridal party last. Carissa and Xen had yet to sit. Everyone started clinking their glasses with a knife, indicating that the groom should kiss the bride. Her husband would not deny the crowd that. He grabbed her around the waist, tipped her and gave her a kiss. The crowd cheered. He then lifted her and helped her into her seat.

"It didn't take much to spur you on," she teased.

"*Koukla*, I'll take every opportunity that I can." A coy smile danced across his lips.

She shook her head.

As she looked across to the tables and guests, she spotted her grandmother and she waved. Carissa returned the wave and weight settled in her chest.

"Are you okay?" Xen asked.

"I'm not sure. I have a niggling feeling."

"What does your gut tell you?"

"I can't quite place it, but I have an ill feeling that something is going to go down by night's end."

"I have security placed around the venue."

"I noticed."

"Someone would have rocks in their head to try anything," Kane added.

"You don't think it just nerves?" Ligi asked from beside her.

"No. This is a heavy feeling rather than a jittery one."

"Well let's stay on our guard," Xen advised.

"Want me to get some guys on the river?" Kane asked.

"Not too close. Ask them to be discreet."

"Will do." Kane got to his feet. "Back in a minute."

"I'm at ease for now."

"Good."

The waiter brought over their meal, and Carissa dug in, but her eyes roamed around the the room and beyond. She hoped that with a teeny chance there'd be no trouble.

Xen put his hand on hers. "Calm, *koukla.*"

A weight lifted from her shoulders.

She'd take the reprieve for now.

THIRTY-TWO

"He who becomes a sheep is eaten by the wolf." ~ Proverb

Reception venue; Charleston, SC
Evening, mortal realm – Day 45

The guests had left, and there were only a few of them now left at the venue. Yiayia and Aunt Paula were talking to Davos whom they too had taken a liking to. Zeus, her father and the other gods and goddesses had also parted for the evening.

Carissa's stomach dropped when she realized a portal had opened. A group of minor gods stepped out.

"What do you want?" she asked

They stepped forward. "We don't want you to return to our domain."

"Who's we?"

"That's none of your business."

"Actually, it is her business. You trespass uninvited and threaten my wife." Xen's security had already moved into place. "Take your cronies and get out of here."

"We're not going anywhere until you swear that you will never step foot on Olympus ever again."

"I can never swear that as my access is linked to Zeus, and if he requests my presence then I have no choice but to fulfil it."

"Lies."

"It's the truth. Ask for yourself."

"You think you're special enough for Zeus to summon you?"

"I don't think but Zeus does.

"*Ekfaino*," she spoke the spell, and her weapons appeared. So did Xen's and his men's.

At the sight of her sword, the minor gods pounced. She blocked a blow and lifted her dress to kick her assailant back.

The portal opened again, and a number of demons came running out.

Everyone joined the fight.

The minor gods stepped back and let the demons take over. Carissa caught the ringleader laughing.

She hurtled a ball of fire in his direction.

He didn't have time to react. It hit him square in the chest. He staggered backwards, howling and gasping. "You bitch. You'll pay." He disappeared into the portal.

The other minor gods kept fighting, but one by one they all receded back where they came from.

The demons however were another problem. Carissa glanced around the room, trying to locate her aunt and grandmother. Davos had pulled them away from the action. A pang of relief rushed through her.

Kirke threw fire balls at some of the demons. They went up in flames with screams filling the rooms.

Ligi and Kelly slashed anyone who came near them, but they didn't need to do that for long because Lox growled back at the demons surrounding the girls. Tithon was at his side. They cleaved through and wiped out the demons.

"Get them out of here," Carissa shouted while blocking another blow. This wasn't how she wanted her wedding to end.

Her anger started to build. "*Pauo*." The demons stopped. "*Diachorizo*." They separated from her friends and family. Then she lifted her hand and bursts of green power hit the demons. They disintegrated to ash.

Kane, Adam and the others all came forward.

"What the hell was that about, Rissa?" Adam asked.

"Unfinished business."

"Seriously?"

"How many of those guys are there?"

"Lots and I'm sick of them, but it's not their doing. They are only puppets."

The realization had only hit near seconds ago that the demons were nothing but pawns to be used every time someone had a beef with anyone in the mortal realm. Hal had used them to get to her, Damion had used them for his own schemes and now minor gods were using them again for their own demented views.

The demon realm needed a shake up, and she would soon be putting in requests for change. They had to stop them from being used as hired guns, but that was going to have to wait.

"Who's controlling the puppets?"

"Good question. I have no idea. I thought it was Damion, but it's not. They seem to follow whoever promises them the mortal plane in an all you can eat buffet."

And there was no way the *Phi Athanatoi* would ever let that happen. Unless they could be redeemed. Something in her gut told her they never could change, they were too far gone. A sickness that was not curable. Lox's men were different. They'd never lost the human side of themselves, and that was what helped them find and break the curse to set themselves free.

"I don't think that's the last of them," Xen said.

"Nor do I," Carissa agreed.

Yiayia and Aunt Paula came rushing toward them.

"Carissa, are you okay?"

"I'm fine, Yiayia." Yiayia barreled Carissa into a hug. "I love you, but we need to get you and *Thitsa* out of here."

Dread filled her. A portal opened and a sword pierced her grandmother through her back. The demon retracted the sword, but he didn't have enough time to dive back into the open portal.

Xen's sword sliced through the air. He took the demons head then kicked him back in the portal.

Carissa's grandmother went limp in her arms.

Rage, hot and burning, filled her. She lifted a hand and shot continuous fire balls at the portal.

"Explode within," she willed the power. The portal started to shrink and screams from inside reached her ears.

All hell broke loose. Paula started wailing and crumbled to the floor. Adam comforted her. Everyone else scrambled to help secure the area. Carissa shrank to the floor with her *yiayia*. Tears, thick and hard, began to fall. "You weren't meant to go like this. Not yet. Not today. Not any time soon."

Her grandmother carefully put her hand up to her face. "*Paidi mou*, my number was already up, and I didn't have much time. At least I got to see you as a bride."

Carissa's eyes blurred and hot tears burned a path as they slid down her face.

"Thank you, Soteria." Her grandmother was becoming delirious and talking nonsense.

Xen was kneeling too. "I've sent the witch to retrieve a doctor."

No sooner had he said it than Kirke materialized with Dr. Aci.

She got to work. Blood flowed from the wound, and they were losing her.

"I'm afraid that all I can do is slow the bleeding. It looks like it hit the liver."

"I have a solution, but I don't know if you want to take it," Xen said.

Carissa met his eyes. "You mean turn her?"

"Yes."

With every fiber of her being she wanted that, however that came with its own price and what if her grandmother didn't want it. She looked down at her *yiayia*. "Do you want Xen to make you like him?"

"No, *paidi mou*, I've had my time."

She started to cough. "Vampire," her other hand looked for his "...look after and treasure my granddaughter. She's the greatest *doro* —gift."

Paula had managed to rip herself away from Adam. "Vetta, don't you dare leave me," she cried, the tears falling thick and fast.

"Oh Paula, one never truly leaves. I'll always be around."

Her aunt's sobs became louder as she sucked in air and hiccupped.

"Yiayia," Carissa sobbed. "Don't leave me yet."

"It is time for me to join your *pappou*."

For this Carissa would unleash all her wrath and give out punishment to those who hired and used demons for any situation. This would be the last time the demons hurt mortals, and in particular, her family. Someone had to pay. And pay they would with her sword.

"Where's my toy boy?" A small smile manifested and then vanished as fast.

Kane kneeled near her and she said, "You'll be happy soon."

"Save your energy," he said, giving her hand a squeeze. "I'd be happier if you'd take Xen's offer."

Carissa caught his misty eyes and pulled her tiny, frail grandmother in her arms.

"My road ends here. Make sure you look after each other."

Her aunt let out another loud wail of tears.

Blood seeped on Carissa's wedding dress. She didn't care. Her *yiayia* took her last breath. Carissa looked up at Xen and he confirmed it. Her heart had stopped. Carissa squeezed her tighter to her chest. The waterfall that leaked out of her eye sockets would not abate. Her grief ripped and shredded her heart to pieces. This she would never forgive. Retribution would be swift.

At some point Xen and the others cleared most of the team out and pulled away her aunt.

Kirke closed the wound with a spell.

Carissa didn't need an explanation of her friend's actions. She knew there would be questions as to her death. With a wave of her hand Kirke also removed the blood stain from Carissa's dress.

The paramedics turned up and so did the police. Jones gave them a run down.

Carissa held on tighter.

"*Koukla*, you need to release your grandmother so the paramedics can look at her."

She shook her head.

"Ma'am, we need to have a look," one of the paramedic's pleaded.

Carissa let go. They checked her grandmother, but they would never really know how she died.

She heard the murmurs. She looked around the room and saw no evidence other than there having been a wedding celebration. Gone was even her sword. How much time had passed, she wondered?

The one person she wanted protected most had become collateral damage for those who hated her connection to the gods. She would find them, and if they didn't fear her yet, they would because she was the daughter of Ares—the spirit of battle that was her father's was also hers.

Xen pulled her in his arms. "We will find them."

She sobbed into his shoulder, and the last thing she remembered as they wheeled away her grandmother was that her legs gave out from under her, but strong arms kept her upright. Xen moved her to a car that had *Just got married* written on it. Inside he handed her some tissues. She took them with a lethargic hand and with heavy movements blew her nose. She dropped her head back in the seat and her eyes fluttered closed.

Xen had taken his bride back to his mansion, and her aunt had been sedated and put in one of his spare rooms. They were both asleep, and he didn't have much time before his rejuvenation sleep pulled him under.

Kane and Adam sat on the couches in his library.

"This changes things." Xen tapped his fingers on the table.

"How do you mean?" Adam asked.

"The rage and anger I picked up in her." He chose his next words to reflect the severity of it. "She'll be like a dog with a bone."

"But there will always be someone."

"There will, but she doesn't realize how many will continually come. It's been evident each time, since Hal, then Damion, that they see her as a way to get to the gods. She's their connection," Kane said.

"We need to find the source," Adam said.

"And I have a suspicion there is a team working on a centralized goal. One we have yet to discover."

"What do we do in the meantime?" Kane asked.

"What we always do. If demons step on the mortal plane, we eliminate them. If any other unearthly creatures try anything, we capture them, question them and deal out a suitable punishment. Somewhere out there..." Xen pointed "...one supernatural knows something. We just have to find them."

Both men nodded.

"I think we all need to get some rest."

"I'm going to have to agree there." Adam rose to his feet. "We're going to have a few rough days."

"I'm expecting it and I will need your help."

"It's all yours," Adam said as he made his way to the door.

Xen came around his desk.

"It goes without saying." Kane got to his feet too.

They all walked out of the library in silence and parted ways. Xen went to his room. Carissa was sound asleep. She hadn't moved from the position he'd put her in. The happiest night of his immortal life was also his saddest. Carissa's *yiayia* would be missed. It wasn't only he who'd developed a liking to the old lady. He knew Kane and Adam both had similar feelings for her. She had been instrumental in raising Carissa. That gaping hole would be difficult to fill.

He made quick work discarding the suit from his body. Then he climbed in beside Carissa. She stirred and mumbled a word he couldn't make out. He caught the glint of her wedding band, which alerted him to the fact he had one too. Silly by vampire law, he was already mated therefore wed. To think that after two-thousand years he could still find it important. He held up his hand and a burst of happiness hit him square in the chest. Then his gaze went to Carissa and his thoughts turned dark. There would be hell to pay.

THIRTY-THREE

"Nothing bad is without something good." ~ *Ancient Greek Proverb*

Xen's Mansion; Charleston, SC
Early evening, mortal realm – Day 48

Carissa contemplated the events of the past three days. They had bled into each other. The arrangements for the funeral were not something that came without a constant mess of tears. When the river of tears eased, anger came in waves. Bursts of power would fly out from the palms of her hands. Xen pulled her back each time, giving her the oxygen and clarity she needed to bring her power under control.

Her father had popped in several times. He and his men were looking for the rogue minor gods. Since he only had her description to go on, he could not adequately pin point them. There were plenty of minor gods with beards and long hair.

Still, that didn't stop Zeus from putting up sketches everywhere. He wanted them found. He had decreed that any god aiding and abetting these minor gods would feel his wrath before he tossed them in the depths of Tartarus.

Carissa sat beside her auntie in silence. Digesting everything, and it all seemed surreal.

"I don't know if I will ever recover from this," her aunt admitted.

"Nor I, *Thitsa*. Nor I." Carissa put an arm around her aunt. Tears began to well in her eyes. They sat there like that for an hour, crying, stopping and then crying again. When her grief subsided, Carissa finally found her vocal cords. "She wouldn't want to see us like this."

"I know, Carissa *mou*. She'd be putting us in our place if she were here."

"Exactly."

"We should try..." her aunt blew her nose "...to gain some composure."

"We should," Carissa agreed.

"I wish she had told us she was sick." Her aunt blew her nose again.

They'd found out after the killing blow that she hadn't had much time to live. Her doctor had called and told Carissa that she had cancer and it was advanced and that she'd refused treatment.

"Or that she gave up any protection for herself for me." Soteria's protection had come through. That sword had been intended for Carissa. She would have survived it though, but not if she were not a Phoenix.

"Are you ready for tonight's viewing?" Xen's voice from the door brought them out of their deep pain.

"Is anyone really ready?"

"No. I doubt anyone ever is. The grief will come in waves, disappear then crash again."

Both women got up slowly. They were dressed in all black and ready.

"It was good of the priest to give us a later time slot," Aunt Paula said.

"It's a quick service tonight. Tomorrow will be harder," Xen replied.

"I know Xenocrates. I went through it all with Alec."

Images from long ago filtered through Carissa's mind, she was younger then but grief for her grandmother punched continuously at her chest. In a haze she and her aunt got into the waiting cars.

The door opened and she shook her head. She'd lost track of time.

They exited the vehicles and stepped into the funeral parlor area. The coffin was open and her legs took her straight there. She looked at her *yiayia* and fat tears rolled down her cheeks. She heard her aunt's deep sobs and pulled her into a hug. Some of Xen's people piled in, and some of Yiayia's friends were right behind them.

The priest commenced the Trisagion—the thrice holy prayers to entreat God to grant rest to her grandmother's departed soul so that it may receive mercy. When he finished they were guided to the open casket to view her grandmother. Carissa's eyes blurred, and she wiped away the tears then leaned down and whispered, *"Someday we will meet again."* She placed a kiss on her *yiayia's* head. Then stepped away to let her aunt have a few minutes. She found Xen and embraced him. Hot tears soaked his black shirt.

The last thing she remembered was being tucked into bed.

A knock sounded at her door. Carissa's eyelids snapped open.

"Carissa. You need to get ready," her aunt's low voice sounded from behind the closed door.

She rolled over to look at the alarm clock on the bedside table. "Twelve fifteen," she whispered to her brain. She needed to get a move on, she'd overslept.

She gave Xen a kiss. He was in his rejuvenation sleep and wouldn't be joining them today.

In a fray of nervous energy she took care of all her bathroom needs then threw on a black dress, heels and did her hair in an upstyle. Ready in record time she bounded down the stairs and made her way to Xen's large kitchen. Her aunt was at the table drinking her coffee but had already prepared one for her. "Thank you, *Thitsa*, you do know I can do that myself."

"I know, but it's always nice when someone does it for you."

She gave her aunt a kiss on the head and sat down next to her, pulling her in for a quick hug and release.

"I'll be going home in a few days' time."

Carissa turned her body on the chair to face her aunt. "There is no reason for you to leave. We have plenty of space, both here and at Yiayia's house."

Her aunt picked up her hand and placed it in hers. "You just got married and have experienced a great loss, again. You will need time with your vampire."

Carissa squeezed her aunt's hand. "Time is overrated, have you seen my life?"

"Yes, you can't say it's boring." Her aunt let out a strangled laugh.

"No, it's not and you're better off here."

"Who's better off here?" Adam's voice startled them both. He walked to the coffee machine dressed in a black suit.

Kane was a few steps behind. "What's going on?"

"Nothing. I just said to Carissa, with Vetta gone, it's time I headed home."

"You're leaving me?" Adam questioned, raising a hand to his heart.

"Only for a little while," Aunt Paula said.

Kane sat down. "Carissa will need you, and you her."

"He's right, you know." It was her turn to squeeze her aunt's hand. "Stay for another month and decide after that."

Her aunt nodded in agreement. "Okay."

Carissa caught the look of satisfaction on Adam and Kane's faces. The lykoi had warmed up to her family, even though she had very few here in the mortal realm. "So what time do we need to be out of here?" she asked Kane.

"Funeral is at two p.m. sharp. Then the burial is at Live Oak Memorial Gardens."

Carissa looked at her watch. "I guess we should get moving. Come on Aunt Paula, let's go give Yiayia our final goodbyes." She bit back the tears that threatened to explode again. She had to try and stay strong. It would be what her grandmother would have wanted from her and her aunt.

They made their way to the waiting cars. Then began their pilgrimage to the Greek Orthodox Church. Once there they climbed out. The hearse was already there. Carissa helped her aunt up the stairs, and they made their way in.

Adam and Kane were part of the pallbearer's team and helped bring the coffin in. Once in place, the funeral services people prepared the coffin.

The casket now lay open at the front. Her grandmother had been positioned so that her feet faced east at the front of the altar. Clusters of pink and white arrangements lined the stairs, condolences from the many who were in attendance.

The priest began to read from the divine liturgy, with hymns and prayers. Every so often there was a pause, and everyone had to stand. The last thing the priest did was give a sermon. He had a lot of good things to say about her *yiayia*. How she had been a pillar of the community in the early days when they had moved to Charleston. The church had been built in 1911 and had an already established and entrenched Greek community. Her grandmother's contribution was evident from the number of people who had turned up.

The priest summoned them to stand and pay their last respects. Hot liquid leaked from Carissa's eyes when she placed one final kiss on her grandmother's cheek. Once the immediate family had done this they were ushered to stand in line and slowly receive condolences from the funeral guests.

When the last guest left the church, they made their way to the cars. They inched away from the church and headed to the cemetery. There they hoisted the casket onto a trolley and made their way to the plot. The priest began with the hymns and lastly a final blessing was given before lowering the casket. When it was lowered he sprinkled it with holy water and wheat, which was prepared by being boiled and strained then flavored with sultanas, pomegranate, mint, sugared almonds and icing sugar. Lastly soil from a bucket was tossed in. The family then took turns throwing in a flower and some soil from the bucket.

Emotionally drained they returned to the vehicles to head back to Xen's mansion for the traditional Mercy Meal. The guests had thinned to half. The smell of cooked fish permeated the foyer when they entered.

It was late and Carissa and her aunt were worn out. Carissa didn't want to stand there and hear what everyone else had to say about her grandmother. That would only make her relive the ordeal. The ordeal of when she couldn't protect the one person she should have protected. What was the point of having power if in the end you lost?

Her duty here tonight was to put on a warm smile and mingle and that was what she did in a zombie manner. Person to person, seeing but not seeing. Hearing but not hearing. "Have you had enough." Xen's voice broke her out of her trance.

She merely nodded.

He wrapped it up early for her, and she and her aunt were ever grateful. She tucked her auntie in by her side. Small tears streaked down her aunt's cheeks. "What will I ever do without Vetta?"

Carissa squeezed her. "I don't have an answer for that because I have the biggest hole in my chest right now."

They stayed like that for a while, and when their tears had run dry for the moment, Carissa kissed her aunt. "Night, *Thitsa*."

"Night."

She made her way to Xen's and her room. Xen was standing at the door. She walked straight to him and into his embrace. His chin rested on the top of her head.

"Let's get you to bed." He released her and opened the door.

She plopped down on the bed then pushed the heels off her feet.

"Stay still." Xen used his vampire speed to undress her. He threw one of his t-shirts over her head then helped her under the covers before jumping in himself. He pulled her into a spooning position.

She let out a sigh then gave in to sleep.

Carissa awoke around 4:00 a.m. and rushed to the toilet. She emptied the contents of her stomach. Xen was at her side.

"I'm sure it's nothing but the grief from yesterday."

"Maybe."

And then he paused for a moment and shook his head.

She retched again.

Again, he paused.

She looked at him with worry. "What is it?"

A small smile spread across his lips. His eyes sparkled.

"Wait, what am I missing?"

"Hold that thought."

He left the room and ten minutes later he was holding a brown paper bag. She had gone back to bed and was scrolling through the photos on her phone.

"Here."

She opened the bag to find two pregnancy test kits. "You're joking?"

"Nope."

She hopped out of bed and a wave of nausea assaulted her.

Xen steadied her.

"Oh, no."

He rushed her to the toilet bowl.

Thank the gods and goddesses for a vampire husband, she thought.

She brought up the tiny contents of her stomach. Again.

"Get me that bag. I need proof."

Xen was back with the contents of the bag in seconds. "Here, *koukla.*"

He rocked on his feet. His joy bursting.

She shoved him out of the bathroom and shut the door. Her hands shook as she reached for one of the two tests.

It took her a minute to read and follow the directions. When she had managed it, she opened the bathroom door. "Now we wait."

Xen said nothing. She caught him eyeing the clock.

"The suspense is killing you."

"Like you wouldn't believe, *koukla.*"

"Trust me, I do."

To get a second chance to be a mom was a big deal and for Xen to be a father even bigger. As a vampire he could have no children, that was until they found Carissa was pregnant the first time. Memories of her past pregnancy surfaced and her limbs shook. That grief was still there. Yet she dared to feel hopeful now. "Let's go check," she said. She got to her feet and so did Xen then she laced her fingers in his. They walked to the bathroom to see if they were given a second chance at parenthood.

In the room Xen stopped dead in his tracks. He'd seen the test and gone into some sort of shock. Carissa feared she may have been stupid enough to have hoped for nothing.

She looked down and saw two very dark distinct lines. "We're pregnant," she announced. She swiveled on the balls of her feet and rushed into Xen's arms.

"I could hear something faint, but I didn't want to get my hopes up." He planted kisses everywhere on her face then gave her one of his panty-melting kisses.

The sharp shrill of her phone had Xen releasing her from their embrace.

"Who the hell calls at this hour?"

He shrugged his shoulders. "Best see who it is."

She made a dash for the phone and picked it up.

"Hello. Is this Carissa?"

The lady asking had a funny accent. It sounded British. Carissa shook her head. No, it was Australian. "Yes, it is. What can I do for you?

"I'm your cousin Phoebe from Australia. Your grandmother had called me about your wedding…" there was a pause "…I wasn't able to make it, and she said it was fine, but I should call you today because you have good news and will need me to help you."

"I'm sorry. I don't understand. My grandmother called you about the wedding and then said I would have good news today?"

"Yes."

"Phoebe, how could she have known when I only just found out myself?"

The silence through the phone was deafening.

After a few beats, Phoebe's startled sigh broke through Carissa's racing brain. By the look on Xen's face, he was thinking along similar lines.

"I'll be on the next flight out, cuz." Her cousin ended the call.

"Did that just happen?"

"Yes, it did."

"That has to be the single strangest phone call I've ever had."

"Well then, let's count it as a blessing. Your grandmother obviously thought you need her help."

Carissa pondered that for a moment. She mimicked Xen's earlier shrug of the shoulders. "Who am I to question help?"

"Exactly. Now Mrs. Lyson, why don't I take you to bed?"

GLOSSARY
OF GREEK
TERMINOLOGY

Alala
　Ancient battle cry.

Aletheia
　Truth.

Anagke
　Force.

Antistrategos
　Lieutenant General

Apolyo
　Set free, loosen, dismiss.

Astrape
　Lightning.

Diachorizo
　Separate.

Doro
　Gift.

Eisai
You are.

Ekfaino
Reveal.

Emphanisi
Appear.

Gamoto
Swear word - fuck.

Hypnosi
Spell of hypnosis.

Kakodaimones
Demons.

Kineo
Move.

Kori
Daughter.

Kori mou
Daughter mine.

Koukla
Greek endearment meaning doll. Used in the same context as saying babe.

Lycanthrope
Werewolves that shift to human form and vice versa.

Lykoi
Wolves.

Lykos
Wolf.

Malaka
Greek swear word for asshole.

Mnemoneuo
Remember, memory.

Mou
My, mine.

Na Zisete
May you live long together.

Nereides
Sea Nymphs.

Orkos
Oath.

Paidi mou
My child.

Paidia
Kids, children.

Pantote
Always, forever.

Pappou
Grandfather.

Paragignomai
Present, arrive at, happen; assist, help.

Pasticho
Creamy baked dish made of pasta, bolognaise, and bechamel sauce.

Pauo
Stop, cease.

Phi Athanatoi
Immortals protecting mankind. Also known as the Athanatoi or just Phi.

Phiale
Bowl, vessel, libation bowl.

Philaso
Hide.

Rigos
Blanket.

Skata
Shit.

Spanakopita
Spinach and cheese pie.

Stifado
Beef stew.

Stous Theous
To the gods.

Strategos
General

Telkhines

Metallurgist, sorcerers.

Thereos
　Close.

Thitsa
　Endearment for auntie.

Tipota
　Nothing.

Tiropita
　Feta and ricotta cheese pie.

Tzatziki
　Sauce made of yogurt with shredded cucumber and garlic.

Vlaka
　Idiot.

Xiphos
　Double edged sword.

Yiayia
　Grandmother.

ALSO BY EFTHALIA

Phi Athanatoi Series

Phantasma: The Awakening

Phantasia: A Bad Day on Olympus

Phoenix: The Rise

The Willow Witch Chronicles

One Wolf Next Door

ABOUT THE AUTHOR

Efthalia is an author of fantasy and paranormal romance. She loves nothing more than getting lost in the world of Greek gods, drool worthy vampires, and knock your socks off werewolves who risk everything for spunky and courageous heroines.

You can find out more about Efthalia on her website at efthaliaauthor.com